# Good Christian Bitches

# Good Christian Bitches

✴

## KIM GATLIN

ⒽⓎⓅⒺⓇⒾⓄⓃ

NEW YORK

An earlier edition of this book was published in 2009 by Brown Books
Publishing Group.

Library of Congress Cataloging-in-Publication Data
Gatlin, Kim.
  Good Christian bitches / Kim Gatlin. — 1st ed.
    p. cm.
  ISBN 978-1-4013-1070-7
  1. Divorced women—Fiction.  2. Suburban life—Texas—Fiction.  3. Church
membership—Fiction.  4. Christian women—Fiction.  5. Domestic
fiction.  I. Title.
  PS3607.A86G66 2011
  813'.6—dc22

2011021175

Hyperion books are available for special promotions and premiums.
For details contact the HarperCollins Special Markets Department
in the New York office at 212-207-7528, fax 212-207-7222,
or email spsales@harpercollins.com.

*Book design by Victoria Hartman*

FIRST EDITION

10 9 8 7 6 5 4 3 2 1

SUSTAINABLE FORESTRY INITIATIVE  Certified Fiber Sourcing  www.sfiprogram.org

THIS LABEL APPLIES TO TEXT STOCK

*To my children, Austin and Lauren, for reminding me that I taught them to take their worst day and make it their best when I needed to be reminded. I love you so much and thank you for the many sacrifices you've made.*

*To Mom, for always giving your wisdom, love, and support— even when it was dangerously unpopular in your circle of friends.*

*To my family, who gives new meaning to "It takes a village." Thank you for all you've done and done and done.*

*To anyone who has ever had their faith in God challenged by the maneuverings of hypocrites. May they ultimately draw you closer to Him.*

*To Christians everywhere who take the responsibility of declaring themselves ambassadors for Christ seriously enough to be mindful of the things they say and do, but more importantly the way they treat people. Knowing others take their declarations to heart and hold them to a higher standard, they realize that when they fall short it's not man who gets the blame, it's God.*

# Acknowledgments

To Rosi, for loving me from day one and leading me to all the right people who hold you as dear as I do.

To Melanie, for walking me out of the dark. This wouldn't be the same book without your wise counsel.

To Fred Gaines, my "Super Fred," for being the smartest guy in the whole world and always having the right answers.

To Mel Berger, for being the second smartest guy in the world and making this happen.

To everyone at Hyperion, especially Ellen Archer, Kristin Kiser, Elisabeth Dyssegaard, Megan Vidulich, Karen Minster, Jill Schwartzman, Sam O'Brien, and designer Victoria Hartman.

To my amazing girlfriends, who have been so supportive throughout this journey. You know who you are and continue to be an enormous blessing in my life.

To David Bower, who has had the joy of being my guardian angel since age twelve. No wonder your hair is all gone. This book would've never happened without you, and I'm so glad you said, "Just write it." Thank you for giving me the courage and ability to write *GCB*.

To Wonly, for going over and above the call of stepfather always. I love you.

To Marc Meijer, for being the best in the world and giving me my life back.

And to "Young Apollo," for knowing me better than I know myself and loving me anyway.

Good Christian Bitches

# 1

✦

Amanda Vaughn, back in Dallas just one day, was going to church. It was a sultry Tuesday afternoon in late September, and the heat and humidity rolled off the Gothic architecture of the cathedral-like edifice in sheets. Amanda descended from her rental SUV, stood before the church that had hosted her elaborate society wedding twelve years before, and wondered if more than a decade of marriage had been some kind of heat-induced mirage.

She wiped her brow, where a bead of sweat was forming. These were the days her beloved grandmother used to refer to as "hotter than young love." Of course, Mimi hadn't been accounting for extramarital heat, Amanda mused, shaking off the painful memories of her ex-husband's infidelities. She stepped toward the main entrance of the sanctuary, tested the door handle, and found it unlocked. Her heart fluttered as she stepped inside. Six blocks from her parents' home, Hillside Park Presbyterian Church was where she had attended services and gone to Bible study ever since she was a little girl, until the day she married William Armstrong Vaughn and they began their new life in Newport Beach—a life that had ended six weeks ago when she filed for divorce.

Barely breathing, Amanda stepped inside the immaculate, vast sanctuary and felt flooded with relief when she saw that nothing had changed—not the décor; not the solemn, quiet feeling she had, an awareness of God's presence; not even the penknife marks in her family's pew that her brother had inflicted decades earlier, and for which he had been thoroughly punished. God reigned in His high heavens and He reigned in the epicenter of His temporal kingdom in Dallas, Hillside Park Presbyterian.

Amanda felt herself drawn to this place. She had left her two children with her mother and come to wander through the church and take a stroll down memory lane. Now that she was here, she wasn't quite sure what to do with herself, which was unusual. She had an hour before she was to meet Ann Anderson, her Realtor, and pick up the keys to her new home. This was the first unstructured hour she had experienced in months. She had picked out a rental house on a previous trip to Dallas a few weeks earlier, but the movers wouldn't arrive with her family's belongings for another day or two, and the children wouldn't be able to start school until the following Monday. She was actually grateful to have a little time to herself after all the tumult of the last days of the marriage—the packing, the good-byes, then the actual move home. This visit to Hillside Park Presbyterian was the first time in months that she had been without an agenda item to cross off her list, without phone calls to return, without something that needed to be done, right then and by her. So she wandered through the church campus in the insufferable Dallas heat, fanning herself with someone's discarded Sunday bulletin. For just a millisecond she found herself missing the cool ocean breezes of Southern California. It might not have ever felt like home, but at least it didn't have humidity that ruined perfect clothes and flawless makeup just a moment after you stepped outside. Amanda opened up a door that led back inside, in part to get out of the heat and in part because she wanted to see the rooms where she had attended Sunday school as a child and then Bible study as a young adult. Once again, she found herself comforted by the lack of change. The carpets looked new, but they were the same dark red that, as a little girl, had always reminded her of the blood of Christ. The same furniture, the same elegant allegorical paintings on the walls, the same frescoes. In more ways than one, she realized, she was home, and the comfort she derived from the familiarity of a church environment went a long way in assuaging the feelings of guilt and shame that accompanied her divorce and move back to Dallas.

Amanda smiled. She had been fearful that Hillside Park Presbyterian Church had been remade into one of the seekers-type megachurches that had sprung up across the country, the kind of place that lacked the austere formality of the century-old Hillside Park Presbyterian—the new kind of place where your children could run around during the service and you could sip Starbucks while the minister intoned a socially relevant sermon televised live on the two super-large, stadium-size wide screens to the left and right of the main stage. That was the kind of church Bill had preferred. A real estate developer, he had grown up Baptist, the kind of church where you went to services three times a week—Wednesday nights, Sunday mornings, and Sunday nights—where the message was that you were damned if you did and damned if you didn't, so it didn't make a damn bit of difference what you did as long as you were saved. He couldn't have run fast enough and far enough from God, and more importantly, from organized religion. The Starbucks-happy megachurch in Newport Beach where Bill and Amanda had raised their children was an unhappy medium between the more formal approach to religion with which Amanda felt comfortable and the intense desire Bill had to inflict no religion whatsoever on the children. Every Sunday, the pastor passed out promises of redemption while the barista served up lattes. But Hillside Park Presbyterian hadn't buckled to the "can I get my redemption with a latte?" trend.

Suddenly, Amanda felt an enormous pang of regret—if she and Bill had lived in Hillside Park and had been part of this church family, they might still be happily married today. But there had been so many reasons to leave. Bill was a fourth-generation Hillside Parker from a very wealthy, very high-profile family, and his father and mother both had certain expectations as well as plans of their own for him. But Bill was determined to be his own man and prove to everyone, especially himself, that he could be successful on his own and without a leg up, banking on the family name every time someone took his phone call.

His father was very conservative and very old-school in his approach to business. Bill, however, was caught up in the real estate frenzy and was much more of a risk taker than his father. It was too small a town, too small a neighborhood, and certainly too small a business community to try and do anything his family would've considered risky without someone letting them know all about it. He wanted his independence, his own identity, and his own freedom from religion. One of his best friends from college was from Newport, and Bill had been out to visit several times over the years. He had always thought it would be the perfect place for him to make a fresh start.

Amanda was more than willing to join him in this adventure. They were madly in love back then, and even though Bill was considered quite the catch, Elizabeth, her mother, had her ways of letting Amanda know she didn't really approve. There was always the hint of "you could've done so much better" as far as Bill was concerned, but Amanda knew that the sad truth was that Bill could've been anyone, and Elizabeth would've put her through the same motions.

She'd always felt the California move was the right one for both of them; they were happy there, she'd thought. Maybe if they'd found a church *like* Hillside Park Presbyterian when they got to Newport? But religion wasn't magic, she told herself. Bill would have spent just as much time running around with single—and married—women in Hillside Park as he had in Newport Beach. He would never have stayed in Dallas— he used to joke that the only reason he stopped when he got to Newport Beach was that the country had run out of land. It amazed Amanda that he had never moved to Hawaii— anything to get as far away as possible from home, his parents, and Jesus Christ. But that was all behind her now, Amanda told herself. She took a deep breath and said a small prayer of thanks that she was back in comfortable, familiar territory, and that nothing, absolutely nothing, had changed. That's when she heard a familiar woman's voice coming from one of the lecture rooms used for Bible studies down the hall. Unless she was mistaken, it was none other than Sharon Peavy, her best friend growing up, a girl who had gone from homecoming queen at her high school to a career in the hospitality industry, working in various five-diamond properties in and around Dallas in marketing and sales. Rumor had it, Amanda knew—and wished she didn't know—that Sharon's career had benefited from extending an all-too-personal brand of hospitality to some of the higher-ups in her company. Sharon was known for having the "best chest" of any woman in Hillside Park, and its origin—natural or store-bought?—had been the subject of heated discussion among men and women for years. Sharon told anyone who asked, and many who didn't, that they were God-given; anyone with contrary evidence had yet to step forward. Amanda checked her watch and saw that it was ten minutes to three. Unless the church had changed its schedule, that meant that a Bible-study class, which Sharon was apparently leading, had about ten minutes left. Silently, Amanda slipped in unnoticed and took a seat in the back of the utilitarian, somewhat ordinary room that had been home to Bible studies for generations of Hillside Park women.

Sharon was talking about the evils of gossip, a topic that both attracted and repelled the ladies of Hillside Park. They knew that it was tough to square their desire to air each other's dirty laundry with their desire to remain true to their Christian witness, but sometimes a story was just too good not to pass along. And since you had the safety net of being saved, a few earthly infractions of spiritual law wouldn't get a girl kicked out of heaven, would they?

"Now before we close," Sharon was saying as she adjusted her Marc Jacobs fuchsia blouse, "do y'all have any prayer requests this afternoon? Mmm?" Amanda smiled at Sharon's familiar twang as a memory from her teenage years resurfaced. At sixteen or seventeen, Amanda had been sitting with her family in church one Sunday morning when the minister's son, who couldn't have been more than twenty-three, ascended the pulpit. A former football hero at Auburn, he had come back to Dallas to assist his father in running the church.

He was surprisingly well-spoken for a football player, dangerously handsome, with an incredible heart for Christ. He delivered a powerful and moving message about God's grace that had brought Amanda to tears. And then suddenly her sister, sitting two seats over, had leaned toward her and whispered in her ear, "I can't stand Sharon Peavy. Whose idea was it to include her for lunch after church, anyway? We've got to get rid of her!"

The sharp contrast between her own rapt attention to the captivating sermon and the fact that her sister hadn't been listening at all had tickled Amanda—she remembered having to cover her mouth with her hand to keep from laughing out loud. And, of course, fearing the roof would cave in.

As it turned out, Amanda's sister wasn't the only one who didn't like Sharon Peavy. It was well known that although she presented herself well, she was really a total mess. The girl simply wasn't marriage material—she had come close a few times, even been formally engaged at one point, but she had never "closed a deal," to use the expression favored in this town full of real estate moguls.

Sharon just couldn't close. That's what Amanda had heard from her mother; she had hardly spoken with Sharon since her own wedding, which was rather odd considering that Sharon had been her maid of honor. You know, a Christmas card once a year and the usual "tell her hellos" through mutual friends over the years. Bill and Amanda had made a point of not coming home very often—or maybe really not at all. They both were so caught up in their new lives in California and then came the children, it was just easier to have the grandparents come to them. On the very rare occasion they came to Dallas, it was usually on their way home from an international flight, and they'd plan it to where they'd literally have one night at Elizabeth's. There was no time to see anyone and it was an easy way to keep her mother appeased, but certainly left no time to see and visit with old friends.

Amanda was always walking a tightrope between Bill and her mother. The wealthier Bill got, the more she approved and the more willing she was to put their past behind them, but Bill had a long memory, and the more successful he became, the less desire he had for Elizabeth's approval or any relationship with her at all. It was just easier on everyone when they kept to themselves in California to enjoy this wonderful new life they'd carefully designed for themselves. Amanda had a couple of friends from high school come visit her in Newport, but for the most part, she'd hardly seen anyone since she'd left home. But that's how things went sometimes. You grow apart. You lose touch. You move on.

In response to Sharon's call for prayer requests, a hand in the back of the room went up. Amanda craned to see who was asking to speak.

It was a woman she didn't recognize, dressed head to toe in the latest couture. She was blond, gorgeous, and in perfect physical condition—a standard-issue Hillside Park housewife. Beside her, Amanda noticed, sat a grossly overweight woman in sweats—not even Juicy or Nike, but cheap, tacky sweats, although she looked as though she was the kind of girl who, when the urge for exercise arose, lay down until it passed. It didn't look as though she had sweated a day in her life, Amanda decided, except maybe over how she'd pay her rent or when trying to remember how to apply makeup on the rare occasions when she was forced to wear it. Amanda immediately felt guilty for judging the woman. The nice thing about Hillside Park Presbyterian was that it attracted a broad socioeconomic range of constituents, and a woman whose net worth was probably a negative number could sit comfortably, or at least relatively comfortably, beside a woman who was clearly and unabashedly Texas rich, and they could study the same Bible together.

"You go ahead, darlin'," Sharon Peavy said, her fingers tapping a quick rhythm on her leather-bound New International Version New Testament.

The blond-haired woman cleared her throat. "I'd like to ask for prayer for my neighbor," she began, "and of course I would never mention her name, out of respect for her privacy."

Anxiously, the women of the room turned, barely perceptibly, toward the speaker. She spoke softly, and it was evidently going to be a juicy story.

"She's been separated from her husband for quite some time, and I'm afraid that her husband's business isn't doing all that well, what with everything going on in real estate right now, and you know financial issues only add more pressure to their problems. She's such a sweet girl, and her children have lived in that house all their lives. It's the only home they've ever known. If something were to happen to her husband's business and they had to sell their house, I just don't know what that family would do. And little Johnny's been best friends with our little Tommy all these years—it would just be tragic if they couldn't make the payments on that nice house anymore, or divorced and had to move." Amanda had forgotten the order of concern when first hearing the news of a failing neighborhood marriage: Do you get to keep your house, was there a third party involved, then "how are your children?"

"Anyway, the reason I want to ask for prayer for her is that this past weekend, the kids were all at her husband's place. I don't know how he manages to keep his head up, living in that dreary little apartment complex right on the edge of Hillside Park, but somehow he gets by." Amanda thought she saw the frumpy woman in the sweat suit stiffen. Maybe she lived there, too.

"Anyway," the blond woman was saying, "we really do have to keep her in our prayers, because while her husband was away, there was another man whose car was there all weekend, and she's not even technically divorced. She must be feeling out of control of her life and distanced from God, since she's acting this way. And I know that the children weren't there, but still, it's not like it's appropriate even then." The woman shook her head sorrowfully and cleared her throat before continuing. "That's just not the right kind of behavior for a good Christian woman, and I know that deep in her heart she must feel the same way, and I know she probably deeply regrets what she's doing. And if her husband's business doesn't turn around quickly, then we all know it won't even matter what she's doing or where she's sleeping or with whom. But I just want to ask all of you to keep her in your prayers."

A contented silence followed the prayer request, and Amanda had the sinking feeling that the women were not using the time to pray for the poor woman in question, bless her heart, whoever she was. It could not have been too hard for the women in the room to determine just for whom they were supposed to be praying. They all must have known the speaker, they all must have known where she lived, and they all must have known who lived next door. Amanda wondered whether the request for prayer was genuine, or merely an opportunity to set in motion a hot item for the gossip circuit. Were the women calling out to Jesus, or were they making a mental list of whom to call on their cell phones once they could get back in their cars?

The situation had everything a Hillside Park housewife could ask for in a prayer request—the collapse of a once-solid neighborhood marriage, the potential availability on the market of the soon-to-be ex-husband, unless he was already spoken for—an alarming possibility, given the shortage of wealthy potential husbands—the acute joy that someone else's perilous financial condition always brings, and the drama of someone else's children's lives on the verge of crisis. It was better than the movies.

The silence ended when another woman put up her hand. Again, Amanda turned in the direction of the hand, trying to identify the prayer-seeker, but she had no idea who she was.

"Mmm-hmm, go right ahead, honey," Sharon said, and Amanda thought she saw a flash of what looked like a hungry grin. The women in the room all seemed to lean forward a tiny bit, ready to devour the latest morsels of misery and unhappiness that the prayer-seeker was about to share with her eager audience.

"I do know a woman who needs your prayer," she began, almost salivating, her eyes glazed ever so slightly with excitement, which she tried unsuccessfully to mask as pity. "Her marriage isn't on the rocks—it's over the cliff, the poor dear. Her husband—well, we really ought to be praying for him, because he knows that God wants every man to walk a humble path and keep his gaze reserved for his wife.

"And I'm sure his heart was in the right place, but the rest of him was all over town, if you know what I mean, and it just about broke his poor wife's heart that he was, well, how can I put it delicately? Ladies, I think you know what I'm trying to say."

The heads nodding and the murmurs of agreement in the room made clear that all of the ladies knew exactly what she was trying to say—the ex-husband in question had been out there bedding anything with a pulse, short of a farm animal.

"It's rough," she continued, her audience of Bible devotees rapt and hanging on every word. "The woman for whom I'm seeking prayer isn't alone in this situation. She does have two darling children, just like the other lady we discussed a moment ago, and their lives have been uprooted by the infidelities and dishonesty that her ex-husband brought into their home."

Amanda, for reasons she couldn't identify, suddenly found herself feeling uncomfortable. The story was hitting a little too close to home. Well, the good news, she told herself, is that I'm not the only one. Sounds like another woman's in the same predicament I'm in. And then she immediately chastised herself for taking satisfaction in the sufferings of another person.

The speaker continued, "She even had to give up her home and the community where she and her ex-husband lived for more than a decade. What her husband had done was pretty much known all over town, and she could no longer bear the shame of it all, and she had to move."

I've got to figure out who this woman is, Amanda decided. I just went through the same thing. Maybe I can be helpful to her. After all, we seem to be in the same situation.

"As I understand it," the prayer-seeker continued, "she and her husband owned a beautiful house in a beautiful neighborhood overlooking the Pacific Ocean, and now she's had to sell that house . . ."

Overlooking the Pacific Ocean? Amanda thought, startled. That's just too much of a coincidence. Who is this woman?

"I mean," the woman was saying, "imagine having a dream, twelve-thousand-square-foot home in Newport Beach, California, and then you've got to sell it in the middle of a down real estate market and then come home with your tail between your legs to Hillside Park, where you grew up . . . and to come back as a renter."

Renting? There was a tiny gasp of horror among the group as the reality of the woman's dismal situation sunk in. Renting was a step up from having a relative let you live in one of their rental properties for free, but not a very big step up. In Hillside Park terms, renters were practically in the same category as the homeless.

Amanda's cheeks flushed, and she was shocked both at her own naïveté and at how well this woman, whoever she was, knew her story. This woman wasn't talking about somebody else. She was talking about Amanda. The gossip mill in Hillside Park was as powerful as ever, Amanda realized to her dismay.

"Fortunately," the woman was saying, "even though she has really been through it, the good thing is that she's come back to Hillside Park, and nobody here in town knows exactly what happened out there in Newport Beach, or why her marriage failed, or just how big a philanderer her husband was, or just how deeply troubled her children are by this tragic turn of events." Amanda's mouth hung open.

"And as we all learned this morning, idle gossip in any form can be so damaging to someone, so it's up to each of us to keep this poor woman's travails in our hearts and in our prayers, and I know that there's not a woman in here who would share these sad tidings with anyone outside the walls of this Bible study."

Amanda just sat there, slowly shaking her head from side to side, too shocked to say a word in her own defense. Not that she really wanted to.

"So as this woman starts her life over," the prayer-seeker earnestly concluded, her mission of character destruction carried out completely and perfectly, "let's pray for her, and for her children, that they may find a measure of happiness in her new life here in the neighborhood, and let's especially pray for her ex-husband, and may he find treatment or counseling for his obvious sex addiction and become the man we know God intends him to be."

Amanda thought she saw at least half a dozen of the women surreptitiously reaching for their Gucci or Chanel bags to get to their cell phones, as if they couldn't even wait to get outside the Bible study before sharing the news.

Frightened, disgusted, and hurt, Amanda quietly rose to her feet and slipped out the door of the Bible study classroom. No one noticed her leave. She glanced back into the room at the stranger who so casually had broadcast the intimate details of her shattered life to this fascinated gathering of women—who were almost certain to share Amanda's story with everyone on their speed dials.

As Amanda turned away from the classroom and headed down the hall, tears streaming down her face, she could hear the group of women intoning solemnly, "In Jesus' name we pray, amen."

## 2

✦

Get your hands off me!"

As Amanda was about to get back into her SUV outside the church, she was startled by the sound of a woman shouting. She turned and looked across the street, where she saw a woman in handcuffs being escorted from a two-story office building by two uniformed members of the Hillside Park Police Department. Hillside Park, strictly speaking, was well within the confines of the city of Dallas, but it had created its own police department almost a century ago and refused to share jurisdiction with or even accept the validity of Dallas police officers within Hillside Park. To Amanda's surprise, the woman was Susie Caruth, her former sorority sister from Southern Methodist University.

"Don't you idiots know who I am?" Susie was shouting.

Amanda slammed the door of her SUV and stood beside the vehicle watching Susie, fascinated. Susie looked exactly the same, except for her western outfit. She looked like a wannabe country music star, which was hardly her normal style. Otherwise, nothing's changed, Amanda thought. But then again, it's not every day that you see a sorority sister from SMU under arrest.

The police, for their part, looked deeply pained. Amanda figured, accurately, that they knew exactly who Susie Caruth was, and more to the point, who her husband was. Edward Caruth came from a long line of Texas-rich Caruths who had made their money in cattle ranching and then real estate in the early 1900s. Edward Caruth had the money to indulge all of his wife's expensive tastes, and it was a good thing that he had a lot of money, because she had a lot of them. The word in Hillside Park was that Susie lacked for nothing except a sense of proportion, common sense, and good taste. Otherwise, she had everything else, and now looked as though she was about to add to her extraordinary collection of things something few other women in Hillside Park possessed—a criminal record.

Amanda took a few steps toward the street so that she could observe the situation more closely.

"Amanda Vaughn?" Susie yelled when she saw Amanda. "Hey! What in the world are you doing here? Can you please tell these men who I am?"

The policemen stared at Amanda, as if perhaps she offered the key to solving the awful predicament in which they found themselves, arresting the wife of one of the most wealthy and powerful men in the community.

Against her better judgment, Amanda crossed the street and ventured closer to Susie, whom she had not seen since Susie's wedding a decade earlier. Edward had generously sent private jets to fetch any out-of-town invitees, which included Amanda and her then-husband. Amanda stiffened at the thought of the wedding, because she had heard rumors later that her husband had been seen at the reception coming out of the coatroom with one of the catering girls. She'd heard both were disheveled, out of breath, and smiling. She bristled at the memory.

"Amanda, help me!" Susie pleaded, the picture of consternation. "These morons are fixin' to take me to jail!"

"Officers," Amanda said respectfully to the policemen. They were a little older than she and Susie, and Amanda thought she recognized one of them from having busted an underaged drinking party at the home of one of the families in Hillside Park when she was in high school. That seemed like a lifetime ago. The police officer didn't recognize her, though, which, in Hillside Park, was actually surprising—the police officers had been around so long they almost counted as friends.

"Ma'am," the police officers chorused, touching the tips of their hats.

It's nice to be home, Amanda suddenly thought. Texas cops were a heck of a lot nicer than the ones out in California. You couldn't even talk to them, especially if you had been driving too fast, one of the few faults to which Amanda readily admitted.

"Tell them who I am!" Susie insisted. The more she fought against the handcuffs, the more they cut into her wrists.

"We know who you are, ma'am," one of the officers said, his tone demonstrating his high degree of discomfort. "That's why we arrested you."

"You can't arrest a woman in her own office!" Susie shouted. "I wasn't doing anything wrong!"

"We were told," the other officer began, "that it wasn't your office anymore, and that you refused to vacate."

"That's the dumbest thing I ever heard!" Susie insisted.

"I'm the Chair of the Longhorn Ball! You just barged into the executive offices of the Longhorn Ball and pulled me out of there as if I were a common criminal! Do you realize you can measure the rest of your careers in law enforcement not in years, but in hours or even minutes?"

The officers clearly didn't doubt her. Amanda had the sense that they would have rather been engaged in a shootout with meth-crazed drug dealers in the worst part of town than to spend another minute embroiled with Susie Caruth in the middle of Hillside Park.

"You're the Chair of the Longhorn Ball?" Amanda asked, impressed. The Longhorn Ball was one of the premier events of the Hillside Park social season. It's an outdoor event, always held in the fall and usually in early September, but the real truth is, the calendar of the entertainment is what dictates what date is chosen. Every Ball Chairman always has a very clear idea of what her Ball year will look like—from the entertainment to the theme, to the foods served, to the special touches she'll add of her own to put her personal signature on the event. It was the only high-profile event where the men didn't have to wear tuxes; they could wear jeans. Everybody loved it because for that one night each year, the wives didn't have to drag their husbands kicking and screaming to a social event. The event sometimes raised two to three million dollars in a single night for charity. Practically anyone of any importance in Dallas attended, bought tables, donated fabulous luxury items for the auctions, or otherwise contributed goods, services, and money to the cause. To say that the event actually raised that much money in one night was actually an exaggeration; planning the Longhorn Ball took a full year. And to be Chair of the

Longhorn Ball was to rise to a position of authority and prominence among the women of Hillside Park that few would experience. The last Ball had taken place just two weeks ago, right before Amanda arrived, and Amanda realized she hadn't heard anything about it. Clearly, she'd been away for too long.

Susie nodded smartly. "We raised five million dollars," she said, her pride evident.

Amanda's jaw dropped. Back in the day, when she had been an active member of the Longhorn Ball committee, the annual event, which featured country music headliners such as George Strait and Willie Nelson, netted close to a million. Five million? That was hard to believe. But then, since she had come back to Dallas, everything was hard to believe.

"Five million!" Amanda exclaimed. "That's amazing, Susie. Congratulations!"

"My husband helped," Susie admitted. "He leaned on a lot of people to kick in some serious cash. Actually, confidentially, and I only tell you this because I've known you so long and you were at my wedding . . ."

Along with only about eight hundred other people, Amanda told herself.

"We really only raised three point six million," Susie admitted. "But since Kelly Hill . . . remember her? She was the Ball Chair the year before? Anyway, she raised four point two million. I could hardly be seen raising less money than Kelly. So my husband kicked in an extra eight hundred thousand. Isn't he a dear?"

"No doubt," Amanda said, and suddenly the insanity of the situation struck her. Susie wasn't just bragging about how much money she had raised but about how much money she and her husband actually *had*—even as she stood in handcuffs between two uniformed Hillside Park cops.

"I hate to interrupt your conversation, ladies," one of the policemen began, his voice somewhat timid.

Susie glared at him, unhappy at having the discussion cut short. It appeared to all present that she had forgotten she was being arrested and had gone back to her usual way of bossing around anyone who had a net worth of under two hundred million dollars, as was surely the case with the two police officers.

"Why are they arresting you?" Amanda asked, glancing again at Susie's western getup. Sometimes people who chaired the Ball got into the ridiculous habit of adopting a western-inspired theme wardrobe, and then acted like they were really living the part at all times. They traded in their usual wardrobes for rodeo attire. It was the cheesy Dallas equivalent of "going native." It was quite a phenomenon, and at the Ball you would see photos of these women in earlier years looking very awkward and uncomfortable in a cowboy hat. Years later they reappeared as Ball Chair, dressing daily like they'd grown up on a ranch and were former rodeo queens.

Susie rolled her eyes. "Oh, it's all just a big misunderstanding," she said matter-of-factly. "Some of the people on the Ball committee keep saying that I was supposed to vacate my office the day after the Ball. But I say that's ridiculous! They can't turn this over to someone else and lose all the momentum I've created. I need to Chair this one more year. I bring in five million dollars? And the committee has me arrested . . . for trespassing? In my own office?"

"That's terrible!" Amanda sympathized.

"You bet it is!" Susie said indignantly. "First, one of these fools broke my nail when he was putting these handcuffs on me. On top of that, when I told him I was going to scratch his eyes out or hit him with mace, he should have known I was exaggerating. Everybody knows I tend to exaggerate. I would never do that to a police officer." The police eyed her warily. Evidently, they thought otherwise.

"Who's the new Ball Chair?" Amanda asked.

"I wanted to do it for a second year in a row," Susie said. "But after the way I've been manhandled, I'm thinking about suing the organization to get my husband's eight hundred thousand back. Actually," she said, dropping her voice to a whisper, "he donated four and a half million. I never really got my act together as Ball Chair, with one thing or another. That's why I want to do it for another year. I figure, I've got the experience, right? And I raised five million without really applying myself. And now I'm thinking about suing the city as well," she concluded, glaring at the cops on either side of her.

"Really," Amanda said, not saying what she was thinking, which was that it was outrageous that anyone would try to be Ball Chair for two straight years. That's just not how things were done, at least not when she had been in town. The Longhorn Ball Committee was made up of one hundred women, most of whom lived in Hillside Park, and most of whom were somewhere between very comfortable and incredibly wealthy, or at least their husbands or family were. There were a few women on the committee who got there by making the right friends, but such a practice was frowned upon by the majority of the group. You could declare an active or inactive status. If you were active, you were involved for at least the first three years of your membership in the hard work of pulling the event together. After that, you could go to inactive status, retaining your membership among the hundred chosen women, but you would not be required to do any work. Amanda had remained inactive during all her years in Newport Beach.

"Has anybody else been Ball Chair two years in a row?" Amanda asked diplomatically.

"No," Susie said, "of course not. But I figure there's a first time for everything. Although, now I wouldn't touch the Longhorn Ball with a ten-foot pole. Officers, can we just get this over with?"

"Honestly, ma'am," one of the police officers began, his tone respectful and reproachful at the same time, "we were actually waiting for you ladies to finish your conversation so we could, um, take you to jail."

Suddenly Susie gave Amanda a look that was both troubled and threatening. "You're not gonna tell anybody they took me out of the Longhorn Ball office in handcuffs, are you?" she asked plaintively. "I'd be embarrassed to death if anybody knew this happened to me."

Amanda thought about the exercise in gossip that she had just experienced in the Bible study.

"Cross my heart," she said.

Susie relaxed. "I knew I could count on you," she said. Then she furrowed her brow. "You back in town?" She tried to sneak a surreptitious glance at Amanda's left hand. "Where's your wedding ring? You and Bill are done, huh?"

"You could say so," Amanda admitted. "The children and I just moved back to Dallas."

"Well, I'm sorry for your pain," Susie said sincerely. "But I guess I can tell you now."

"Tell me what?"

"Your husband," Susie said. "Okay, your ex-husband. He made a pass at me."

"What?! When?" Amanda asked, surprised. Then she instantly asked herself why she was surprised.

"The day of your wedding."

"At my wedding?"

Amanda's ex had always said that he never understood what Edward saw in Susie. Bill said he thought she looked like a monkey. He didn't even find her attractive, Amanda thought, shaking her head. Good riddance, she said to herself, totally disgusted.

One of the police officers gave Susie a look.

"All right, officers," Susie said, in a voice that expressed her weariness. "I guess my work for the Longhorn Ball falls into the 'no good deed goes unpunished' category. You might as well go ahead and shoot me now, if that's what you've got in mind."

"We were just going to take you down to the station," one of the police officers said. "We won't be shooting anybody today."

"That's unless you try to mace us in the cruiser," the other one said, only half in jest. The police officers gently guided Susie down the path toward their black-and-white.

"Would you be a dear and call my husband at the office?" Susie called to Amanda over her shoulder. "Let him know I might need to be bailed out."

"Um, sure," Amanda said, thinking surely Susie knew she wouldn't know how to begin to try and reach Ed, but if it made her feel better to think so . . .

"I'm glad you're back," Susie added. "Let's have lunch and catch up."

"I'd love to," Amanda said. She watched as Susie chewed out the officers as they placed her into the backseat of the police car.

Welcome to Dallas, Amanda thought, shaking her head again. Welcome home.

# 3

✴

Amanda watched the cruiser fade into the distance, in shock at what she'd just witnessed, trying to process the arrest of a sorority sister. She checked her watch. A quarter after three. She had to be at the Realtor's at three thirty to sign the papers and pick up the keys to her new home. There was something unsettling about the idea of renting in a community where you grew up and the only people who rented were executives doing two- or three-year stints with multinational companies, social climbers, and divorcées. So often, people would move to Dallas, discover Hillside Park, and if they didn't like their past, create a new one, or at least a more respectable one. In Hillside Park, renting implied a lack of seriousness of purpose about life. If you were renting, could you really be trusted? People would even sometimes say, "Well, she's renting," as if to summarize in a single word the lack of financial stability of the individual under discussion.

Nevertheless, it made no sense for Amanda to buy right away, and she knew it. She had plenty of money, thanks to her late father; that wasn't an issue. She had her own family money from oil, gas, and banking interests, and would have whatever the lawyers worked out for her with Bill (and that would be substantial). But she wanted to get reacquainted with the neighborhood before she made a purchase of any kind, since she'd been away for so long. She couldn't imagine living anywhere but Dallas, and within Dallas anywhere but Hillside Park, so it wasn't a question of whether or not the neighborhood appealed to her. Of course it did. It was still Mayberry—okay, Mayberry with a lot of zeroes after it. It was a place where kids rode their bikes to public school, and public schools were so well-funded that the Texas legislature, led by that socialist Ann Richards after she talked her way into the Texas governor's mansion—God rest her soul—had actually passed a Robin Hood–style luxury tax on the community, forcing it to share its wealth with impoverished school districts throughout the state. Indeed, Texas was dotted with small towns where the public schools, paid for with hard-earned (or easily clipped, it didn't matter) Hillside Park dollars, were frequently much newer and nicer than the homes that surrounded them.

It was actually hard to figure out a good reason to leave Hillside Park. At any time, for any purpose. The community certainly had all the churches anybody could ask for, as well as three country clubs—the second and third of which had been founded by individuals blackballed at the first and then the second—three shopping areas with all the high-end stores to which anyone could aspire, office buildings (so that the professionals in its midst could have commutes only as long as it took them to jog to their offices), a movie theater, and one of the finest universities in the Southwest, all within its fabled borders. It was said that the two most popular sports in Hillside Park were golf and illegally subsidizing the university football team.

Amanda crossed the street, got back in her car, and headed

for the real estate office of Ann Anderson, located across from the Starbucks in Hillside Park Village. Ann Anderson's grandfather had started the agency in the early 1920s, when Hillside Park was little more than lot lines and a huckster's dream. The original Anderson, Dan, had settled in Dallas after having been railroaded out of half a dozen towns from Indiana to Kansas, where his rampant real estate speculation had ended up taking serious money out of the pockets of the locals while leaving nothing but plot lines and sticks in the ground. Dan Anderson was planning on the same activity in Hillside Park, but then he realized that in a city like Dallas, in the midst of its oil boom, there was more money to be made legitimately in real estate than fraudulently. So Dan actually stuck around long enough not only to create a consortium to develop Hillside Park, but also to reap the financial and social rewards that came to those in Dallas, or those anywhere, who somehow managed to turn a little bit of money into a whole lot of it. Dan Anderson married a daughter of one of his first home buyers, a roughneck-turned-oil-gazillionaire also named Anderson. The "double Andersons" and their progeny had dominated the Hillside Park social hierarchy ever since, to the point where the daughters of the family kept their own names when they married, long before movie stars and television anchorwomen adopted the same habit. It was a short drive from Hillside Park Presbyterian to Anderson Realty in Hillside Park Village; it was a short drive from anywhere to anywhere else in the neighborhood, which was one of its charms.

Amanda glimpsed herself in the rearview mirror. I must look horrific, she told herself, running a hand through her humidity-dampened hair. Again she found herself missing the cool ocean breezes of Newport Beach.

To Amanda's surprise, the office was practically empty. Real estate was hitting a slow spot, which meant that a whole bunch of people in the community who had been flipping properties for fun and profit were now stuck with unoccupied rental houses, underoccupied apartment buildings, and even a few office buildings. Nobody was going to go belly-up, though. It wasn't that kind of place.

"Hello," Amanda said to the receptionist. "I'm looking for Ann Anderson." The receptionist smiled, clearly agreeing this was the only place to buy a house in Hillside Park.

Certainly, there were plenty of other agencies from which to choose, but it seemed unpatriotic to go anywhere else. And besides, if you didn't list your house with Ann, or if you didn't buy from her when you were upgrading, you and your spouse would pay such a high social price that it didn't make sense trying to save the one or two percent discount other brokers offered. Not buying or selling with Ann Anderson was like not responding to a chain e-mail and sending it on to six more people. A husband's business would dry up, his tee times at the club would mysteriously vanish, and restaurants would somehow lose his reservations. Not to mention their names disappearing from every social mailing list on the planet.

As for the wife, it was even worse. Ann's mother, Catherine, even in her eighties, was still the grande dame of Hillside Park social matters, and she was still the ultimate arbiter of those who were "good people" and those who were not. You didn't get anywhere in life, or in Hillside Park, by crossing the Andersons. And since the firm was so well-connected, the Andersons always did a great job of representing their clients, because they had more buyers and sellers than the rest of the agencies in the neighborhood put together. Put that all together and it would never have occurred to Amanda to go elsewhere.

Ann had helped Amanda, by long-distance phone and e-mail, in locating an appropriate four-bedroom home to rent for a year or two while Amanda figured out what the next direction of her life would be. To her credit, Ann had been extremely discreet with regard to information about the collapse of Amanda's marriage and her return with her children to Dallas—she hadn't told more than a dozen people, which, in Hillside Park terms, is about as close as a person can come to depositing a secret in Fort Knox. That's probably how they made the connection in the Bible study, Amanda realized. One of Ann's dozen divas she'd confided in had not kept her confidence. They say a woman's loyalty only lasts as long as it takes her to hang up and dial again.

"I'm sorry," the receptionist, a plain-looking woman in her early twenties, said over her dark-rimmed glasses. Ann had a thing about not hiring attractive young women. They kept getting snatched up by the male home buyers, single or otherwise. It just took too long to train new ones. "She's out with a client."

Amanda checked her watch. They were supposed to meet at three thirty, and it was three thirty. "I was supposed to meet her right about now," Amanda said, surprised and slightly miffed. The receptionist gave her a conspiratorial grin.

"It's some guy from Kentucky," she confided. "They're looking at ranches."

"Oh," Amanda said, nodding, as if she was supposed to take some sort of comfort from the fact that Ann was out with a heavy hitter and not with some Regular Joe just looking for a house.

Anybody who was wealthy enough to buy a ranch could afford to command Ann's time anytime.

"When's she getting back?" Amanda asked.

The receptionist shrugged. "I don't know if she's getting back today," she admitted. "They're halfway to Plano."

"I'm supposed to pick up some keys from her," Amanda said, her sense of amusement about the whole thing, such as it was, rapidly fading. "Didn't she say anything about me?"

"Let me get someone who can help you."

I'm being treated like an outsider, Amanda thought, and she definitely didn't like it.

"Yes, yes, I'll help her," a voice familiar to Amanda called out from a cubicle halfway to the back of the agency. "I know all about it."

I know that voice, Amanda told herself. I just can't place it. I've just been away too long.

Suddenly Heather Sappington emerged from the cubicle and slithered down the hall. Once again, Amanda thought she was imagining things. The last time she had seen Heather had been fifteen years earlier, at a Longhorn Ball where Heather had gotten famously drunk and had danced solo with a cowboy hat, doing something that resembled a dirty-cowgirl stripper routine. She was last seen that night kicking and screaming, being literally carried off by a security guard who, by day, was a lineman for the SMU football team. Rumor had it, and a highly accurate rumor it was, that once he had carried her off to her car, she returned the favor by bringing him back to her place, a somewhat dingy two-story apartment she shared with her ninety-four-year-old grandfather on the other side of the acceptable boundary line of Hillside Park.

Certainly, neither Heather nor the security guard was seen

again at the event, even though their departure took place around ten p.m. and he and the rest of the SMU football team—along with off-duty Dallas cops patrolling the perimeter of the event on horseback—had been hired to be there until two a.m. A neighbor of Heather's said that he was awakened by a large man barely fitting into a sport coat carrying a bag of clinking empties past his home; his first thought was that the guy had murdered Heather's grandfather and stolen his beloved coin collection. When the police stopped him a few blocks away, it turned out that all he had in the bag were empty vodka bottles that Heather had asked him to remove on his way out.

The next morning, Heather, looking only slightly worse for wear, appeared in her usual pew at Hillside Park Presbyterian, praying earnestly for salvation—or maybe praying that the football player would keep his promise to call her again sometime. The only clue to the fact that she might have had a longer or more tiring night than the rest of the congregation was the fact that she was the only one out of the 1,100 penitents present wearing sunglasses indoors. But that was Heather, Amanda realized. A bottle of vodka in one hand and a Bible in the other; there wasn't a single Bible study or party she had ever been known to miss. She was just as famous for passing out the Rabbit, a battery-operated sex toy, her personal favorite made famous on *Sex and the City*, to her single girlfriends as she was for giving sets of coffee mugs bearing different Bible verses on each to her married friends.

"Oh my gosh," Amanda said, trying to look happy to see Heather, whom she had never really liked. That night fifteen years ago was only the first episode that came to mind, but there were many others. Amanda felt that if you were going to be a party girl, be a party girl. If you were going to hold yourself up as a fine Christian woman, be more mindful of the behavior you demonstrate—but how you could serve two such radically different masters never made sense to Amanda.

Heather came rushing over to Amanda, gave her a hug and a few air kisses, and studied her from top to bottom.

"My, my. So you're back in Dallas!" Heather exclaimed, and Amanda sensed that Heather was trying to restrain her sense of glee that yet another marriage had bitten the dust.

"I guess I am," Amanda said, with an aw-shucks tone of voice, as if to say, that's life—not all marriages last forever.

"You poor, poor dear," Heather said, with an uncontrollably insincere tone. Amanda tried to remember what that German word she had heard in college was, the one that meant taking pleasure in the pain of others. Schadenfreude, that was it. If you looked it up in the dictionary, you would see Heather's face right next to it.

"Ann told me all about it," Heather said, and then she back-tracked. "I mean, about you coming by to pick up keys," she added quickly. "That's really all I know."

Amanda nodded wearily. "Don't worry about it," she said. "I just got back from Bible study at Hillside Park Presbyterian, and they're already praying for me."

"And your darling kids," Heather added, and then she winced. "Children," she corrected herself. "I just can never remember to say *children* instead of *kids*. I'm never gonna get this." Amanda knew exactly what she was talking about. There were certain conversational rules that applied in Hillside Park, and if you didn't follow them, people would question whether you really even belonged in the neighborhood. One of the conversational giveaways to a non–Hillside Park childhood was the use of the word *kids* instead of the proper word *children*.

Among the mothers of Hillside Park, children were children, kids were goats, and people who didn't know the difference didn't belong.

"You can't worry about things like that," Amanda assured Heather, and suddenly she found herself asking why she was so interested in the feelings of a woman who was perhaps the ultimate gossip machine in the community. Amanda found herself surreptitiously glancing at the ring finger on Heather's left hand, which sported a remarkably large engagement ring. Heather, embarrassed, caught her looking.

"It didn't work out," she said sadly. "He's a good man and all, but we just weren't right for each other."

"Was this something just recent?" Amanda asked sympathetically.

"Oh, no, no," Heather said dismissively. "Norm and I broke it off, like, more than two years ago."

"Norm?" Amanda asked. "Norm who?"

"Norm Hunter," Heather said, surprised that Norm needed a last name to be identified. He was only one of the leading cosmetic surgeons in the Dallas–Fort Worth area.

"Norm Hunter?" Amanda asked, shocked. "I didn't even know he was divorced!"

Now Heather shrugged. "He wasn't exactly *divorced* divorced," she admitted. "But he and Jane were separated, and it didn't look like their marriage was going to survive, and he proposed to me."

"While he was still married to Jane?" Amanda asked, not getting it.

"They hadn't been living together for more than a year," Heather said defensively. "I didn't, like, bust up that marriage, if that's what you're thinking."

Amanda put a hand up. Hold it right there.

"Whoa," she began. "I wasn't accusing you of anything like that. It's just a lot to take in all at once. I had no idea Norm was even divorced."

Heather, calming down, studied her. "You sure have been out of the loop for a while," she said.

Amanda nodded. "You've got that right," she said. "I'm sure I've missed a lot."

"No doubt."

"You never gave the ring back? I don't mean to be rude, but . . ."

Heather grinned. She held up her hand for Amanda to admire. "Ten carats," she said proudly. "I call it Ira, like I-R-A— get it?" She giggled. "An engagement ring's a gift, right? Why should anybody have to give back a gift? After all, he broke off the engagement."

"I always thought . . ." Amanda began, but she bit her tongue. Suddenly she vaguely recalled hearing that Heather had been through three such engagements/near misses, and come to think of it, Heather had kept the rings on those occasions as well. The saddest thing was, she remembered hearing that with all three men, Heather might as well have had a tag in her ear. They were men who would have settled for anybody—they just couldn't stand to be alone—and yet they still passed on Heather.

"But enough about me," Heather said with a wicked grin. Clearly, she didn't see her situation as so pathetic and proudly felt that if getting over highly successful ex-fiancés were an Olympic sport, she would have had a host of gold medals to go with those diamond rings. She fancied herself a regular Hall of Famer.

"Don't you just look amazing, and after all you've been through!" she gushed, turning the conversation back to Amanda.

Amanda thought she detected a trace of envy embedded in the compliment. They stood for a moment in awkward silence.

Finally, Heather sighed. "I've really got to go—I have a doctor's appointment in ten minutes. I've got the keys on my desk. I'll be right back." And with that, she went slinking back down the hallway, in a curve-hugging dress that looked better suited for dinner than office attire. But then again, Heather was always in audition mode for her next engagement ring. Amanda was about to ask her whether Ann had known all along that she wouldn't be able to be at the office to meet her, but suddenly it didn't matter. She just stood there and waited for Heather to come back and give her the keys.

# 4

✦

Ten minutes later, with the keys to her temporary new home in hand, Amanda pulled up to the sweeping circular drive in front of her parents' house. She cut the motor and paused a moment to take in the magnificent, seven-bedroom house where she had grown up. She thought for a moment about the limousine that had taken her from the house to Hillside Park Presbyterian on the day of her wedding. She felt like something of a failure to be coming home now, after a failed marriage, to start her life over again.

There was something inside of her that had always hoped the damage in her marriage, great as it was, could have somehow been repaired. Of course, Bill wasn't interested in healing. It was going to be his way or the highway. He also knew he had enough money to find someone who was willing to live like that in exchange for his lifestyle—someone who would simply turn a blind eye to his bad behavior in exchange for his charity. And it wasn't going to be Amanda, that was for sure. No way.

Now, taking possession of the keys to her new place somehow made the whole thing more real. Gotta make the best of it, Amanda told herself. This is a much better place for the children anyway.

And with that, she got out of her SUV and headed into the house. Parked next to the front door was a new black Mercedes Maybach with paper license plates—a car that cost at least three hundred thousand dollars. Amanda had always had a thing for black Mercedeses. She'd asked for one for her high school graduation gift and had fully expected to get one. When her parents presented her with an eighteen-carat gold Rolex, complete with diamond face and diamond bezel, she threw the watch at her father and stormed out of her graduation dinner. But Amanda was a different person back then, and after all, it was the 1980s.

"Mom didn't tell me she was buying a new car," Amanda said to herself, admiring the vehicle. "Ooh, I love it!"

Amanda headed inside, where she was immediately greeted by her two children, Will, twelve, and Sarah, nine. Will was his father, Bill, reincarnated as a sixth grader—the same shaggy blond hair, the same mischievous eyes, the same half smile that gave people the sense that father and son alike were somehow getting something over on an unsuspecting world—which, half the time, they were. The resemblance between father and son was so uncanny that Amanda frequently had to remind herself not to take out her anger and frustration over her husband's bad behavior on her son. Will had just discovered the skateboarding and surfing culture of Southern California, and leaving it behind for landlocked, uncool Dallas was, to his young mind, nearly a mortal blow.

"I hate this place!" he shouted, enraged, by way of greeting. "There's nothing to do! Dallas sucks!"

Here we go again, Amanda told herself.

"I've asked you never to use that word, Will," she said calmly. She simply didn't have the energy for a struggle. It never went well under the best of circumstances. And besides, today it was just too hot.

"Dad uses it all the time," her son countered. His father was his hero and he worshipped the ground he walked on.

"I'm not Dad," Amanda said, trying unsuccessfully not to raise her voice. Sarah approached and gave her a waist-high hug.

"Why'd'ja have to take us away from Dad anyway?" Will asked, obviously ready for battle.

Amanda was exasperated. If your father hadn't had the morals of an alley cat, she wanted to tell him, you'd be skate-boarding this very minute on Balboa Island. But she wanted to be extremely careful not to say or do anything that could affect Will's relationship with his father. It was bad enough that the boy was going to be fifteen hundred miles away from his dad, unable to see him on a regular basis. The last thing Amanda wanted was to be accused of poisoning the relation-ship between the two of them.

"We've been over this a thousand times," Amanda said wearily. "It just didn't work out between Daddy—your daddy and me. I wish the truth were otherwise, but it's not."

"Well then, let's make it a thousand and one times," Will sassed back. "Dallas sucks. This house sucks. I hate it here."

"You haven't even given it a chance," Amanda said mechani-cally, but she just didn't have the energy to match his anger. She tousled his hair. "You'll see."

The boy recoiled from his mother's touch. "I hate when you touch my hair like that."

"Okay, Will," Amanda said, trying not to let the thing es-calate. But with Will, as with his father, escalating anger could happen in an instant.

"Did you get the keys, Mommy?" Sarah asked. She was nine years old going on twenty-five, physically a mix of Amanda and Bill, with long, straight blond hair and Amanda's green eyes and warm, self-deprecating smile. It broke Amanda's heart that Sarah didn't have a daddy to live with, and Amanda had given over many hours in a therapist's office discussing whether it might be better to keep the marriage intact for the sake of the children. Ultimately, Amanda had decided that a precocious child like Sarah, who heard everything and missed nothing, would be far more confused—even damaged—by her father's philandering if she had to witness it up close. Amanda couldn't have Sarah growing up thinking that this was what a happy, healthy marriage looked like. That was the final straw in making the decision to get the divorce and move back home.

"I got 'em," Amanda said.

"That's so great!" Sarah exclaimed with an excitement that Amanda didn't understand, but for which she was grateful. At least someone was happy about their new life. "When are we moving in?"

"It all depends on the movers," Amanda said. "They're supposed to be here in the morning. We could realistically be in the house by tomorrow night."

"And none too soon," came a voice from the hallway. It was Amanda's mom, Elizabeth Smith. "These kids are more than I can bear," she said as she strode into the room. "Well, just Mister Tough Guy over there."

Will gave a half smile. Nothing could make his day like proof from adults that he was driving them crazy.

"Hi, Mom," Amanda said. "It's just for one more day."

"I know," Elizabeth said, waving a hand dramatically at her grandchildren. "It's just not something I'm used to. Especially not in this heat. It's so hot and dry the trees are whistlin' for the dogs."

Elizabeth was a tall, thin, graceful sixty-two-year-old from one of Dallas's leading banking families, and she had married into one of Dallas's leading oil families. For forty-one years, she had been the dutiful CEO's wife, traveling with her husband, Ed, to far-flung locales in the Middle East and South America, as Ed oversaw both his family's oil interests and her family's banking interests. Elizabeth's priorities had always been marriage and family, church, community service and philanthropy, and golf. She had played to a two handicap since college and the first floor of her home was practically littered with trophies and other testaments to the championship nature of her golf game. Ed had died three years earlier while piloting his private plane on a mission trip in Mexico; due to mechanical failure, the plane had crashed into the side of a mountain and Ed's body had never been recovered.

Elizabeth had never quite been the same since the loss of her beloved husband. She was a member of the generation that put sacrifice and marriage above all else, and that included ignoring the rumors, mostly substantiated, of Ed's wandering eye. To his credit, Ed never became involved, even in passing, with any woman in their social circle. He had the decency to keep his philandering a relatively private matter, and out of their own backyard—commendable, as many men weren't that discreet. Elizabeth was the kind of woman who assumed that this was something all men did, and there was no point throwing a hissy fit about it. For this reason, she had a hard time understanding why her own daughter would have ended a marriage to an otherwise perfectly nice man simply because of this one manageable issue. This was an unspoken—or at least mostly unspoken—argument between the two of them.

Since Ed's sudden passing, Elizabeth had found herself on the receiving end of the attentions of half a dozen or more Hillside Park millionaires and even billionaires, some of whom were married, some of whom were not, who offered to take her anywhere from dinner at the Mansion on Turtle Creek to fabulous faraway places.

Elizabeth had turned down all of these invitations. After forty-one years of marriage and putting up with one man, she was not about to begin putting up with another. She loved knowing she had the security and flexibility to make that decision.

"Children, go play," Amanda said. "I've got to talk to Gigi."

"Gigi" was a name Elizabeth had chosen for herself while Amanda was still pregnant with Will. She couldn't stand the thought of being stuck for life with one of those "old lady" sounding grandmother names, so she had quickly chosen her own. She worked hard at staying as beautiful as she'd always been famous for being, and Gigi was the only name that really fit her.

"Can I stay and listen?" Sarah asked. "I'll be quiet."

"That'll be a first," Will said with a sneer.

"That's enough," Amanda said firmly. "Will, I don't want you teasing your sister. And Sarah, no, you can't listen. This is a conversation for grown-ups."

"Awwww!" There was nothing better in Sarah's world than listening to a conversation between grown-ups. It was better than TV.

"If you're going back into the media room," Elizabeth told

her grandchildren in a tone that brooked no snappy comebacks, "you'd better keep your food and drinks off the furniture! You hear me?"

The children dutifully nodded and ran off toward the media room, which featured a wide-screen TV almost as large as a screen at the local multiplex.

"I just had the most bizarre day, Mom," Amanda said. "You got any coffee on?"

Elizabeth studied her daughter, ushering her toward the massive kitchen. "I might. You weren't gone more than a couple of hours. What happened?"

"What didn't happen?" Amanda said, shaking her head slightly as they reached the kitchen.

Elizabeth poured coffee. "Oh, by the way. A couple of your girlfriends called. They heard you were back in town and wanted to get together with you, take you to dinner. Nancy McRae and Diane Taylor."

Nancy and Diane. These were two of Amanda's friends from grade school. They had even come out to California to visit. They had both been dear friends and confidantes through the whole divorce struggle.

"I'd love to see them," Amanda said with a sigh. "I just need a couple of days to get my head on straight. There's so much insanity in my life right now."

"I'll put them off for a few days," her mother said, using her thumb to work out an impertinent smudge that had mysteriously appeared on the glossy granite countertop. "So what kind of insanity are you talking about?"

Amanda was extremely grateful for the opportunity to unload. "I stopped in at Hillside Park Presbyterian," she began, her voice rising at the end of the sentence as if she were asking a question, "just to look around? And the girls there in the Bible study—they were actually praying for me."

"They were praying for you?" Elizabeth poured two cups of coffee into the china pattern she had discovered on a business trip with Ed to Paris. "Did I ever tell you the story about how your father and I got this china out of the country?"

"Half a dozen times," Amanda answered. The last thing she wanted to do right now was to hear the story of how her parents had bribed a French official and given a box of Cuban cigars to a French customs officer to get this eighteenth-century coffee set out of a dusty, dingy museum and into their Dallas home. It was a great story, but not one that bore repeating right now, at least not in Amanda's mind.

"Somehow, somebody got ahold of everything going on in my life, and I couldn't believe it, but I swear those women were praying for me. I don't know how sincere it was, but they certainly did a great job of letting everybody in Hillside Park know all about my dirty laundry."

"Lettin' the cat outta the bag is a whole lot easier than puttin' it back in," Elizabeth quipped, adding unhelpfully, "You know, if you'd stayed married, they wouldn't have had anything to talk about." She leaned against the counter with her arms folded. "If I told you once, I told you a thousand times—never leave a provider."

Amanda rolled her eyes. "Thanks, Mom. I knew I could count on you for support."

"I'm sorry. I guess you and I are never going to see eye to eye on this whole thing. Is that all that happened? Some of the women were praying for you?"

"There's more. I was stepping out of the church and I looked across the street, over to where the Longhorn Ball offices are? And I saw Susie Caruth, in handcuffs. Two Hillside Park police officers were taking her away."

"That doesn't surprise me in the least," Elizabeth said matter-of-factly, picking an invisible speck of dust from her spotless white blouse before carrying the coffee cups to the huge kitchen table. "Did I ever tell you how your father and I brought this table back from Borneo?"

"Only one hundred times," Amanda said drily. Was her mother just as self-obsessed as always, or was Elizabeth starting to lose it? Amanda felt a chill as she envisioned a future in which her mother would tell her repeatedly of the origins of every stick of furniture in their homes here in Hillside Park and at the ranch. But then Amanda realized that's pretty much all her mother had talked about for the last twenty years. It would be pointless to fear she'd ever be diagnosed with Alzheimer's—little would change.

"I had a feeling they would have Susie arrested," Elizabeth said.

"What do you mean?" Amanda asked, surprised that her mother would find it so normal that one of the leading socialites was in police custody.

"You've been away," Elizabeth said, as if that represented some sort of mortal failing on Amanda's part. Amanda knew that her mother had never been happy that she had forsaken Dallas for the wilds of California. In some sense, Amanda suspected, Elizabeth believed that her daughter had gotten exactly what she deserved for making so rash a move.

"She practically single-handedly destroyed the entire Longhorn Ball," Elizabeth explained, sipping her coffee while keeping her back perfectly straight in the kitchen chair. "She ran that thing like it was her own personal fiefdom. She had committees, but she completely ignored everything they recommended. She just did everything her way, and she alienated practically everybody in the city. Nobody wanted to donate anything to the auctions. Nobody wanted to buy tables. Nobody wanted to underwrite the thing. She was so high-handed that a lot of people wanted to just quit the Longhorn Ball altogether."

"You're kidding. I always thought she was a little more level-headed than that."

"I don't know where you ever got that idea." Elizabeth acted as if it were common knowledge that Susie had always been a colossal pain in the ass. "Have you ever seen her order lunch? She makes waiters want to quit their jobs and go work in factories or something where they don't have to deal with the general public. And now she's dressing like she's somewhere in the Wild West. Special orders everything from catalogs. From catalogs! I mean, my God!"

"I know, the dreaded western-inspired-theme-dressing curse of the Longhorn Ball Chairwoman." Images of former Chairs paraded through Amanda's mind—women in alligator belts and python boots, women in leather halter tops who were too old or heavy to wear them, even women in regular dresses topped off with concho belts. She shivered at the thought. "But why did they have to have Susie arrested?"

"As I understand it, Susie got the idea in her head that she could stay on and run the Ball a second time, especially after she'd 'raised'"—Elizabeth used air quotes—"four point one million dollars. Heck, she didn't raise any four point one million. Sometimes she even says it's five million. I'm like, at least get your story straight.

"Her husband gave three and a half million, and there

were a few bucks in the till from the previous year. I don't think anybody gave a dime to the Longhorn Ball last year. Susie claimed she had commitments for major donations that never appeared. They had two parties a week—a Longhorn Ball record—mostly given by retailers. Normally the Longhorn Ball wouldn't have even accepted auction donations from most of these retailers, as they were hardly Longhorn Ball material. But she'd allow them to host a party in exchange for, say, a ten-thousand-dollar donation. They'd have the party and never send in their check, and Susie wouldn't pursue it."

Again, Amanda knew exactly what her mother was talking about. It's considered very smart marketing for high-end retailers to compete for what had been, prior to Susie's year, the few, coveted opportunities to host events for these groups, as these women were definitely their target market. It is considered an honor, almost a coup, to be granted this privilege, but it comes with an equally impressive price tag—usually in the form of a significant auction item, as well as the large cash donation. The two parties a week were excessive, but the worst thing was that many weren't the type of retailers they would've normally even asked for a silent auction item. When these lesser known, or worse yet, "pedestrian" type retailers would never send in their check after hosting a party, Susie was so irresponsible and unorganized, she wouldn't pursue it and still sent them their sponsorship packages complete with Ball tickets.

"She sold auction packages that she didn't have contracts for. Once the buyers had paid, she couldn't provide the goods or services because they were not officially procured donations. She was trying to curry favor with everyone from maître d's to retail salespeople, so she gave away more free passes than she sold Ball tickets. She then provided false figures of expected guests to everyone, including the valet parking company, the caterer, and even the company that provided those golf-tournament-style portable restrooms—all in hopes of saving a dollar or two. They ran out of food and drinks, the lines for the ladies' room were thirty minutes long, and it took forever to get your car. The outcome was a total disaster, as it embittered longtime supporters, sponsors, and vendors.

"Not to mention," Elizabeth went on, "that for the first time in Ball history, the Chairman was drunk, dancing on a table at the end of the night. You know the saying, the higher a monkey climbs up a tree, the more you see of its ass? She was hoping to clean up her mess by chairing a second year in a row. After all that, she had the audacity to think she could hang on to her position for another year. The nerve!"

"But I still don't understand why they had her arrested," Amanda said, taking a sip of her coffee. As self-absorbed as her mother was, it was just nice to be sitting in the kitchen of the house where she grew up, listening to gossip. At least it was gossip that wasn't about her, Amanda told herself. That was refreshing.

"The Ball committee took a vote," Elizabeth continued. "They passed a new rule that said that no individual could run the Ball two years in a row. They had to go to that extreme measure because Susie wouldn't have let go of that thing if they'd held a gun to her head. And then Susie hired lawyers, and I mean junkyard-dog lawyers—can you imagine, hiring lawyers to go up against the committee of the Longhorn Ball? This is supposed to be volunteer work. It was insane! And her lawyers actually took the thing to court, claiming that Susie was grandfathered into chairing it for a second year because the vote to pass that rule had been taken after she had already committed to running it again." Elizabeth smacked her palm against her forehead. "I swear, that girl. The engine's running, but nobody's been driving for God knows how many years."

Amanda grinned for what felt like the first time since she had left California. She hated to admit it, but it was satisfying to hear of another woman who had made a bigger mess of her life than she had. How encouraging.

"So what happened then?"

Elizabeth gave a disgusted look and had another sip of her coffee. "The committee hired lawyers of their own, and they got an injunction, or whatever you call it, against Susie staying on. They even had the locks changed, and when Susie wouldn't vacate the office, they got an injunction to get her thrown out of there, too. She wouldn't go, so the committee called in the police to get her out of there. I guess that's when you happened on the scene."

"I guess," Amanda said. "So who's going to run the Ball now?"

"Beats me. That Longhorn Ball is so messed up, I don't think you will find anyone who's willing to take it on."

"Oh, and that's not all," Amanda interjected, pleased and not feeling guilty to have a gossipy tidbit of her own. "You'll never guess who's working at Ann Anderson's office."

"Heather Sappington," her mother said, stealing her thunder.

"You knew that?"

"Of course I knew that," Elizabeth said indignantly. "Why would you think I wouldn't know that? Ann's mom and I have been friends forever."

"Why would Ann hire her?"

"I don't know," Elizabeth said, waving a hand dismissively. "Pity more than anything else. That girl just can't get a man to marry her. Propose, yes, but marry her, no."

"I don't even see what men see in her," Amanda said. "I don't mean to gossip—"

"Well, I do. That girl has quite a reputation for being wild. You know what they say about Heather, 'Bible in one hand, vodka bottle in the other.' Good men like women who are spiritual, but they can still be amused by a pro-series party girl. With Heather, they get both in one package. But I guess the package gets tiresome, because she gets as far as the engagement party, but she never makes it to the altar." Elizabeth rubbed at a dim spot on her china coffee cup and shook her head. "She may know how to work it," she added, "but she's about as pretty as homemade soap."

Amanda couldn't help but smile. "Is it true that she kept the rings from each of the men she's been engaged to?" she asked. It wasn't in her nature to inquire into other people's private business, but there was something so pleasant about sitting with her mom and chatting, having an amiable conversation for the first time in longer than Amanda could recall. *God'll forgive me, I hope,* she told herself.

"She cashed in the first couple of rings," Elizabeth said conspiratorially, "and I think she lived off the proceeds for a few years. Somehow she really gets guys to pony up when it's time to go to the jeweler."

Amanda nodded. "That rock on her finger I saw today was pretty incredible."

Elizabeth grinned. "You mean Ira?"

Both women laughed. "I've met Ira," Elizabeth said. "He's a pretty impressive guy, isn't he?"

"Yeah, but I swear, Mom, I'm not tryin' to be ugly— putting a ring like that on Heather's finger is like puttin' perfume on a pig! I mean, what are these guys thinking?"

"It's not ugly, it's true!"

They laughed again.

Then Elizabeth turned quiet, as if someone might be eaves-dropping. "You know she's got a problem with diet pills. She's always running off to some doctor or other to get another pre-scription. I hear she's got like six different doctors writing scrips. Of course, the fact that she drinks like a fish on top of the diet pills only adds color to all her reported 'episodes.'"

"I think she mentioned she had a doctor's appointment to-day," Amanda said with a nod. Suddenly she thought of some-thing off-topic. "Mom, that black Mercedes in the driveway—you didn't tell me you were thinking about a new car."

"I wasn't. It's actually for you." Elizabeth's tone betrayed a sense of wonder. "I wondered when we were going to get around to this subject. Is there something you'd like to tell me?"

"What? No! For me? What do you mean it's for me?"

"Some young man from the dealer came and dropped it off while you were out. Said it was a welcome-home gift for you."

Amanda's jaw dropped. "A Maybach? That's quite a welcome-home gift. Who could it possibly be from?" she murmured.

"There was a card," Elizabeth said, sauntering into the living room to get it.

Amanda sat there, amazed. A car? For me? A welcome-home gift? Her first thought was that her ex might have given it to her as a way of saying "no hard feelings," but that made no sense. There were plenty of hard feelings—enough to last a lifetime.

Coming back into the kitchen, Elizabeth handed her an envelope, which Amanda tore open. The card read: "I heard it would be a while before your car was shipped from California. Welcome home. Let's celebrate at Al's at 7:30."

The card was unsigned.

Elizabeth looked expectantly at Amanda, waiting for an explanation of the mystery suitor's identity.

Amanda shook her head slowly. "I didn't know that any-body even knew I was back in town. But after today's Bible study, I guess I shouldn't be surprised."

"Somebody out there knows and likes you," her mother said, her tone tart again. "And judging by that car outside, a lot."

"I guess."

"Looks like Gigi's going to be babysitting tonight," Elizabeth said, putting on a martyr's face.

"Looks like you are!" Amanda said, getting up to go back outside. She wanted to get a second look at that car.

⟡

## 5

So much to talk about, so little time. As soon as Heather had given Amanda the keys to her rental home and went to one of her six doctors to get a new prescription, she called Sharon Peavy, leader of the Bible study, and made plans to meet at the Starbucks at Hillside Park Village as soon as Heather could get off work.

They met at a quarter to five and ordered lattes, which sat before them at a table Sharon chose, right where the picture windows looked out on the Hillside Park Village parking lot. The Starbucks was beloved because it had such a magnificent view, from its floor-to-ceiling picture windows, of the entrance to the parking lot. That might not sound like much, and in fact, there was absolutely nothing scenic about it. But it did allow those sitting in Starbucks to gaze out on the cars coming in and out of the outdoor shopping mall, the oldest and most prestigious in Dallas with all the top-name boutiques, and see who was driving what, and with whom, and where. Indeed, the table Sharon had chosen was ground zero for Hillside Park gossip, because there were few things more interesting than who was driving, shopping, dining, or just simply hanging out with whom.

"Well, well. Guess who's back in town?" Heather asked quietly, scanning the coffee shop to see if there was anyone present whom she would not have wanted to hear her brand of talk.

"Mmmm, Amanda Vaughn," Sharon said, in the same conspiratorial low tones. "Oh, honey—I heard all about it at Bible study."

Heather reached for her latte. Then, realizing that the last thing she wanted was a two-hundred-degree beverage on a one-hundred-degree day, let it sit there. She spun the cardboard holder around the cup and bit her lip.

"I just gave her the keys to her house this afternoon," she said.

"Which house?"

"The Harrington place. Four bedrooms, fabulous kitchen looking out onto the family room/play area—"

"Solarium, media room, six thousand square feet," Sharon finished for her. "Mmm-hmm. I saw the listing."

Heather looked puzzled. "That's a five-million-dollar house!" she exclaimed. "No offense, but what are you doing looking at houses with that kind of price tag? You can't really afford it, can you?"

Suddenly she wondered if maybe Sharon had won the Texas lottery, or perhaps she had a new sugar daddy who could be persuaded, somehow, to give her the down payment on a new house. Maybe if he was real wealthy, high-profile, and married, she could wrangle him into buying the house for her in cash. For a moment, Heather's hopes rose about Sharon's potentially higher socioeconomic status. That would be a pretty nice commission for Heather.

But Sharon shook her head. "A girl can dream, can't she?"

she asked, a little embarrassed by just how much she knew about the Harrington property. She tapped her foot uneasily against the table's metal base and looked away. The house had sat on the market for eight months because its owner, Tom Harrington, had been a little too emotionally attached when setting the asking price. So few nice houses came on the market in Hillside Park that many buyers were happy to pay a premium just to live in the neighborhood—it was that desirable. But Tom's timing had been poor, and he had slapped that luxury premium on the asking price just at the point when the market was starting to head south.

Sharon knew about the house for another reason. In her mind, Tom Harrington represented perfection in a man. He was wealthy, he was kind, he was a great husband by all accounts, he was very good-looking, and when he stood on his wallet, he was ten feet tall. She had always had a thing for him.

Not everyone was as impressed with Tom Harrington as Sharon and Heather, however. Years ago, when everyone had just been out of college a few years, Tom made a business investment with the friend of a friend. They seemed like nice enough people—they were horse people, after all—but it turned out that they were involved with much more than just horses. It seems their business, Pegasus Horse Transport, became well-known for flying more than just horses. Tom and his partners were rumored to be huge drug traffickers and had earned themselves the nickname "The Cowboy Mafia." When it was discovered there was more to their business, people immediately began to defend Tom, saying he had no idea any of that was going on and if he had, he would've never tolerated it. He hadn't been involved in the day-to-day operations and rarely, if ever, made the quarterly meetings—he would often just conference in. But many others weren't so quick to let him off the hook. If he didn't know what was going on, he was just as guilty because he should've been more involved, then. Eventually, there were many arrests made and Tom was never even questioned, much less considered a person of interest, but to this day, many people questioned whether or not he was aware of what was happening at Pegasus. In a neighborhood as conservative as Hillside Park, anything drug-related isn't easily forgotten.

Heather nodded sympathetically.

"Did you see Amanda?" Sharon asked. "How does she look?"

"She looked amazing," Heather said, shaking her head slightly, as if she couldn't believe it, as if she was horrified by the thought of it all. "You'd think that somebody who had been through the kind of traumatic stuff she's been through would look like hell. But she looked incredible. Thin, fit, beautiful, perfectly dressed—just drop-dead gorgeous. No wonder they say all the boys in high school used to call her 'hell in high heels.'"

Sharon nodded slowly, digesting the bad news that Amanda looked great, and sadly remembering those painful high school days.

"Oh, perfect. That's all we need," she said, dejected, "another attractive single woman here in Hillside Park. This one's potentially the most dangerous of all. It's not like she started out like the rest of us." She furiously smoothed out the wrinkles in her hand-me-down Givenchy skirt. "It kills me to think she's gonna end up just jumping from lily pad to lily pad."

"She's not exactly single," Heather said helpfully, testing the temperature of her latte again. Still too hot to consider drinking.

Why she had ordered latte on a hot day like this, she had no idea. She didn't even like lattes. But they just sounded so sophisticated. And besides, everybody knew lattes had fewer calories. "She's still technically married."

"Sure, darlin', but not for long," Sharon said, staring out the window at a Bentley she did not recognize. "Who's that?" Surely there wasn't a man who drove a Bentley in this neighborhood that she didn't know.

Heather followed her gaze. She studied the car and looked at the license plate, hoping for a clue. It was a Texas vanity plate that read "TH"—something. She couldn't catch the rest of it as the car blew past.

The women quietly chorused the initials to themselves, trying to conjure up an identity to go along with the letters.

"Oh, oh! Tom Harrington," Heather suddenly exclaimed. "That's the guy whose house Amanda rented. He developed half of Mexico, you know."

"Mmm. I sure wish he'd hurry and get around to the other half," Sharon cracked. Then, on a more serious note, "Is he still married?"

"Yup," Heather replied. She patted her dry lips and debated whether to apply more lip gloss.

"But is he happy?" Sharon asked sarcastically.

"Unfortunately. By all accounts."

They both laughed hysterically at their own wittiness.

Sharon nodded philosophically as her fingers tapped out a frustrated rhythm on the plastic cup lid. "Too bad. I've always had a thing for him. But what about Amanda? I mean, she does have two children."

Heather frowned. "A boy and girl," she said. "But nobody

old enough to be interested in her is going to be scared off by the idea of kids. And I hear they're really nice kids."

Sharon nodded her agreement. It was too bad—if only Amanda's son were the type that you were inclined to ask "And what prison will you be going to one day, young man?" as opposed to "What college are you planning to attend?" or, if her daughter were the type that it was impossible to predict until the last minute whether she was going to turn out to be a pole dancer or CEO, well, that might scare off a suitor or two. It always helps when the new, hot divorcée in the neighborhood is known to have children who act like they've been raised by wolves.

"After Bible study," Sharon began, "I went out for coffee with a bunch of the girls, and although they were being very polite about it, you could tell that even the married ones were none too happy about Amanda being back in town. Most of their husbands had huge crushes on Amanda through high school. They're afraid their husbands are fixin' to jump on the bandwagon, or at least fantasize about life without them."

"You really think there's going to be a ton of men interested in Amanda—married or otherwise?" Heather knew the answer was definitely yes.

Sharon waved a hand in the air. "Why not? She's got the whole package. She's gorgeous, she's rich, she's available, and she's got time for a relationship because she doesn't have to work and her children are old enough to be in school all day."

Heather stiffened, pressing her lips together.

"I didn't mean that as an insult, honey," Sharon said, quickly taking Heather's hand. "I have to work, too, you know."

Heather rolled her eyes, as if to say, "Forget it, let's just move on."

"But even the best marriages are cyclical," Sharon continued. "People go through ups and downs—good times and bad. A wife isn't always emotionally available to her husband. At a time like that, even in a good marriage, a good man might be interested in getting his emotional needs met elsewhere. Not to mention his physical needs."

"Where'd you get all that?" Heather asked, surprised at the wisdom of her friend's psychological observations.

"Dr. Phil," Sharon admitted. "But you have to admit it makes sense."

"It does at that . . . that it does."

They lapsed into silence, both thinking about Dr. Phil. Now, that would be a real catch, if he ever came on the market. And he does spend a lot of time in Dallas, Sharon thought to herself. He may be married, but is he happy?

"Don't you think she'd be too traumatized by what happened in her marriage," Heather mused, "to start thinking about getting involved with another man right away?"

"You'd think so," Sharon said brightly, fussing with the sleeves of her blouse. "I hear Bill was an absolute serial adulterer. I hear he was a huge player and got his DNA all over half the women in Southern California."

Heather studied Sharon. "Weren't you and Amanda best friends when you were growing up?"

"Oh, we'll always be close and very dear to each other. I just say that out of love and concern for Amanda. There's a difference between nosy and concerned," Sharon concluded, feigning sincerity.

"I thought so," Heather said. "Anyway, even if she were

traumatized, we can't really count on her to stay traumatized for too long. And then what? She's just going to take attention away from every available single woman here in Hillside Park."

"And maybe from, some of the unavailable women too." They chuckled.

"Did you hear about Susie?" Heather asked, changing the subject.

Sharon's eyes went wide. "I heard she was arrested, if that's what you mean."

"She sure had it coming, you know," Heather said, squeezing more gooey gloss onto her lips. "After the way she pretty much declared herself Chairwoman for life of the Longhorn Ball. I can't believe how shortsighted she was."

"Who's going to run the Ball now?" Sharon asked. "I can't imagine anybody who'd want to go anywhere near the damn thing, it's so messed up. After Susie, the finances are so twisted, it would take a T. Boone Pickens to save that ship."

Heather nodded. "Normally, it's a full-time job for the Ball Chair, just lining everything up—the entertainment, the donations for the auction, underwriting, and coordinating with the committee chairs. It's gonna be a minimum eighty-hour workweek every week, just to undo the damage Susie did."

"I can't imagine anybody wanting that job now," Sharon pondered. "You're right—it's a full-time job under the best circumstances, but you'd have no time for anything else all year after this mess."

"It's too bad Amanda couldn't be Chair of the Longhorn Ball," Heather said jokingly. "That would certainly take her off the social circuit. She wouldn't even have time to think about dating, let alone be able to keep a man's interest."

"That would be a great solution," Sharon agreed. "Keep

Amanda all tied up with the Longhorn Ball. Between that and her children, you're right. She wouldn't pose a threat to anybody."

The women sat in silence for a long while, thinking about how wonderful it would be if Amanda had the distraction of the Longhorn Ball to keep her from developing a social life.

"Wait a minute," Sharon exclaimed after a few minutes. She stopped tapping her fingers and laid both hands flat on the table. "Who says she can't be the Chair of the Longhorn Ball? She's still a member, isn't she?"

Heather thought for a moment. "We've gotta find out," she said, sitting up straight in her chair. "If she's been on inactive status this whole time, she could certainly go active and Chair the Ball."

"We need to get our hands on a member directory. All the members are listed."

"There's one in my office!" Heather said, triumphant. "All the best real estate offices have a copy. Let's go!"

"I think we might have just solved a major problem!" Sharon said, smiling. They quickly left Starbucks, dashing across the parking lot toward Ann Anderson's office. They ran past the surprised receptionist down to Heather's cubicle. Flipping through stacks of paper—Heather was a "keeper" who tended to hold on to every piece of paper or document with which she came into contact—she found a copy of the Ball directory. Excitedly, with Sharon peeking over her shoulder, she paged to the back, where the names of all the inactive members were listed. There was Amanda's name.

The women looked at each other and grinned. "Problem solved," they chorused.

"But how do we get her to do it?" Heather asked, glancing

at her watch. She had an after-hours appointment with a doc-in-the-box for another prescription of diet pills.

"Hmmm. You sure this is such a good idea?" Sharon asked, sounding doubtful for the first time.

"It's an awesome idea," Heather replied confidently. "But let's think for a minute. How can we get her to say yes?"

# 6

✦

At a quarter to seven that evening, Elizabeth came downstairs from her bedroom and found, to her great surprise, Amanda making hamburgers for the children, who were watching music videos in the living room.

"You're still here!" Elizabeth exclaimed. Amanda glanced at her, as if to say, "You got that right." Elizabeth eyed her daughter, who was wearing the same outfit as earlier in the day.

"Surely you're not going to Al's dressed like that?" she asked, putting her hands on her hips in emphasis of her surprise and disapproval over her daughter's wardrobe choice.

Amanda said nothing, continuing to focus her attention on dinner for the children.

"Don't you realize what time it is? If you're getting to the restaurant on time, or even fashionably late, you better get moving."

"I'm not going," Amanda said quietly, aware of the fact that her decision would set off shock, even outrage, in her mother's mind.

Predictably, Elizabeth exploded. "Are you crazy?" Her voice was loud enough for both children to hear.

Will and Sarah glanced up from the television screen.

Will had little interest in a brewing argument between his mother and grandmother, but Sarah was all ears. Quietly, she crept from the living room couch where she had been sitting to the doorway leading into the kitchen, hoping to eavesdrop.

"Young lady," Elizabeth continued, in a tone of voice that instantly reminded Amanda of how happy she had been to leave Dallas with Bill; it brought back the hundreds of run-ins she had had with her mother while growing up. "Do you realize what an opportunity this is? Somebody obviously thinks the world of you! Somebody—and we don't know who it is—is clearly very financially secure and is clearly very interested in you! And you're not even going to bother?"

"Mom, not in front of the children," Amanda replied wearily. She peeked around the kitchen doorway into the living room, where Sarah stood, listening attentively, not surprising her mother.

"Okay, guys, why don't you watch in the media room until your grandmother and I have had . . . had a chance to talk?"

Will gave a resigned, uncaring look. "Whatever," he muttered, turning off the TV and ambling out of the room. His sister gave her mother a pleading look, begging permission to stay for the fireworks, but Amanda would have none of it.

"Hit the trail, young lady," Amanda heard herself saying, a phrase that her mother had said to her countless times. That was alarming.

Reluctantly, Sarah tore herself away from the controversy and followed her brother to the media room.

Now that the children were out of earshot, at least in theory, Elizabeth cut loose. "Are you insane?" she hissed. "A guy sends you a car—a Mercedes—a black Maybach, your favorite color for a car, and you won't even go meet him to say thank you? Is that how I raised you?"

Amanda, about to respond, first marveled at the way her mother could globalize an issue, turning it from simply a matter under discussion into a referendum on her entire career as a parent. She checked on her hamburgers before she spoke. The last thing she wanted was to get into an argument with her mother, especially about her personal life. She knew it would be only a few moments before the subject would turn from the mysterious suitor with the black Mercedes to why she left Bill in the first place.

"Mom," she finally said quietly, "doesn't it seem a little over-the-top to you to give somebody a three-hundred-thousand-dollar car as a way of inviting them out to dinner?"

Her mother shook her head. "When your father was trying to get my attention, he used to fly me in a helicopter, which he landed at Vanderbilt Stadium, on the fifty-yard line, to take me to dinner with him in Knoxville, where he was working on a project. I was just a college student, but that's how he did it." Elizabeth angrily plucked a crumb off the kitchen table and tossed it into the trash can. "What's wrong with a man trying to impress you or show you how interested he is?"

"If he's so interested," Amanda countered, immediately regretting that she was getting drawn into a discussion she did not want to have, "why is he so interested in keeping his identity a mystery?"

"You can spend a lot of time trying to figure out how men think, and you'll always be wrong. That's because they're so much simpler than we are. They don't think half the time. They just want what they want and then they go for it. And this guy obviously wants you."

"This is too strange," Amanda said, genuinely perplexed. "Unless he's been going to women's Bible study, he has no idea what's going on in my life. And even if he did, who would want a woman coming off a divorce with two children and a crazy ex-husband? Who'd want to get involved with someone like that?"

"Maybe he doesn't want to get involved. Maybe he just wants to . . . spend some time with you." She smiled and winked at her daughter.

Amanda shrugged as she flipped the hamburgers. "If you want to spend time with a woman, you can generally do that for a lot less than the price of a Maybach. Appearances can be deceiving. I think we've all learned that the hard way." She gave her mother that knowing look.

"That's just negative thinking," Elizabeth replied, her tone dismissive. "I'll finish the hamburgers. Just throw something on, do something with your face and hair, and get your butt on over there." A crafty smile suddenly broke out on her face. "Unless you're just playing hard to get."

"I'm not playing, and I can't be gotten," Amanda said flatly. "I've got no interest in this guy, or any other guy. I just want to get my life back together. Why is that so hard for you to understand?"

Elizabeth's smile slowly faded as she realized that her daughter truly wasn't going out to meet the mysterious car-giver, whoever he might be.

"You don't have to have dinner with the guy," Elizabeth said, exasperated, making one last run at getting her daughter to rethink her position. "Just have a drink. Thank him for the car. See who it is. Aren't you dying to find out?"

"Honestly, Mother, no," Amanda said, sliding the burgers off the grill and onto buns. "I don't even want to know who it is. I just don't want anything to do with the whole subject of men right now."

"Well, you'll have to start thinking about it eventually," Elizabeth said. "It's not like you're getting any younger," she continued, unwilling to quit. "And, who knows, by the time you decide you are ready, this great catch could be long gone."

Amanda was incredulous. By her mother's standards, all a man needed to qualify as a great catch was that he could afford to give away a Maybach!

"That may be, but who says it has to be tonight? I'm moving in the morning—assuming that truck shows up. Don't you think I've got enough on my mind without starting a social life? I'm not even legally divorced."

"In this town, that's never stopped anybody."

"Mom, I'm not going, and that's that. And the car is going back to the dealership in the morning. I don't need anybody's charity."

"I'm not talking about charity—" Elizabeth began, but Amanda cut her off.

"I seriously can't believe you," she said heatedly. "My whole life, I've listened to you and your friends gossip about women who accepted or even solicited extravagant gifts from men. You always deemed it inappropriate to accept certain gifts from any man who wasn't your husband.

"Whether it was over-the-top jewelry, boob jobs, furs, cars, homes—whatever—you used to say there was a name for girls like that, and it wasn't 'sweetheart.' I remember when Nancy McRae was engaged to, what was his name . . . Derek Tarver. And he bought her a new Mercedes as a wedding gift, but he gave it to her a month before the wedding. And when she called the wedding off at the last minute, her daddy called Derek to ask what he'd paid for that car and then he sent him a check. You and all your friends hailed that as the right thing to do!

"Now you want me to accept a car even more expensive than that from a complete stranger? I don't understand what has happened to you since Dad died. You would have never encouraged this behavior before."

Elizabeth's eyes widened. "Stay out of my damn business! And are you kidding? You're not keeping the car?" she asked, stunned.

"Why should I?" Amanda asked, going to the refrigerator and taking out a head of lettuce and a couple of tomatoes for a salad. "I don't even like sedans. I like the SUV I'm driving right now. Even if it is a gas guzzler," she added, mostly to herself. "In Newport Beach you'd have thought I was a heretic for not having a hybrid."

"Trade it in," Elizabeth implored. "An SUV's a lot cheaper than the car he gave you, so you could make a few bucks on the deal."

"Mom, I'm not looking to make a few bucks."

"Well, between the trust your daddy gave you and other investments he made on your behalf, plus the fact that you're certainly going to make enough off your divorce, it's not exactly like you're unwilling to take money from a man."

For Amanda, that did it. "Okay, that's it, Mom. I've had it! This discussion is over! I don't need this aggravation from you! It's not like you didn't inherit a ton of money from *your* father and you never worked a day in your life while you were married to Dad!! And we're talking about my father and my soon-to-be ex-husband here—this guy's just some random stranger with an inappropriate way of showing he has a crush on me! I don't know who gave me that car. I don't care who gave me that car. I'm not trading it in for an SUV, and what I do in my private life is none of your damned business."

A thin smile played at the corner of Elizabeth's lips. She had gotten to her daughter, which, in some ways, was her whole point in having this conversation.

"You sure you're not going?" she asked, knowing exactly what the answer would be.

"Of course I'm not going," Amanda said, tired of the whole discussion.

"Well," Elizabeth said mischievously, "I am." She scooped the Maybach keys off the kitchen table, picked up her purse, and marched out of the kitchen.

"Mom, you most certainly are not! And not in his car!" Then Amanda saw Sarah, who had crept back into the living room and who had obviously overheard the entire conversation.

"Sarah, didn't I ask you for a moment with your grandmother?" she asked her daughter, irritated.

Then, to the receding figure of her mother, "Mom, don't you dare go!"

"Try and stop me," Elizabeth said with a laugh. She was out the front door before Amanda could move.

A moment later, Sarah, Will—who had wandered into the living room to see what all the commotion was about—and Amanda heard the sound of the Mercedes engine starting up. They looked out the window. Elizabeth was on her way. As sweet Mimi used to say, "If the people who love us didn't love us when we were bad, nobody would ever love us." She had to have been referring to her own daughter.

✦

## 7

At eight o'clock that evening, Sharon Peavy and Heather Sappington arrived at the doorstep of Darlene Cockburn, widely considered one of the most powerful women in Hillside Park. At sixty-seven, Darlene had changed husbands over the previous three decades approximately as many times as the United States had changed presidents, and, just as many Americans had little good to say about their succession of presidents, neither Darlene nor people in her social circle had all that much good to say about her various husbands.

The best thing that Darlene, or anyone, could say about her first four husbands was that they either died (the first and the third), or were deported because of tax and fraud matters (number two), or went to prison (number four). Before their demise, disappearance, or loss of freedom, each had managed to enrich Darlene's personal fortune by anywhere from tens to hundreds of millions of dollars, giving her the financial wherewithal to become one of the community's leading philanthropists and power brokers. A word from Darlene was all it took for an individual to become socially prominent or a social pariah.

Her fifth husband, a retired admiral with a background in engineering, maintained a separate residence in Fairfax,

Virginia, close to his lobbying interests, his fox-hunting farm, and a wide variety of mistresses, whom Darlene monitored by means of various private security agencies, with the thoroughness and at times the ruthlessness of the KGB.

Darlene knew at all times what her husband was doing and, for that matter, whom her husband was doing. She stored all this information in a file in a wall safe in her living room, behind a Matisse abandoned by the husband who had been deported. He had been an art collector of note before most of his collection was seized by U.S. Treasury agents in partial satisfaction of a tax debt—and it didn't help that he was in the country illegally, of course. Darlene considered the documentary material in the wall safe a retirement plan that more than offset the prenuptial agreement husband number five had made her sign, although she had need of one worse than he did. The home was a 1930s stone Normandy Tudor with arched stone walls and an entry foyer leading to a main foyer and then to an expansive living room with an eight-foot-high wood-burning fireplace. Another fireplace, almost as high, dominated the vast dining room. The kitchen and the adjacent full-service butler's pantry were enormous, very catering friendly, and looked as though they had the capacity to feed a small army. The floor-to-ceiling bookshelves on two of the living room walls—complete with removable staircase on a rack—contained thousands upon thousands of books, none of which had ever been opened. They were strictly for show, of course.

"Are you sure this is a good idea?" Sharon, sounding shaky, asked Heather as they lurked on Darlene's porch.

"Making Amanda Chair of the Longhorn Ball? I think it's a fabulous idea. Don't you?" Heather responded.

Sharon, still harboring a measure of doubt, rang the doorbell. A moment later, a liveried manservant, a hot, blond-haired young man in his late twenties, opened the door. Recognizing the ladies, he ushered them in.

"Miss Darlene is upstairs," he said, pointing them toward the cavernous living room filled with incredibly valuable, and incredibly uncomfortable, eighteenth-century French furniture. "I'll let her know you're here."

The women seated themselves on silk-covered sofas and waited. Heather crossed her legs, which was somewhat difficult in her skin-tight dress. Sharon tapped her foot against Darlene's absurdly expensive antique rug. She still had misgivings about the whole thing.

"This is nuts!" she finally exclaimed. "What if she does a good job? Then everybody'll love her. Not just the men."

Heather shook her head. "No, no. It's impossible. Susie screwed up that Longhorn Ball to the point where nobody will walk away from that thing in one piece. Not only will Amanda be jammed from sunup to sundown, she'll get complete credit for the thing failing for a second year in a row. It will be an absolute wrist-slitting experience for her, and it might completely do her in. Not that we really want to, like, kill her," she added quickly. "Still, on the heels of her other recent failures—it's brilliant." They heard a noise on the stairs. "Okay, here's Darlene. We've got to sell her on this!"

Darlene Cockburn flitted down the plantation-like grand staircase robed in Oscar de la Renta's finest, a flowing cerulean shantung dress. There was something dramatic and yet earthy about Darlene, as if she understood that her whole over-the-top house, five marriages, and vast fortune were all somehow part of a grand private joke that only you and she shared. She was nobody's idea of beautiful, and her addiction to cosmetic surgery had made her eyes look like she was in a catatonic state, her lips looked like a baboon's ass, and her breast augmentation had been so overdone, she looked like there was a butt on her chest.

In Dallas, plastic surgery is considered nothing more than good grooming. Women who don't have the funds to have a little work done now and then, or those whose need for surgery is so great that their tabs at the surgeon might resemble the national debt, are considered the "unfortunates." Those girls were forced to play it off like they don't understand why women do those things. They pretend to be superconfident in their looks, acting as if they don't feel the need for surgery. Everyone jokes about the fun-house mirrors the unfortunates must have in their homes—the ones that tell them how beautiful they are, although compared to the ones with a maintenance budget, they're virtually invisible. Most Hillside Park women managed to stay in the well-maintained, aging-well zone. The opposite extremes—the unfortunates and the over-fortunates— were, fortunately, few and far between, but Darlene was definitely one of them.

Despite Darlene's overdone face, there was something undeniably sexy about her, even at age sixty-seven, and if her ex-admiral husband ever decided to remain permanently in Virginia with his harem of spied-upon girlfriends, neither Darlene nor any other woman in town doubted that she would very quickly line up husband number six.

"To what . . . do I owe the unequivocal pleasure?" she asked in her studiously breathy voice, which most people referred to as her "Sunday school voice." Darlene had a way of melding words together to invent her own language, while punctuating her speech with arduous breaths and silences.

She wafted into the room on Alexander McQueen stilettos with pencil-thin heels. Immersed as she was in perfecting her ethereal entrance, she narrowly avoided missing the final step. Undaunted, she glanced at her guests to make sure that they were sufficiently impressed with their surroundings—which, to be fair, they were—air kissed them both, and seated herself on a yellow divan.

"Good Lord, Darlene. You're more beautiful than ever," Heather gushed. Flattery had definitely always gotten Heather everywhere.

"Mmm-hmm," Sharon concurred, fidgeting with her faux Hermès bracelet.

"We both know that better not be true," Darlene said, casting a majestic smile on her subjects. "But as you know . . ." She exhaled deeply for one of her dramatic pauses. "I do so love to hear the expression of it, however erronical."

Away from Darlene, Sharon liked to tell other women that Darlene's vocabulary and syntax made her sound as if she were trying out for a road company of *Cat on a Hot Tin Roof*, but there was something so endearing about Darlene's affectations that, as the expression went, even people who didn't like her . . . liked her. Not everybody could pull off the five husbands, the house, and the liveried houseman—and rumors involving him and Darlene were rampant—but somehow, she did. Her many husbands were always age appropriate—but when it came to trainers, chefs, and house managers, she was a regular cougar.

"Darlene, you know Amanda Vaughn is back in town," Heather stated.

Darlene nodded. "So I've heard. And I also heard that somebody gave her a brand-new Maybach," she noted with a breathy sigh, extending an arm as if she were introducing a famed performer on the red carpet. "As a welcome-home gift, or a 'please, date me first' gift. As of yet, we haven't quite decided."

"You're kidding!" Sharon was beside herself with jealousy. "A Maybach? Who in their right mind would do a thing like that?"

Heather swallowed hard. A man with his mind already set on Amanda, she thought. This was just the kind of thing she had been afraid of. Men were already competing for Amanda's affection, and she hadn't even moved into her rental home.

"How . . . how does she get men to do that?" Heather asked, amazed. "I've never had a guy buy me a car."

Sharon threw her a patronizing look. "I've had guys get me cars," she said, a trace of pride in her voice.

"Yeah," Heather cracked, "and you had to spend more time in the backseat than in the driver's seat in order to keep it."

"That's not true," Sharon replied, stung. Then she smiled. "Look, if a gentleman opens a car door for you, the least you can do is get in. Whether it's the front seat or the backseat. Right, girls?"

They all snickered.

Then Heather became earnest, getting down to business. "But that's exactly why we're here. Amanda just got here. If a guy is already buying her a Mercedes, where's it going to stop? I mean, there are so many great girls in this town who are having a hard enough time finding someone. If the men're all gonna be focused on Amanda to the exclusion of all other women, what are the rest of us supposed to do?"

"Well," Darlene replied, stroking the edge of the divan, "what can you do about it? She's young, she's pretty, she looks great—"

"Have you seen her?" Heather asked, surprised. "How do you know all that?"

"I've heard it from a cavalcadium of different people," Darlene wheezed, making a sweeping gesture with her hand to indicate her vast social network. "She looks fantastic, none the worse for wear, considering what she's been through. I'd have presumed that, after a nasty divorce, she'd come plodding back into town looking rougher than a night in jail." Darlene chuckled at her clever use of cowboy slang before growing serious again. "But au contraire, mon petite amours." She sighed, unaware that she had just addressed her two guests as lovers. "Sounds like she's managed just fine."

"Mmm-hmm. That's exactly what we're talking about," Sharon said, pressing her fingertips tensely against her thighs. "If she's already doing so well without even trying, what's it gonna be like once she's back to feeling like her old self again?"

"Wait a minute, girls . . . hold on," Darlene said. "She won't be interested in a relationship for a while. She's just been through a horrifically ugly situation and an even uglier divorce. Maybe she's gonna want to stay on the sidelines for a while. Regroup. Put herself back together emotionally, instead of just . . . throwing herself into another relationship."

"I don't remember you ever doing anything like that," Heather noted tartly.

"That's true, darlin'," Darlene replied with a grin, "but not everybody is like me. Some gals can stand those empty-bed blues."

"Where's Rick?" Sharon asked, remembering her manners. "Virginia?"

"Alas, my dear . . . Rick was number four," Darlene gently corrected. "Greg is number five. And yes, he's up in Virginia.

What he's doing is his business. And what I do . . . is mine."
She shot a wicked glance toward her manservant, who, embarrassed, quickly looked away. The exchange was not lost on either guest.

"We have an idea for Miss Amanda," Heather said.

"But I don't think it's a great idea," Sharon said, backpedaling. "I think we're just borrowing trouble."

"Sharon!" Heather said, annoyed. "We agreed we were gonna present a united front."

"What is this all about?" Darlene asked, very much amused. "What are you two plotting, and what is it that you can't agree on doing to Amanda?" She threw her hands out and held them at an awkward angle, waiting for a response.

Heather cleared her throat. It was now or never. "We thought that maybe, maybe Amanda should be, ought to be . . ." She swallowed hard. "The next Chair of the Longhorn Ball."

Darlene looked puzzled. "What?" she asked, in a booming vibrato that belied her usual studied breathiness. "She hasn't lived in Dallas in ages! How would she know whom to ask for what and why?"

"Mmm," Sharon said, trying to follow Darlene's muddled syntax. "That's just the point—she wouldn't know what to do."

"Exactly!" Heather exclaimed. "It's a full-time job anyway. And this year, whoever takes over has to dig out from the mess Susie made. And then on top of that, since Amanda's a total outsider at this point, it'll take her even more time to figure out who's who and what's what in Hillside Park these days. It's just perfect."

"Perfect for what?" Darlene asked, not getting it. "What exactly is to be gained by putting Amanda in charge of the Longhorn Ball? Judging from the way you two are talking about this . . . mendaciousative scheme," she intoned, silently congratulating herself on such an excellent word choice, "it sounds as if you want to cast a net of troubles in her wake, not give her social life a boost."

"Oh, it's a boost, all right," Heather said quickly. "Let me explain. If she's Ball Chair, especially this year, when there's such a messy mess to clean up, it's gonna take every working minute of every working day. Sharon and I were thinking that there's no way Amanda would have time for a social life on top of raising her kids, fighting Bill in court, and running the Ball, blah-blah-blah. And if she doesn't have time for a social life, then men'll quit showing up at her doorstep with new cars or jewelry or airline tickets or who knows what else they'll throw at her, just to get a little attention from her. It's the best way to keep her occupied and unavailable, don't you think?"

Darlene looked lost in thought, then finally nodded. "I sure wish I had thought of a similar strategy back when I was married to Sidney," she said, referring to hubby number two. "If he'd been distracted with something, maybe some charitable thing, he wouldn't have had time to get all mixed up in that tax shelter thing, whatever it was. He was cute. Crooked as a dog's hind leg, and a convicted felon to boot . . ." Darlene paused to heave a laborious sigh. ". . . but cute. Whenever Greg neglects me, which is eighty-five percent of the time, I always have half a mind to just get on a plane and go down to Costa Rica and see how Sidney's doing."

"How is he doing?" Sharon asked. "Still single?"

"He's in jail in Costa Rica, actually," Darlene said in an even voice, "for drug smuggling. And the only visitation he gets is through a pane of glass. So unless you want to talk to him on a telephone with that glass between the two of you, you may want to find a different man, precious."

"Touché," Sharon conceded.

"That's all that remains of her French major at SMU," Heather cracked.

"That was uncalled for!"

"Well, girls," Darlene said, breaking up the squabble, "I think the two of you have an excellent idea. Keep her busy enough with the Ball, and she won't have time for men. I've never let my philanthropic endeavors interfere with the pursuit of my romantic life, but I might be a little bit different."

"Oh, I think we'd all have to agree," Sharon said, grinning, "you're a little bit different, all right."

Darlene stood and nodded humbly toward her guests, pressing her palms together in a display of perfect piety. "You must permit me to make a few phone calls," she said. Heather and Sharon took their cue and stood to go. "I can't make any promises, but I will see what I am able to arrange," Darlene continued. "I find the idea very appealing. A threat to one woman is a threat to all of us. I like Amanda, but she's got to be neutralized, and what better way than by being Chair of the Ball? And it's not like anybody else is dying to do it, right?"

The three women shared a conspiratorial laugh.

"Roland, see these ladies to the door," Darlene commanded, gesticulating with such grandiose vigor that she smacked him soundly on the chest as he approached. Roland grimaced. Darlene, completely unaware, turned to him with a devilish smile. "And then draw my bath, will you?"

She gave Sharon and Heather a knowing wink.

Sharon and Heather winked back, and Roland saw them

out. On the doorstep once again, Heather turned to Sharon. "I think we've solved our problem."

"I don't know." Sharon seemed dubious. "I think we may be creating more problems than we're solving." She paused, then spoke in a whisper. "You think she's really sleeping with her manservant, or butler, or whatever you call him?"

Heather flashed her a wicked grin. "Um . . . wouldn't you?"

# 8

### ✦

Amanda was sitting in the guest room of her mother's home around nine forty-five, watching an old Humphrey Bogart movie but not really paying attention to it, when her mother finally came back from the restaurant. Amanda had had a tough time getting Will to bed—he had let loose with a long string of angry objections to the move back to Dallas, the divorce, and the fact that he wouldn't be able to see his father quite as often. Amanda's heart was broken for her children, and they remained her biggest concern.

Eventually, she had gleaned from her son's angry monologue that there was a girl in the middle of this, some little surfer girl Will had become very smitten with, and an additional source of the boy's anger was the fact that he had been cut off from her. It's amazing how quickly a relationship can seem like oxygen, Amanda thought as she listened to her son, and it was just as amazing how quickly you could suffocate on the $CO_2$ a bad relationship produced.

"Are you still up?" Elizabeth asked as she came in.

"Barely," Amanda admitted. "How was my date?"

"A no-show, just like you," Elizabeth replied, glancing at the screen. "He's no Humphrey Bogart, I'll tell you that."

"He didn't show?" Amanda asked, surprised. She sat up a bit on the chaise longue.

"That's what I'm telling you," Elizabeth answered, sinking down into the other chaise and watching the screen. "Neither of you showed up for your first date. You guys think alike, so I guess it's a pretty good sign you're made for each other."

Amanda thought for a moment. "How could you be sure that he never came if you don't know who you were looking for?"

"I might not have known who I was looking for," Elizabeth reasoned, "but I sure knew *what* I was looking for. Single white male, forty to sixty years of age, affluent by the look of his clothes, positioned at a discreet angle to the front door so that he could see who was or was not coming into the restaurant."

"Sounds like half the men in Dallas on a Saturday night," Amanda noted with a grin.

Her mother thought about that for a moment and nodded. "Good point. A lotta guys out there lookin' for somethin', but I don't think it's love."

They shared a laugh, the first break in the tension between the two women since Amanda had come home two days earlier.

"I know I've been kind of mean to you," Elizabeth said.

Amanda sat up a little straighter. "What are you talking about?"

"When I was sitting in the restaurant . . ." Elizabeth began. "Actually, I need to be very frank with you. I had a little bit of time to think. And a couple glasses of wine to help me think. And I realized I've been furious with you and haven't masked it very well, ever since you came home."

"There's a shocker," Amanda replied sarcastically. "I've been thinking, what did I do to deserve this?"

"You didn't do anything. It's me. I haven't been angry at you. I've been angry at myself."

"What are you talking about, Mom?" The Bogart movie went into commercials, so Amanda hit the mute button.

"Your husband did the same stuff mine did. I can't even believe I'm talking to you like this. My own daughter."

Amanda waited. This was a level of openness from her mother she had never seen before.

"Well, we're all adults here," Elizabeth went on. "My husband had the same wandering eye Bill does. But I tolerated it. And I really hated myself for it. It just seemed like the deal that a lot of us made back then. You marry a guy, and he provides you with this great lifestyle. Which I already had, but still. I guess you can never have enough.

"And then what does he do? He figures he can mess around with any girl, or all the girls he wants, because he's earned the right. And the more money he makes, the bigger his right to go screw anyone and anything. Single women, married women, airline stewardesses, secretaries, babysitters or nannies, knotholes in elm trees, whatever. You know what I'm saying?"

Amanda nodded slowly.

"It's disgusting, when you think about it," Elizabeth continued. "I mean, it's not quite prostitution on our part—okay, on my part—because I'm not providing sex for money. It's kind of reverse prostitution—he's providing money so that he can go off and have sex with whoever he wants, whenever he wants. I never thought about it that way, but that's what it comes down to. It's what my mother always told me. Never leave a provider."

"I guess that's kind of how it is," Amanda agreed. She didn't know what was more surprising to her—the fact that her mother was being so open with her, or the fact that her mother was making so much sense. Both were new experiences for her.

"Mom, I always kind of knew Dad was . . . well, not exactly faithful to you. Let's just say I always knew Daddy was 'a hard dog to keep under the porch,' as the old saying goes. But I never thought I'd marry the same kind of man; although, Bill is far worse than Daddy ever was . . . At least I hope Daddy wasn't as bad."

"It's a shame," Elizabeth said. "But it seems like too many women in Hillside Park tolerate it at some point in their marriages. I mean, I know there are a lot of husbands who are faithful, don't get me wrong, but maybe those guys are faithful because they're just not that interested in sex. I know there's a difference in surviving an affair and saving your marriage, which I'm all for and think you should try to do, but that's completely different from what I'm talking about. Of course, there are some men who really can walk the line. I've just never known many of them. Or known many women married to them. It's just . . . endemic."

"Endemic?" Amanda repeated, surprised. She'd never heard her mother use that word before.

"I'm not as dumb as I let on to be," Elizabeth said. "I like it when people underestimate me. I can get away with a little more that way. I guess that's how I've gone through life. But I think I really underestimated myself. I think I deserved more than a man who basically cheated on me my entire life. But it's not something I felt like I could ever afford to let myself think about.

"It's just one of those thoughts that comes into your head

and then you do everything you can to think of something else. And then you move back home, because you won't accept that same life with Bill that I had accepted with Ed, well, it just did me in. It just got me thinking. And then all of a sudden here comes Mr. Black Mercedes and it doesn't even dawn on you to go out and see who it is, even just for sport. I mean, it would have been the perfect opportunity for you to just do something—have a fling, take a weekend in Mexico with him—"

Amanda's eyebrows went up. This was definitely a level of intimacy she had never experienced with her mother, and she wasn't entirely sure she was comfortable with it. But here it was, so she just had to deal with it. "Or maybe God was putting him in your life so that you wouldn't be another forty-something, lonely divorcée, chasing after what available men there are here in Hillside Park like the rest of them. At least I had the dignity to get out of the game when Ed died. But I tell you, there's no dignity in the way these women chase these men or compromise themselves to maintain a certain lifestyle. Believe me, your dignity is something you just might need later.

"And the men know it, and that's why they feel no need to make a true commitment. You didn't do that. You wouldn't even go to the restaurant and see who it was. And I really believe you're not even going to keep that car. Am I right?"

"You're right," Amanda said softly. She was amazed—her mother was actually honoring her for a choice she had made. That was something different. On the other hand, maybe she had grown up a little bit out in California, away from the stifling confines of Hillside Park. Maybe her choices were a little more honorable than they might have been in the past, when she had done exactly as she pleased, with whom she pleased, when she pleased—which is why her relationship with her mother had never been that great to begin with.

"I just think what you did tonight . . ." Elizabeth said, leaning slightly toward Amanda, just enough that Amanda could smell the alcohol on her mother's breath. "I thought it was really cool. You're tough as a boot, kiddo. And you quitting Bill because of the way he was sleeping around on you? I wish I'd have had the courage to do what you've done when I was your age. I don't know what we would have done as a family, but it probably wouldn't have mattered, because your father was away so much anyway. But at least I wouldn't have been putting up with all that dishonesty and deceit, playing that charade of the perfect Hillside Park family, knowing that that fool husband of mine was doing some stewardess in Barcelona or Houston or wherever the hell he was."

"Mom," Amanda said gently, a bit embarrassed for her mother by now, "don't you think maybe you ought to get to bed?"

Her mother thought for a moment.

"I'll tell you what I think," she began, and Amanda braced herself—her mother had been telling her what she was thinking for the last ten minutes, and it was more honesty than the two of them had shared in the last twenty years. It was almost more than Amanda could bear.

"I believe he was sitting in his own car, the whole time, waiting to see if you would show up. Because anybody who's got the kind of money—no, that's not true. Tons of men who have that same kind of money wouldn't think twice about plopping themselves down at the bar at Al's, waiting to see what the selection of ladies will be on the menu this evening. So that's not what he did. He was too cool for that.

"Anybody who drops off a hundred-thousand-dollar car—I

don't even know how much it costs. Two hundred thousand? Three hundred thousand? I'm old-school. It's hard to imagine anybody paying that much money for a car. But still. It was an incredible gesture on his part to give you the car, and it was even more impressive that he didn't sit in plain view in the restaurant, flirting with all the other women in the bar until you came in, like many men in this town would have done."

"Mom," Amanda said, shocked to hear such talk from her mother. But then, her mother had always been a pretty straight-shooting woman, and she probably talked this way with her friends. The only difference was that now she was sharing her innermost feelings with her daughter.

"I'm okay," Elizabeth said, waving a hand. "I know, you're shocked to hear Mommy talking like this. But we're all adults. You can take it. I've been angry at you these last couple of days, but the reality is that I've been really angry at me. For living that lie. I don't know where you got the gumption to stand up for yourself, but I admire you for it. And I wish I'd had it, too."

"You were hardly the only one, Mom. Dad was definitely the rule back then, not the exception. A guy really had it all—a beautiful wife, wonderful family, awesome career with great financial success, multiple homes, expensive cars, and, oh yeah, a rockin' mistress on the side that everyone knew was his, to discourage any possible legitimate suitors. So many of them did it in Dad's time, and some still do; they just aren't as arrogant about it."

They were silent for a moment. "You're really gonna return that car?" Elizabeth asked finally.

Amanda bit her lip. She said nothing.

"You're not gonna trade it in for an SUV? You could, you

know. And you'd get a bunch of cash back, too. I'm sure Mr. Black Mercedes wouldn't mind, whoever he is."

"I can buy my own SUV, Mom," Amanda said quietly.

Elizabeth nodded admiringly. "You're a good girl, Amanda," she said, yawning. "This heat just wipes me out completely." She pointed at the wide-screen. "Movie's back on. I like Bogart. Not that I would have liked being married to him. It would've been a part-time job. Well, maybe I would have. Why don't you put the sound back on?"

Amanda glanced over at her mother, awestruck by the direction the conversation had taken. She actually felt relieved to put the sound back on; the conversation had been a little too revealing for her comfort level. And yet, it was the kind of talk she had always dreamt of having with her mother. She hit the mute button and the raspy voice of Humphrey Bogart returned. A moment later, Amanda saw that her mother had fallen asleep and was snoring like a bear.

Amanda watched the rest of the movie, secretly wishing she had a bucket of popcorn with lots and lots of butter. Forget SoCal tofu—if there were ever a time in her life for Orville Redenbacher, this was it. What a day, Amanda thought, letting out an exhausted yawn as the film credits rolled across the screen.

# 9

✦

Sharon Peavy knew she was not the perfect woman. She knew she was moody, insecure, flawed, and hard to stay in a relationship with, or at least that was the feedback she had gotten from men over the years. But she had read enough self-help books and been to enough relationship seminars to know that she was lovable just the way she was, and that if one man said no, there would always be another man coming up quickly behind him to say yes—so she'd been told.

But the older she got, the longer the dry spells between men seemed to be. Sharon was well known as a "covert competitor." The stories were legendary. She was the type that was always competing with someone for someone or something, but her opponent was never aware they were anything but the dearest of friends. When women who've never had to play that game encounter someone like Sharon, they end up hurt, deceived, and betrayed, but walk away from the experience just being very grateful they've never had to hone those skills and that they weren't the type to have to try and make someone else look bad in order to try and make themselves look good. But Sharon had perfected this long ago and was truly a master of the game.

She was also self-evolved enough to know that her attractiveness to men wasn't entirely spiritual, and that they were not drawn solely to that tiny kernel of lovability that she possessed. She knew that a lot of men were interested in her simply because, in addition to all her other fine points—a great sense of humor, an adventuresome nature, and pretty eyes—she had absolutely, positively perfect boobs. Some said she had the very best rack in Dallas.

The truth was they weren't store-bought, they didn't need an assist from a Miracle Bra, and they had never been surgically enhanced. They were naturally, absolutely perfect, and she was exceedingly proud of the fact that it was common knowledge they felt real. At the gym, on the rare occasions when she went there, she frequently saw women in their twenties glancing admiringly and curiously at her, and she would look right back at them. Those girls might have been ten or fifteen years younger, but they had nothing on Sharon Peavy—or so she had convinced herself.

She was also one of those women who would be the first to complain about how she hated it when men wouldn't look her in the face because they were too busy staring at her chest, but she dressed to show it off anyway. So when Sharon needed something—companionship, attention, affirmation, or information—she knew that all she had to do was show some cleavage and the world was hers. Most men would say that Sharon had a great body and a face to guard it with. Most women just considered her hard-looking. One particularly disenchanted suitor had told his buddies that without makeup, Sharon looked rougher than a truck stop waitress. But even he couldn't deny that she had a great body.

And she knew it could get her places. As she arrived at the

Mercedes dealership the morning after her and Heather's chat with Darlene, Sharon wore a revealing, scoop-necked electric-blue Dolce & Gabbana top she had "borrowed" from a Hillside Park friend. She didn't want to buy a car—she was determined to find out who the gentleman was who had bought Amanda her car.

She parked her four-year-old BMW, a gift a boyfriend had given her in a fit of perfect-body-inspired generosity, power-walked across the parking lot, and approached the first sales-man she could find and asked for a manager.

"Dean," the salesman said, "she needs your help."

With his eyes focused squarely on Sharon's chest, Dean dropped his jaw. He found himself unable to speak for a moment.

"She doesn't need anything," he finally said. "She's perfect the way she is." And then to Sharon, brightly, "How may I help you, ma'am?"

"I'm from the head Mercedes office in Stuttgart," Sharon said authoritatively. "Could we talk in your office for a moment, please?"

Dean blinked several times, trying to reconcile the idea that this most attractive woman had anything to do with the head office.

"I left all my business cards on the plane," Sharon lied. Somehow the comment galvanized the still-awestruck Dean into action.

"Right this way, ma'am," he said, leading her past the long-ing glances of the other car salesmen to his private office.

Once seated, Sharon thought about doing the Sharon Stone "crossing and uncrossing of legs" thing, but Dean was obviously already so flustered that that might have sent him over the edge.

"How are—how are things in Stuttgart?" he asked.

"Great." Sharon tried to think for a moment about how things really were in Stuttgart. She'd never been, but she'd once dated a German. In her time, she'd covered most of the categories. Her German ex had been scrupulously hygienic, and come to think of it, he had pitched a fit about the dangers of air pollution.

"Smoggy," she added as an afterthought. "Very smoggy. Especially this time of year."

Dean nodded knowingly, as if intimately familiar with the subject of seasonal smog in Stuttgart. "We have that same problem here in Dallas, ma'am," he said, groping for common ground.

"Mmm, I'm sure you do," Sharon murmured. Then she got to the point. "Well, I'm sure you're wondering what I'm doing here. Basically, Stuttgart sends me around to all the dealerships as kind of a secret shopper, but not really."

Dean struggled both to simultaneously follow what she was saying and keep his eyes off her chest, neither of those an easy task. "Well, I'm not really a secret shopper, in the sense that I'm not shopping for a car." Sharon's explanation served only to pitch Dean into a greater state of confusion and despair.

"What I'm trying to say is . . ." Sharon started to think that maybe she should have come up with a simpler story. ". . . Is that I'm supposed to look at a random transaction y'all have completed in the last twenty-four hours? And just make sure everything was up to the standards that we at Mercedes try to instill in our dealerships." Dean and Sharon exchanged a look of great relief—Sharon delighted that she had actually gotten her story straight, and Dean grateful because he finally understood, at least on some level, what she was talking about.

"You just want to make sure that we're satisfying our customers," he said, translating Sharon-speak into something that he could understand and explain to himself.

Sharon brightened. "That's it exactly!"

"Um, sure. We've delivered about a hundred cars this week—I could get you all the QED reports you want, or phone numbers of the customers, or anything."

"We've chosen at random," Sharon said, going back to her story, emboldened by the success she had already achieved, "for our study a black Maybach. And we're trying to focus specifically on black Maybachs that have been delivered to residential customers in the last twenty-four hours. Do you have any vehicles like that that might have been delivered in the last twenty-four hours?" She tried to sound professional.

Dean was flustered, fantasizing so heavily about taking Sharon into a dark corner of the repair shop that he could barely remember the question. "Um, I'm sure we have. . . . I'm not really in charge of the deliveries. But I could make a phone call for you. I could find out exactly that information, ma'am, if you'd give me a moment to make that call."

Sharon smiled, angling herself at Dean in such a way that he found it truly impossible to keep his mind on his business.

He swallowed hard. "Ma'am, let me just get Yolanda on the phone, and I can get you that information," he said, his voice starting to crack like an adolescent boy's.

Sharon smiled primly. Unbelievable, she thought, this is actually working.

Dean reached for his phone, misdialed, misdialed a second time, then waited a moment as the phone rang on the other end.

"Is Yolanda there?"

Short pause.

"Could you find her, please? This is Dean. I've got a quality-control person from Mercedes of Stuttgart here in my office, and we've got a quick question for her." Long pause.

Dean glanced at Sharon, and then for safety's sake, restricted his gaze to the calendar in the blotter on his desk.

"Yolanda! I'm sitting here with—I'm sorry, your name was?"

Sharon came up short. She hadn't even thought of a name to give. If she gave her real name, someone in the dealership might recognize it. After all, she *was* "somebody" in Dallas. She rapidly looked around the office for something to clue her in and noticed all the "Top Sales" awards on Dean's walls.

"Sharon . . . Sales," she said as convincingly as she could.

Dean nodded. "Like I said, I'm sitting here with Sharon Sales? Of the Stuttgart office? She's a QC specialist and she wants to know if we've delivered any black Maybachs in the last twenty-four hours."

"I need to see the paperwork," Sharon said.

"She needs to see the paperwork," Dean repeated, then listened.

He put his hand over the mouthpiece and turned to Sharon. "We delivered two black Maybachs yesterday—one to downtown Dallas and one to a residence in Hillside Park. Do you want the paperwork on both?"

Sharon thought quickly. She tried to make it sound as random as possible when she spoke. "What if we just did . . . the home delivery one in . . . what was that neighborhood you mentioned? Hillside Park?"

"It's one of the nicer neighborhoods here in town. It's just over Brookshier Road."

"That would be ideal," Sharon agreed.

Dean smiled with relief. It was just too much to be sitting alone in his office, even though it was a glass-walled office, with Sharon Sales from Stuttgart. Mercedes was known for springing quality-control experts on its dealerships, but the combination of sex and power that Sharon exuded was just too much for Dean.

"Thank you," he told Yolanda. "She'll be right there."

"I'll take you back to Yolanda's office," he told Sharon as he hung up, relieved to move her down the line.

Sharon, however, wasn't relieved; she didn't want to carry her charade to another person. "I don't understand," she said, confused. "Can't you get the records for me? I just need to see the bill of sale."

"It's a different department," Dean explained apologetically. "You know how it is. We just sell 'em. Yolanda's group does all the record-keeping associated with delivery, warranties, the rest of it. I'm sure it's the same in every dealership."

"Oh, of course." Sharon nodded rapidly, as if she had the slightest idea what she was talking about.

"Right this way, then, Ms. Sales," Dean said, standing up to escort her out of his office and then down the hall.

Sharon followed, disappointed. Who was this Yolanda, anyway? Was she going to buy the idea that she was Sharon Sales from the Stuttgart office?

"That's Yolanda right there," Dean said, opening an office

door and pointing. He gave her a little wave. "Yolanda, this is Sharon . . . Sales. She's the QC from Stuttgart. Well, good luck, and safe travels." He then got himself out of there as quickly as he could.

"Um, hi," Sharon said in her most professional voice— which wasn't all that professional, even she had to admit. "I'm Sharon Sales? From the Dallas office? I mean, from the Stuttgart office?"

Yolanda did not stand to greet her guest. Yolanda, a no-nonsense Latina born and raised in San Antonio, had little use for the self-important Dallas women who breezed into the dealership, bristling with impatience, ill-concealed racism, and stacks of their husbands' hard-earned cash. To her practiced eye, Sharon looked like just one more Hillside Park wannabe.

"I left my business cards on the plane," Sharon explained, flustered by Yolanda's steely gaze.

"No doubt," Yolanda said, not giving anything away. Sharon broke eye contact then, noticing that Yolanda's blouse scooped even lower than her own. Great.

"I won't be but a minute of your time," she said, trying to sound as professional as ever. "I'm from—"

"Stuttgart," Yolanda said, her tone dripping with disbelief. "You want to see the bill of sale for the black Maybach we delivered to a residence in Hillside Park yesterday. Is that correct?"

Sharon, uncertain about what to do with herself since she had not been invited to sit down, gave a nervous nod.

"I'm sorry," Yolanda said after checking her records. She put her elbows on her desk. "The car was purchased anonymously for cash. There is no name on the bill of sale. Do you still want to see it?" Her tone challenged Sharon's entire sense of authority. Sharon, flustered, felt what little control she had over the situation rapidly ebbing away.

"I—I don't know," she stammered. "For cash? With no name?"

"And in any event," Yolanda replied, eager to put this conversation to an abrupt end, "the transaction has been rescinded. The car was returned to the dealership earlier this morning. Would you like to see the car? I can assure you there was nothing wrong with it."

"That—that won't be necessary," Sharon averred, backtracking slightly.

"Did you say your name was Sharon . . . Sales?" Yolanda asked, making a note on a yellow pad.

"Yes, b-but . . . I'd better go now."

"I think that's probably a good idea," Yolanda agreed, studying Sharon's whole game, which she had to admit, was remarkable. "Let me guess. You're checking up on your husband because you think he bought his girlfriend a Mercedes. Is that correct?"

Yolanda fixed her steady, terrifying gaze on Sharon, who was speechless.

"I wouldn't worry about it," Yolanda told her. "I'm sure you'll be able to get another husband in no time. Have a nice day, Ms. Sales."

Sharon meekly backed out of the office and practically ran out of the dealership, clicking her Dior heels on the highly polished showroom floor and nearly tripping as she ran. Once back in the safety of her gently aging BMW, she slammed the driver door. "Shit!" she yelled as loud as she could. Fortunately, she was out of sight and earshot of Dean, Yolanda, or anyone else at the Mercedes dealership.

Sharon yanked her cell phone out of her purse and called Heather.

"What's up?" Heather said, bypassing "hello" or any other greeting.

"The guy bought it for cash," Sharon said angrily. "And she returned the car! She didn't even keep it. Now we'll never know who bought it." Silence.

"Shit," Heather finally said.

"You got that right." Sharon was furious that Yolanda had figured her out. If only Dean could have gotten the information. "I'm late for work. This is so screwed up."

"I know you're disappointed you didn't get the 411, honey. But this will make you feel better. Guess who the next chair of the Longhorn Ball is gonna be?"

"Amanda Vaughn?" Sharon's mood quickly turned around.

"Shush-shush. Mum's the word for now," Heather said. "But it's all been cleared by the powers that be. We just have to get her to say yes."

"Awesome! Well, it's safe to say we just ruined her whole next year."

"Don't worry about the car thing," Heather said.

"What car thing?" Sharon answered, her unhappy visit with Yolanda already receding into foggy memory. "She's not gonna have time for anything anymore. She's gonna be way too buried with the Ball."

"Call me later. We need a plan. That guy really, like, paid cash for the car? And she returned it?"

"Right on both counts."

"I can't believe it! What is she thinking?" Heather asked. "I have to say that Amanda's got a little more backbone than we thought. I kind of can't help admiring her." There was a long pause. "But I mean, we'll take her down," she added quickly. "Not to worry."

"I'm not worried in the least," Sharon said. In a much better frame of mind now, she clicked off the call, folded the phone back into her purse, started up the Beemer, and happily headed to work.

# 10

✦

This house sucks!" Will pronounced in his angriest voice as Amanda did her best to direct the movers to unload the furniture into their new home. It was another sweltering, humid afternoon, and between the stress of trying to figure out where to put stuff while contemplating her new life and dealing with her belligerent son, Amanda felt at the breaking point.

"Will," she said wearily, "for the hundredth time, please don't use that word. It's just so inappropriate."

"It's totally appropriate!" he said with a snarl. "It's exactly how I feel, and it's exactly the truth, which makes it appropriate, and you know it!"

Amanda glanced around the house. Okay, so it was only six thousand square feet, and it looked out on a view of other, equally large homes, instead of twelve thousand square feet looking out on the Pacific. She felt a pang of guilt that her son's sense of values could be so skewed. Granted, she had grown up in a house larger than the Harrington home they were renting, but her values were pretty down to earth. Where exactly did Will get his attitude about life, so deeply rooted in entitlement? That's not how kids were when she was growing up. But then she thought, maybe they were and she just never realized it. Who knows how these things happen. Still, she couldn't help but think her son's outbursts were way out of line.

"Where does this box go?" one of the movers asked, and Amanda sighed, staring at it and trying to decide exactly what its contents might be. She had been in such a hurry to pack and move that she had neglected to label many of the boxes. Dozens of brown boxes, with who knew what inside them, littered the living room floor. She shook her head. It would take months to unpack everything, and then after a year or two they would move on, so she'd have to go through the whole process all over again. Next time she'd hire a service instead of trying to do it all with her housekeepers. On the other hand, next time she wouldn't be running from her ex-husband, desperate to start a new life for herself back home and put the past behind her.

"Just put it in the living room with all the others," she said, resigned to her fate of spending an endless stretch of days trying to turn boxes and boxes of possessions into something approaching a normal home for her family.

"Can I go swimming?" Sarah asked cheerfully. "I love our new pool!"

Leave it to my daughter to find something good in all this, Amanda thought. "Of course, honey," she said. "Will, you can go with her if you want."

"I don't want to go swimming, Mom," he said, scowling. "I'm just gonna skateboard on the front steps. Our landlord should've put in a skateboarding ramp instead of that dumb pool."

"Will," Amanda said, trying to mask the exasperation she felt, "the movers are trying to use those steps for the boxes and the furniture."

"Well, then, maybe they can find another entrance," Will replied testily. "I live here, not them."

Just at that moment, a Jaguar pulled up to the house. From it emerged Heather, who had been driving, holding a beautiful flower arrangement, and Sharon, holding a large object covered in tinfoil.

Amanda scratched her head, trying to figure out why the two women were coming to visit right now.

"We're the welcome wagon!" Heather sang out, prancing up the sidewalk in an outlet mall Calvin Klein sheath that clung to her narrow hips. She had taken a couple of extra diet pills and was a little more wired than usual, which was saying something.

"We baked you a pie, darlin'!" Sharon added as she moved boldly toward her former best friend, having sufficiently recovered from the debacle in Yolanda's office to regain her usual cheery state.

"Yum-yum," Heather said, patting her stomach and then frowning by force of habit. "We just wanted to say welcome home. We want it to feel like you never left."

"That's so sweet," Amanda said, touched and yet suspicious, then immediately upset with herself for feeling that way. Why couldn't she just accept a nice gesture at face value? Maybe, she thought, because Sharon had been leading the Bible study where she had been prayed for—or was it preyed upon?

"I seem to remember you having a fondness for chocolate pecan pie," Sharon said. "I know my grandmother's was your favorite. I've attached her recipe."

Amanda had to laugh at the fact that Sharon was so clueless, she didn't even get it that most people hoped the famous Peavy family recipe would've long since been forgotten. The story of Sharon's grandmother and her now famous chocolate pecan pie was a legend in the neighborhood. It was said that Grandmother Peavy's pie was so good that the recipe was not only jealously guarded, but coveted. Very few received the recipe, and those who did paid a tremendous price—and never in dollars. Grandmother Peavy gave out the recipe only as a last resort, when she wanted a favor from someone or wanted to influence someone's thinking. Over the years, she'd shared it with no more than half a dozen people, and always with the stipulation that the recipient had to cross her heart and promise to never share it with another. They all went to Hillside Park Presbyterian together, so the provision was easy to enforce. For years, recipe recipients marveled that no matter how hard they tried, or how often they made it, no one could ever seem to quite master the recipe like Grandmother Peavy. It was truly a phenomenon, and many attributed her luck with her being blessed for all her good deeds. For many, many years, she taught Sunday school, volunteered in the nursery for the early service once a month, and helped out in the pastor's office once a week. She was almost a saint. So, of course, no one could justify disclosing the secret recipe. One year, in an attempt to "honor" her grandmother, Sharon snuck a copy of the famous pie recipe and submitted it for publication in the much-anticipated church cookbook. You can imagine the shock that ensued when it was discovered by comparing the recipes that the original called for real butter, not margarine, and one-half cup more sugar than the version Grandmother Peavy had given out over the years.

Oddly, when these same lucky people followed the new cookbook version, it tasted exactly the same as Grandmother Peavy's. Poor old Mrs. Peavy had a heart attack and died just days after the cookbook came out. Though everyone had a different theory regarding Sharon's true intentions, to her credit she had wept throughout her grandmother's entire funeral service. In fact, it was the last time anyone remembered having seen Sharon Peavy cry. Amanda grinned. She hadn't had a slice of chocolate pecan pie in her entire sojourn in California, and it was her favorite. She accepted it graciously.

"That's really so sweet of you, Sharon. Thank you. How have you been, anyway?"

"I've been fine, honey. You know how it is. This, that, and the other. I don't know why I never picked up the phone and called you all that time you were out West."

"Phones work both ways," Amanda admitted sheepishly. "I could've called you."

"Let's not be strangers," Sharon said. "You're here, you're back, your children are here, and I just want to be close again. I can't see why it can't be like you never left."

Amanda nodded. On one level, it really felt as if she had never left. The heat, the humidity, the homes—all that was the same. Even Sharon strutting around half-dressed all the time. She had been the same way in high school. When you've got it, flaunt it, I guess, Amanda thought.

"What a beautiful home!" Heather gushed, and Sharon nodded in agreement.

"We're really lucky it was available," Amanda said. "It's just a couple blocks from my mom's, so I can keep an eye on her, and she can see her grandchildren easily. A lot more easily than getting on a plane to Southern California."

"We missed you!" Sharon exclaimed. Amanda couldn't tell whether she was being sincere or not. Then she thought of one of her ex-husband's favorite sayings—that the hardest thing in the world to demonstrate is sincerity. Once you can fake that, you've got it made. And she asked herself again, Why am I being so suspicious of these women?

"Would you look at all this stuff," Sharon said, looking around at the mess. "I guess you'll be unpacking those boxes for a long time, mmm?"

"I know. I feel like I'll be unpacking forever."

Sharon felt that old familiar jealousy for Amanda raising its ugly head again. How could two people who were so close end up so differently in life? Sharon hadn't made such poor choices. She was always a victim of circumstance. And look at Amanda. Those beautiful children, this home, these beautiful things everywhere. If Sharon were to ever get lucky enough to move from her aunt's house, all she'd need is a friend with an SUV willing to make two trips.

"I can't believe how busy I am," Amanda said, rolling her eyes. "Between taking care of the children and getting these boxes sorted away, I don't think I'm gonna have time for anything else. Not for a long time, anyway." Heather and Sharon exchanged glances, and Heather cleared her throat.

"Actually, Amanda," she said, "there is something we wanted to talk with you about. Is this a bad time?"

Amanda shrugged. "It's about as good as any. I may get distracted every so often if a mover needs to ask me where to put something, but otherwise, I'm all yours. What's up?"

"It's the Longhorn Ball," Heather said.

"What about it?" A mover held up an unmarked carton for Amanda's consideration. "Beats me. Put it anywhere. Living room, I guess."

The mover nodded and continued up the stairs, barely missing contact with Will and his skateboard.

"Will," Amanda said, raising her voice, "could you please find somewhere else to skateboard right now? Why don't you skate over to Gigi's place and watch a video?" That was one of the great things about the neighborhood—you could still feel comfortable sending your children off by themselves, as long as it was within Hillside Park. Amanda had never felt safe sending her children anywhere around Newport Beach, because there was so much traffic zipping around, and also because everybody just seemed so crazy. At least compared to Hillside Park, anyway. Although who knows, Amanda thought—maybe they're just as crazy here, too. Maybe they just feel more of a need to hide it here, unlike in California, where you can be as crazy as you want and nobody seems to care one way or the other.

"We were talking about the Longhorn Ball," Heather said, a trace of impatience in her voice. She wished she'd remembered to reapply her lip gloss. Those diet pills always left her feeling parched and dry.

"Oh, of course," Amanda said wearily. "It's just too much to keep track of, between the children and the boxes and the furniture. Okay. What about the Ball?"

"We're wondering if you'd be interested in taking more of an active role," Sharon said delicately. "We know you've been an inactive member all these years."

Amanda thought for a moment, then shook her head. "I'd love to, but I don't see how. At least not this year. I've got so much going on right now, what with the children and the house. I think I'd better stay inactive. I don't even know anybody anymore. I wouldn't even know who to ask for what. You know what I mean?"

"Sure, sure. We know what you mean," Heather said, dig-

ging in. This was obviously going to be a harder sell than either she or Sharon had anticipated.

"We were thinking," Sharon began, choosing her words
carefully, "about the fact that, well, you know the Longhorn
Ball is in shambles right now."

Amanda bit her lip. "I know that something happened yesterday with Susie," she said, wanting to walk the fine line between staying out of other people's business and satisfying her
curiosity about what had happened. With everything going on
in her life—the mysterious black Mercedes, the unexpected
heart-to-heart with her mother, Will's anger, and the business
of the move—she had forgotten all about Susie.

"Poor Susie," Sharon said, making a clucking sound.

"I tell you what," Heather said. "I think the chief of police
of Hillside Park is going to be looking for a new job."

"A new career, you mean," Sharon said with a snort. "And
not in law enforcement. I think Edward Caruth is gonna make
sure he never gets near another badge or gun anywhere in the
fifty states."

"Uh-huh," Heather agreed. "Anyway, Susie's okay. But she
definitely left everybody in Hillside Park with a bad taste in
their mouths about the whole Longhorn Ball. So the question
is . . . how do you get the Ball back to where it was?"

"I wouldn't know. I've been out of the loop for so long,"
Amanda said.

"Well, the way you make anything better," Heather said,
answering her own question, "is with great people. It takes
great people to restore a great institution . . . to . . . greatness.
Right?"

"Right," Sharon chimed in, although she sounded a little
less convinced, to Amanda's ear, than Heather.

"Where's all this going, ladies?" Amanda asked warily. "If you'd like me to write a check, I'll be happy to. But I don't—"

"Let me cut to the chase," Heather interrupted. "We all love, love Susie. She made a lot of money—made, collected, extorted—who really knows? But she left dead bodies everywhere. She messed everything up, and now the whole thing's just . . . a disaster! I heard from some of the girls in the office that all the records of donations from previous years are lost. The Pediatric Foundation's madder than heck at us, even though we gave them more money than ever. They may not even want to be associated with us anymore. So there's a lot of fence-mending that needs to be done. And the question is, who's best to take on a job like that? Who's got credibility with everybody in Hillside Park—all the businessmen, all the wives, all the corporate interests? Who hasn't been tarnished by this whole thing?"

"Everybody in town is so disgusted with Susie," Sharon added, "because of her high-handed attitude. Just about everybody involved with the whole thing is saying, 'I don't want anything to do with it.' Somebody's got to take on the responsibility of making sure that one of the most important events on the Dallas social calendar, not to mention one of the most important philanthropic events in the city of Dallas, doesn't dry up and disappear."

"Somebody who's solid and level-headed," Heather said. "Somebody who's been away from town for a while, and therefore didn't get caught up in the whole crazy thing with Susie. Someone who is an insider and grew up in Hillside Park, and knows how *we* do things here, but someone who isn't tainted by what went on last year."

"'We,' Heather?" Amanda had to laugh at her undeserved

ownership of the neighborhood. Suddenly it dawned on Amanda what they were asking her to take on.

"You want me," she began slowly, "to be Chair of the Longhorn Ball?"

There was a smash in the background, and Amanda yelled to Will, "For goodness' sake, Will! You nearly knocked over that mover! Okay, that's it! I've had it! If I have to ask you one more time to stay out of these people's way, you're gonna be grounded until Jesus comes again, and I mean it!"

Her son glared at her. Heather studied her carefully. Sharon toyed anxiously with her flashy Pomellato ring, trying in vain to spin it around a pinky that had swelled from the heat.

Amanda shook her head. "I can't do it. I can't even begin to express how honored I am that you would ask, what with my being back in town just a couple of days and everything. But surely there have to be dozens of more qualified people than myself. I don't know anyone anymore. I don't know who runs what business. My ex-husband didn't do business in Dallas. Thank God for that. But still. In fact, I can't think of anybody less qualified to run the thing than me. Even if I had the time, which I don't. I just have to say no."

Heather and Sharon glanced at each other. They were expecting a rejection on the first ask, and, veteran salespeople that they were, they knew that selling only began when the customer said no. Someone once told Heather that she was such a good saleswoman, she could talk anyone into anything. Considering her natural expertise, she wasn't too worried about Amanda Vaughn.

"For thirty-three years," Heather began, in a speech that she had prepared, and in tones so ringing you could almost hear background music as she spoke, "the Longhorn Ball has been, like, the most important philanthropic event for the women of Dallas. We've raised close to forty million dollars for pediatric care and scientific research. I know we've improved the quality of life for many. You're very fortunate in that you've got two healthy children right here. But you and I both know that we've seen a lot of people go through a world, just a world of pain—"

Amanda put her hand up.

"You're killing me over here!" she exclaimed, laughing. "I know the Ball does a ton of good work, and I feel the same way you do. I'd hate to see it go away. But I just don't have the time or the mental energy right now. I'm honored that you asked, but you're going to have to ask someone else. I don't even know if I'll have time to serve on a committee, let alone be Chair. Especially in a year where there's so much damage control and repair to do. I have enough of that in my personal life, as I discovered in Bible study yesterday."

Now it was Sharon's turn. They figured if the "sick children" thing didn't get to Amanda, they'd have to try an alternate route.

"There's another reason to think about doing it," Sharon said, leveling her shoulders and ignoring as best she could the fact that Amanda had given them a big, fat, flat-out no. "You're just getting reestablished here in Hillside Park. It's tough. It's got to be lonely. I'm gonna fess up and tell you the truth. A lot of women know you from growing up here—a lot have moved in and established themselves since you left and don't know you at all. Some are gonna perceive you as a threat, because you're pretty and you're young and you've got your own money— you're quite the catch, and you're the newest single girl in the neighborhood. And this would just be a great way for you to show people here in Hillside Park that you're here to contribute. You're not after anybody's husband, you're not after anybody's boyfriend, you're who you are—a great lady with the same deep sense of community your family has."

Amanda studied Sharon, and found herself realizing that she'd given Sharon the benefit of the doubt for way too long. How could they have been so close back then? Maybe they were both different then—or more alike. The marriage to Bill had definitely been a sobering experience and had helped Amanda get her feet on the ground in a way that she might not have been able to understand in the past. But this was a very strange selling point.

"Let me see if I've got this right," Amanda said, trying not to sound curt or dismissive of the woman who had been her best friend all those years ago. "You want me to be Chair of the Longhorn Ball not just because it's a good cause and somebody needs to rescue it from what happened this past year, but because it's a way for me to prove to the women of Hillside Park that I'm not after their men? Is that what you're saying?"

"Not exactly," Sharon said, backpedaling furiously. "What I meant was—"

"I understand what you meant," Amanda said, shaking her head wearily. "It's exactly what you said. You're saying people are going to perceive me as a threat. I'm saying not everybody thinks like that. Like you. And if people want to think the worst of me, let them. There is nothing I can do about that. I just don't have time to worry about it. Ladies, I really appreciate the pie, the flowers, the hospitality, and the invitation, but it's just not for me. Okay?"

Sharon and Heather looked grimly at each other. They had taken their best shots, and they had failed.

"Will you at least think it over?" Heather asked hopefully.

Sharon cut in to give it one more try. "Amanda, everyone just loves you so much and has always had so much respect for you and knows you to be a wonderful Christian girl from a nice Christian family. They know you'd treat people well, you're organized, and you were quite the fund-raiser when you lived here before—always a good steward of the donors' money. You have great leadership skills. It'd be a fun year for everyone coming out of that disaster."

Amanda shook her head, but her mind was already on the movers. "Let's have lunch sometime, girls," she said. "I just have to turn my attention back to what's goin' on over here. Thanks for coming by. I appreciate the visit. I really do! Bye, y'all."

She was irritated by the tactics of her unannounced and uninvited guests. Amanda never had been able to stand being ambushed, and this was a perfect example of why. She called out more orders to movers carrying in Sarah's bed.

Heather and Sharon, dejected, said their good-byes and trudged down the steps toward the Jag.

When they got inside, they took a last look back at Amanda directing the movers. "The nerve of that girl," Heather said, reaching for her tube of lip gloss as she started the car. "She's gonna be much tougher than I thought."

"I don't know that we'd be able to get men to lose interest in her if she were running a small country," Sharon said. "She's so damn strong. She's confident, and she looks great. She wasn't even wearing any makeup."

"She's strong enough to stand up to the two of us," Heather said with grudging admiration. "Time to figure out a Plan B."

"I guess we'll have to." Sharon glanced down at her cleavage. At least she was superior to Amanda in that department. "You got one?"

"Nope. Not a one, not a single one. She turned down a free Mercedes. And she turned down being the Chair of the Longhorn Ball. I guess some people just can't even begin to know how to be happy."

"We'll think of something, sweetie," Sharon said consolingly.

"You got that right," Heather said. "She's not gonna get away with this, no way."

"Ain't no way in hell," Sharon grumbled in determined accord.

They sped off to rethink Amanda's demise.

✦

## 11

Dinner for Amanda, Sarah, and Will consisted of pizza at a neighborhood Italian place that had been a favorite of Amanda's while she was growing up. It felt comfortable and familiar, even though the décor was tacky and hadn't been updated since it was opened. The place was reputed to be a mob hangout, but since crime in Dallas was more disorganized than organized, there was little evidence for that claim. It was more of a local joke than anything.

Amanda couldn't help but notice the four older women seated at a nearby table who kept staring at her and talking to one another. They were all well-dressed and had beautiful faces, but each of them was slightly to considerably overweight and they all wore their hair much longer than was really appropriate for women their age.

About the same time she noticed the women, Nancy McRae, Amanda's sweet girlfriend from high school, popped into the restaurant dressed in a simple but elegant Tory Burch tank and slacks.

"Oh, my gosh, Nancy!" Amanda exclaimed, rising from her seat.

"Amanda! Welcome home! I called your mom—didn't she tell you?"

Amanda, who had just about decided that everyone here had either not changed a bit for the better, or left, was very excited to get reacquainted with Nancy. Nancy was drop-dead gorgeous, smart as a whip, and had a heart of gold. In addition to having a great sense of humor, she was a great wife and mother. Her husband was the ultimate good guy. He was handsome, successful, crazy about his wife, and a doting father. They were just the kind of people others felt good to be around.

"She told me," Amanda answered, her tone apologetic, as she and Nancy hugged. "I've just been so busy unpacking."

"I'm just so happy to see you. You look great."

"No, you look great. As always." Amanda dropped her voice to a whisper. "Do you recognize any of the women at the table behind me?"

Nancy glanced in their direction. "No, why?"

"They kept staring at me and talking about me and weren't even the least bit discreet about it. They were so obvious, it was just rude!"

Nancy, taking a seat at Amanda's table, waved her hand dismissively.

"Oh, honey, they probably just heard you were home. It's all over town that you're back. And I'm sure they were talking about you and have already decided they hate you, but who could blame them? Those women look like rejects from auditions for *Hairspray*. They represent the generation of stereotypical Texas women that you and I are so desperately trying to live down." They both laughed, realizing they weren't quite free from judgment, either.

Sarah and Will, who till now had remained uncharacteristically silent, giggled.

"You guys remember Nancy," Amanda said by way of introduction.

"Hi, Ms. McRae," the children chorused.

"Nice to see you two back where you belong," Nancy told them. "Do you like this restaurant?"

Sarah said she liked the place well enough, but Will pronounced his two-word condemnation, "It sucks!" on everything from the décor to the waitstaff to the food itself.

"Well, he's honest!" Nancy said, suppressing a grin. "Let's talk, okay, sweetie?" She gave Amanda a kiss on the cheek and got up to leave. "Hang in there. Don't let the gossips get you down."

"I'll call you," Amanda promised.

Dinner and the remainder of the evening were trials for Amanda, thanks to the unfriendly stares and Will's grumpy attitude. But then she drove by a skate park the town fathers of Hillside Park had thoughtfully provided for skateboard-addicted adolescents like Will. His eyes practically popped out of his head when he saw the ragtag collection of stoners, X Games wannabes, and other young people. Suddenly Will had a reason for living, especially when he noticed that some of the skaters were actually girls. Amanda promised they'd check it out next weekend.

The family had something of an adventure before bedtime, finally locating bedding in the thirtieth of the fifty or so boxes strewn across the living room floor. Amanda felt a measure of fear and depression as she imagined what her days would be like going forward. It would be getting the children up and ready for school in the morning, easy with Sarah and a nightmare endeavor with Will, followed by days alone in the massive house, unpacking boxes, and then angry evenings with Will, trying to get him to bed, so they could start the whole miserable routine all over the next day. For the first time since she had left Newport Beach, Amanda wanted to cry. After the children had gone to sleep, she came back downstairs to see if she could make some headway on the unpacking. The more boxes she unloaded, the more she felt as though she had gone to her own yard sale and overpaid for everything.

Her cell phone rang around nine p.m. It was her mother. "You still awake?"

"That's a yes," Amanda said, staring at the boxes everywhere. "I'm such an orderly person that the idea of going to bed with all these boxes half full just makes me crazy."

"With all that stuff you've got," Elizabeth said, "I don't know what possessed you to go to Neiman's and buy everything in the store. But you obviously did, because a bunch of clothes from Neiman's was delivered to my house this afternoon."

Amanda, puzzled, flopped down on a couch in the living room, realizing from the stinging pain in her behind that she had seated herself on top of Will's Game Boy, which she removed and stared at disdainfully. Children have great eye-hand coordination and the strongest thumbs in the world, she thought, but if it weren't for skateboards, they would probably get no exercise at all.

"Mom," she said, turning her attention back to the phone, "I didn't order anything from Neiman's."

"I don't know whether you ordered it or whether you went

there and picked it out, but you got a bunch of stuff, and that's that. Want me to bring it over?"

Amanda sighed. She was about to tell her mother that she was exhausted, that it could wait until morning, and that the idea of bringing even one more material item into a house so overwhelmed with clothing, pots and pans, furniture that didn't fit rooms, and rooms scattered with boxes would make her physically ill. But then suddenly she realized that her mother was actually trying to reach out to her, and that as tired as she was, a visit would be most welcome right now.

"If it's no trouble," she said, brightening for the first time that day. She was not normally a down or depressed person. But the divorce, the move, and above all, her constant run-ins with Will had begun to take a toll.

"Oh, it's a bother, all right," Elizabeth answered. "But I'll manage it. Give me fifteen minutes."

"I'll need a hand," she said, when she arrived at Amanda's door.

"A hand? Is there a lot of stuff?"

Elizabeth gave her daughter a look that was both accusatory and bemused.

"You could say that," she said without further explanation.

Amanda, intrigued, followed her mother out of the house, down the big lawn, and to her mother's Range Rover. Its passenger and backseats were jammed with boxes. "What's this?"

"You're not serious! The back is full, too. And this is just the first load."

"First load?" Amanda blinked rapidly. "What do you mean, first load?"

"It's going to take at least four trips for me to get everything from my house to yours. Why they couldn't have just delivered this stuff to your house in the first place, I'll never know."

"What the—" Amanda was all but speechless.

"Are you just gonna stand there," her mother asked, placing her hands on her hips, "or are you gonna help me unload?"

For the next hour, mother and daughter unloaded boxes into the already overfilled living room. Every ten or fifteen minutes, Elizabeth went back home for another load. In all, thirty cartons of various sizes, shapes, and weight had arrived from the venerable Dallas department store.

Once it was all inside, the tired women surveyed the haul. "A little retail therapy?" Elizabeth asked.

"I swear to you, Mom," Amanda said, staring awestruck at the boxes, "I've had no contact whatsoever with Neiman's. Not today, not since I got back . . . frankly, not in the last ten years."

"Then where do you buy your clothes?" Elizabeth asked, genuinely confused, as if there were no other place to shop in the United States.

"Neiman's isn't the only place to buy something to wear," Amanda insisted with a roll of her eyes.

"Well, for me it is," Elizabeth insisted regally. "And that's blasphemy, coming from a Texas girl!"

They dug into the first box. It contained half a dozen Chanel dresses, each more perfect than the last. Both women gasped. This box alone had to contain twenty thousand dollars' worth of clothes.

"Oh my God!" Amanda uttered.

"Un-f'ing-believable!" Elizabeth exclaimed, reeling. Amanda shot her mother a startled glance; she had never heard her mother use any expletive, in any context, ever. "Aw, for good-ness' sake," Elizabeth said, sighing. "It's only a word."

They moved on to the second box, which contained eight pairs of Manolo Blahnik shoes.

"I'll tell you what's so bizarre," Amanda said, shaking her head slowly. "All these things are exactly my taste. There's not a single thing I'd return. And they're just the right size, too."

Elizabeth's eyes narrowed as she studied her daughter. "You're not sending all this back, are you?"

"All of it," Amanda answered, in a tone brooking no argu-ment. "It doesn't belong to me. First thing in the morning, I'm calling Neiman's. They can send a truck and they can get all of this out of here. In fact, I wouldn't mind it if they took another ten or twenty boxes with them," she joked, making a sweeping gesture at all the moving boxes scattered about.

"Amanda, are you out of your mind . . ." Elizabeth started to let her have it. But all of a sudden, she stopped. "Why am I not surprised?"

"No, Mother, I haven't lost my mind, but Bill certainly did his best to try and take it. Was there a card?" Amanda asked. "I'm assuming this stuff is all from Mr. Black Mercedes."

"If it is," Elizabeth mused, "if you turn him down for din-ner and he sends you all this stuff, what would you get if you turned him down for a weekend in Cabo? A new house?"

"I don't need a new house, and I don't need boxes of stuff from Neiman's, no matter how . . . okay, no matter how perfect it all is. I just don't get it." She turned directly to her mother. "Mom. If a guy is so interested in me, why can't he just pick up the phone?"

Elizabeth thought for a moment before, unable to resist, tearing into another box. "Maybe he's in the CIA," she said, removing half a dozen cashmere sweaters—and not the crummy-quality cashmere making the rounds in the last few years but the real thing, buttery soft to the touch. "And he can't reveal his identity." Amanda laughed. "Or the witness protection program."

Then they both hit on the probable real answer. "Or maybe he's still married," they chorused.

The likely reality of the situation sunk in. They silently retreated to the couch, which Amanda scanned for Game Boys and other foreign objects before sitting down.

"The whole thing is a little over-the-top," she said.

Elizabeth nodded, still cradling the half-dozen sweaters as if they were a small, multicolored, extremely soft child. "Surely he's not married," she said hopefully.

"He's certainly got separate bank accounts if he is," Amanda reasoned. "I can't see any woman standing for her husband ringing up a hundred thousand dollars' worth of women's clothing and accessories at Neiman's without an explanation."

"On the other hand," Elizabeth countered, "you do get the Neiman's InCircle points. A hundred thousand points—you could really get something with that."

"Yeah, like a tiny piece of Waterford, as I recall," Amanda scoffed. "Is there a card?" Amanda asked again.

"Wait, I see one," Elizabeth answered, producing a tiny card, which looked miniscule and ill-proportioned compared with the size of the bounty it accompanied.

It read, in a woman's script: "Missed you last night. How's Friday at Javier's, eight p.m.?"

"Looks like a woman's handwriting," Elizabeth noted, scrutinizing the card. "Maybe that's why I didn't see a guy at the restaurant last night. Maybe there's a woman interested in you!"

"Oh, great! I can already hear them praying for me in Bible study over that one!" Amanda said dismissively. "I'm sure it was just one of the salesgirls who wrote the card. He probably didn't want his handwriting as an identifier."

"Maybe he's got his DNA on some of the clothes. We could take it to a lab."

Amanda raised an eyebrow.

"I don't mean in a Bill Clinton sense," Elizabeth said, rolling her eyes. "I mean, maybe he just touched things. When he was picking them out."

"I'll tell you what's so bizarre. He knows my taste in cars. He knows my taste in clothes. I don't know whether to be flattered or just plain creeped out."

"Can't you just keep one itty-bitty sweater?" Elizabeth knew full well the answer was no.

"No, not just one itty-bitty sweater. And don't you be thinking about keeping one for yourself. Before you leave, I'm going to frisk you, like you were a blackjack dealer in Vegas. What came from Neiman's goes back to Neiman's."

"How did an unscrupulous woman like me ever raise such a sensible daughter like you?" Elizabeth tousled her daughter's hair.

"I ask myself the same question every day."

"How are your spirits? This move gettin' you down?"

Amanda glanced at her mother warily. Throughout Amanda's entire childhood, Elizabeth had been so self-involved that any awareness of her daughter's feelings would have come as an outrageous surprise to Amanda—as it did now.

"To tell you the truth, Mom, it does have me down a little bit. All I have in front of me, really, is just taking care of the kids and unpacking all this . . . crap."

"You need something to get you out of the house. Maybe you could get involved with some charitable thing. Get on a committee or whatever."

Suddenly Amanda remembered the conversation she'd had earlier that day with Heather and Sharon. "Oh yeah . . . Mom, you're not going to believe this," she said. "But Heather Sappington and Sharon Peavy? They stopped by this afternoon. They want me to get involved with the Longhorn Ball."

Elizabeth, surprised, turned to study her daughter. "The Longhorn Ball! I wouldn't go near that thing, after what Susie did to it. I don't even think it's going to survive."

"They asked me to be Chair."

Elizabeth looked stunned. "Why on earth would they do that? I know you'd do a fabulous job, but you've been out of the loop for, what is it, twelve years! Why would they ask you?"

"Beats me," Amanda said with a shrug. "I mean, I had the exact same reaction you did. And I also figured that between the children and the unpacking, I wouldn't be coming up for air for a long time."

"So what did you tell them?"

"I told them no."

Elizabeth nodded, and the women sat quietly on the couch, both lost in thought.

"It would be good for you, you know," Elizabeth said suddenly, still stroking the cashmere sweaters.

"What would? Being the Chair of the Longhorn Ball?"

"After your father died," Elizabeth said in a serious tone, "I was at my wit's end. They came to me and asked me if I'd want to get involved with the Diamond Ball."

The Diamond Ball was *the* leading charitable organization in Dallas, run by women in their forties, fifties, and beyond. It had even more cachet in Hillside Park than did the Longhorn Ball.

"At first, I thought it was a terrible idea," Elizabeth continued. "I thought I just needed to mourn the loss of your father and be off by myself. It turned out that having something worthwhile to do and having those wonderful women to talk to was the best therapy I could have imagined. I think it really helped me bounce back a whole lot sooner than I might have otherwise."

Amanda pondered her mother's words. "You really think I should be Chair of the Longhorn Ball?" she asked. "I've been away for too long, things change in twelve years."

"Not in Hillside Park," Elizabeth assured her. "You'd be amazed at how little has changed. People are still people. Money is still money. The neighborhood's still in the neighborhood."

Amanda let out an exhausted sigh. "I don't know. Susie must have messed it up pretty badly if there's not a woman in town who's willing to take this on."

"Well, I can't argue with any of that. But look at it this way. If you don't do it, probably nobody will, and that'll be the end of the Longhorn Ball. This'll be a great way for you to get reacquainted with your old friends, meet the people who have moved in since you left, and generally have something to do other than just sit around this big ole house and think. That's what I was doing after your daddy died, and it damn near drove me crazy."

"I understand that Susie's husband gave pretty much every dollar they took in," Amanda said, taking the idea seriously for the first time. "Whatever I did, it would be an improvement from last year."

"It's kind of perfect," Elizabeth noted. "There'll be no expectations. It's kind of a win/win proposition."

Amanda shrugged. "Okay, maybe you're right. I guess I've lost my mind, but what the heck! It's not like I've got anything better to do with my time. I know the unpacking seems like it will last forever, but I know it really won't. And I just can't stand the thought of being idle."

Elizabeth patted her daughter's shoulder. "I think you made an excellent decision. And I'll give you a hand with the Old Guard."

The Old Guard were the women Amanda's mother's age who served as informal but undeniable social arbiters of Hillside Park. Darlene was one of them, and so was Amanda's mother, along with a few dozen other women, all of whom possessed great wealth, status, and indeterminate age. They ran the town.

"I may not bring in four million like Susie did," Amanda said, warming to the task, "but it won't be a total disaster."

"It'll be great. I know you'll do a great job. So, why not give me just one little itty-bitty sweater as a way of saying thank you for giving you such great advice?"

Amanda shook her head firmly. "It all goes back. If Mr. Black Mercedes, hundred-thousand-dollars-from-Neiman's, witness protection program, CIA, married guy wants to ask me out, he can just pick up the phone like a normal person."

"You're tough," Elizabeth said admiringly.

"Not half as tough as you are," Amanda said with a smile.

"I'm going home," Elizabeth said. "I've got to be ready for whatever your boyfriend sends you in the morning."

"I'm gonna call Heather. Tell her I changed my mind. Unless she already found some other poor, unfortunate, willing victim to take the thing on."

Elizabeth stood to leave. "I can tell you as sure as I'm standing here," she assured her daughter, "there's no woman in Hillside Park foolish enough to do what you're about to do."

"Guess I'm just taking one for the team then, huh, Mom?" Amanda asked playfully.

"Guess you are at that, honey." Then Elizabeth's expression turned serious. "Just brace yourself, is all I'm saying."

# 12

✦

Sunday morning at Hillside Park Presbyterian, Amanda had the uncomfortable feeling that people were staring at her. Every time she glanced around the sanctuary to see if anyone was indeed looking in her direction, she thought she kept catching people glancing away from her, looking down at their hymnals or otherwise pretending not to have been studying her.

"Am I going crazy," Amanda whispered to Elizabeth, "or are people staring at me?"

"Even the paranoid have real enemies."

"Thanks."

"Anytime."

When Amanda was growing up, her parents had always taken the family to the same restaurant, Geno's, for brunch practically every Sunday after services, and it was to Geno's that the family headed now. Contrary to its Italian-sounding name, the restaurant served nothing but Texas food, heavy on fried chicken, corn on the cob, mashed potatoes, fried okra, and the best chicken-fried steak north of the Guadalupe. Sunday wasn't Sunday without peach cobbler at Geno's. Wayne, the movie-star-handsome maître d', who hadn't changed in the twelve years Amanda had been gone, recognized her immediately. He ushered the family, who had not bothered to make a reservation, past dozens of other groups and couples—some of whom had been waiting a full hour to be seated. Wayne gave them the same table they had occupied throughout Amanda's childhood.

She had to admit, it felt great to be home. Will, staring around the restaurant, was on the verge of opening his mouth when his grandmother cut him off.

"Don't tell me, let me guess," Elizabeth said sarcastically. "This restaurant sucks. Am I right or am I right?"

Will, his thunder stolen, could do nothing but nod un-enthusiastically.

"No Hooters girls to stare at, huh, little man?" Elizabeth stuck the knife in a little farther.

"Mom, let up on him," Amanda said, studying the menu, which hadn't changed, except for the prices, in all the time she had been gone. "He's just twelve."

"Fair enough," Elizabeth said, studying her grandson's shaggy blond hair and California good looks. "He's a good-looking kid, I'll say that."

"Just like his daddy," Amanda noted with a sigh.

"This is practically all carbohydrates and hydrogenated fats," Sarah said disdainfully, studying the menu. "Can you get anything organic here?"

Elizabeth stared at her granddaughter. "How old are you?"

"Nine," Sarah answered, confused. "Gigi, don't you know how old I am?"

"I never heard of organic till I was over forty," Elizabeth said.

"Maybe that's why your skin is so wrinkled," Sarah said innocently.

Elizabeth looked furious. Amanda tried hard not to laugh.

"They were living in a different culture," she explained to her mother.

"The only culture in Southern California is yogurt," Elizabeth replied, peeved.

Sarah, for her part, had no idea why her comment had been taken as an insult by her grandmother and as a reason for laughing by her mother. In California, or at least in Newport Beach, everybody ate organic.

"Beef is protein," Amanda told her daughter. "When I was growing up, I always liked to eat the pot roast at Geno's on Sundays after church."

Sarah wrinkled her nose at the idea of beef. "Do they have anything here made of soy? Like the veggie burger you made me the other night?"

"Darlin'," Elizabeth said in a serious tone, "this here is cattle country. Please don't say *soy* where anyone can hear you. Okay?"

Sarah, bewildered, looked at her mother for clarification. Amanda just waved a hand. "Sarah, honey, things are a little different here. People pay a little less attention to what they eat or where it comes from."

"No kidding," Sarah said, scanning the diners. "They've got more fat people in this restaurant than they do in all of Newport Beach."

"That's enough," Amanda said, unable to stifle her laughter. "It feels good to laugh. I feel like I haven't laughed in months."

"Have any plans for how you're going to run the Ball?" Elizabeth asked, just as the waiter came to take their order— chicken-fried steak for Elizabeth, pot roast for Amanda, chopped sirloin for Will, and a chicken Caesar salad for Sarah.

"I've got no idea at all about how to run the Ball," Amanda admitted. "The biggest thing I've ever organized was my wedding, and that was a long time ago. And I had a wedding planner to help with that."

"I'm sure there are good event planners who could give you a hand with the Ball," Elizabeth said. "I could look into that, if you want."

"That would be great. I wouldn't even know who to ask here."

"Sarah's right," Will said suddenly, looking around the restaurant. "Gigi, why is everybody in Dallas so fat?"

"I'm not fat!" Elizabeth said indignantly.

"Mommy says that's because you smoke like you're on fire," Sarah said.

Amanda reddened. Elizabeth shrugged. "Well, out of the mouths of babes. I guess I could cut down a little bit."

"Children in Southern California are just different," Amanda said apologetically.

"They're sassier, I'll grant you that. Any news from Mr. Black Mercedes?"

Amanda shook her head. "Honestly, I was looking around the church, trying to see if I saw any men staring at me. I thought I saw a lot of women looking in my direction, but no men."

"I'm sure he's not going to quit now. Men love it when you play hard to get. And on top of that, you still have a gift card from Neiman's for ninety-eight thousand dollars in your purse."

Amanda had returned everything to the store. Usually with a credit that large the store opened an account for the client; however, because Amanda's divorce was pending, she wasn't able to open any new accounts in her name until it was final.

So instead, ever-helpful Neiman's had provided her with the gift card.

Will's eyes widened. "You have a gift card from Neiman's for ninety-eight thousand dollars?" he asked, awestruck.

Amanda had a policy of never lying to her children unless it seemed like a good idea. "Yes, I do. Somebody gave me some things, and I sent them back to the store."

"But ninety-eight thousand dollars' worth?" Sarah asked, equally astonished. "Somebody really likes you!"

"It isn't Dad!" Will said.

"You got that right," Amanda said, sadly unsurprised by her son's smart mouth. It's exactly the same thing Bill would have said, had he been there.

"What are you gonna do with the gift card?" Sarah asked.

"Yeah, what are you gonna do with the gift card?" Elizabeth echoed. "Buy yourself the his-and-hers suits of armor from this year's Christmas catalog? Since you didn't want all those nice sweaters and dresses."

"You can buy suits of armor at Neiman Marcus?" Will asked, intrigued. "Cool! You can't find anything like that at Nord-strom's."

"Or his-and-hers helicopters," Elizabeth said. "Or a diamond-studded personal spa set. Maybe you can get Neiman's to donate something to the Longhorn Ball. Or maybe you can auction off the gift card! Mr. Black Mercedes just wants you to be happy, right?"

"The gift card is going back to the store tomorrow morning," Amanda said firmly. "Right after I enroll you guys in school."

"School sucks," Will declared.

"If you don't stop saying that word," Amanda said, "I'm going to wash your mouth out with soap and then send you to military school. I'll make sure you don't see another girl until your eighteenth birthday."

"Awww, Mom!" her son whined.

"Seriously, Amanda," Elizabeth steered the conversation back to her subject of choice. "Have you given any thought to how you're going to run the Ball? Where you're going to get started? What you're going to do your first day?"

Amanda shook her head as the waiter brought lunch. "No idea," she admitted. "I'll consider my first day a success if they don't lead me out of the office in handcuffs, like Susie. Come on, guys. Let's just stop talking about the Ball and Mr. Black Mercedes and Neiman Marcus, and let's just eat. Okay?"

## 13

Sunday night, after Will and Sarah had gone to bed, Amanda stayed up until two in the morning, trying to get as many moving boxes wrestled to the ground as possible. By the time she collapsed in bed for five hours of dreamless sleep, she had unpacked two-thirds of the boxes in the living room and all of her clothes upstairs.

Another day or two and she would have the whole job finished, she told herself. Although that day would not be Monday, because Heather had texted her late Sunday night that they should meet at the Longhorn Ball office at ten a.m. Monday so that Amanda could get started in her new role as Ball Chair.

On Monday morning, Amanda walked a sullen Will and a quiet Sarah the six blocks from their new home to Hillside Park Middle School, which, to Will's delight, seemed to have fourteen hundred students riding fourteen hundred skateboards. Will, board in hand, rolled directly into the mass of students and only reemerged when he realized he didn't know what classroom to go to. Sarah looked doubtfully at the other students. In a concerned tone, she whispered, "Mommy, there are so many fat kids!"

Amanda was about to object to her daughter's use of the word *kids*, when she looked around and realized it was true. The epidemic of obesity that she kept reading about in magazines appeared to have skipped over Newport Beach, where, it seemed, you could grab any ten adolescents and pull together an Abercrombie & Fitch ad. But here, in the middle of the country, the kids were definitely bigger in the middle.

"I'm sure you'll find some other students who are just as committed to healthy eating as you are," Amanda said, squeezing her daughter's hand. She wondered why in California people worshipped healthy carbohydrates more than they worshipped God. She vowed to concentrate on redirecting Sarah's obsession on weight and dieting.

The paperwork didn't take long to complete, and Amanda thought she recognized a few of the administrators from when she had attended the same school twenty years earlier. They looked just as old now as they had then, although they must have been in their twenties or thirties then. When you're young, everybody looks old, and old is old whether you're in your twenties or your seventies, Amanda decided. It wasn't until you got a few years under your belt that you were able to make distinctions.

Will and Sarah disappeared into the crush of students, and Amanda walked home to get her rented SUV so she could drive the mile and a half over to the Longhorn Ball office to meet Heather.

An hour later, at ten o'clock, after finding herself unable to resist the temptation to tussle with a few more kitchen boxes, Amanda arrived punctually outside the Longhorn Ball office. There, in the exact spot where she had seen Susie led off by two Hillside Park gendarmes just a few days earlier, stood

Heather Sappington, chatting on a cell phone, unaware of Amanda's approach till the very last minute.

"Oh-oh, there she is!" Heather exclaimed, her tone, to Amanda's ear, somewhat guilty. What's that all about, she wondered.

"Good morning!" Heather sang out, a little too cheerfully for Amanda's taste. She never trusted anyone who was cheerful at ten o'clock on a Monday morning. She certainly never was.

"Good morning," Amanda replied, her tone somewhat more businesslike. "I appreciate your coming down and taking time out to give me the keys."

Heather shook her head. "No, it's you who everybody appreciates," she gushed. "Taking on such a big job. It really is so sweet of you."

"Well," Amanda said, wanting to shorten the conversation and not knowing why, "we'll see how sweet everybody thinks I am if I can actually pull this off."

"Oh, I've got no doubt you'll do a fantastic job," Heather said, a little too patronizingly in Amanda's opinion. Heather reached into her dated Prada handbag and pulled out the keys for Amanda.

"Good luck!" Heather said, giving her an air kiss. And then, under her breath, "You're gonna need it."

Amanda, puzzled, nodded thanks.

"Gotta run, sweetie! Ann'll be waiting for me. And I've got to make a doctor's appointment."

"How'd that deal go," Amanda asked, curious, "the one with that guy who wanted to buy a ranch last week?"

Now it was Heather's turn to look puzzled. "What ranch? Ann never told me anything about a guy trying to buy a ranch."

"But there was—" Amanda began. She cut herself off, realizing that she had been played. "Never mind, it isn't important."

"Whatever. Anyway, gotta get to the office. Call me if you need anything. Bye."

Amanda watched her all but sprint toward the Jaguar parked at the corner opposite the church. Amanda found herself wondering how exactly Heather managed to own a Jaguar, given her presumed level of income, but Heather had all sorts of ways of making nice things appear in her life. It was really none of Amanda's business, and she knew it. She turned around and faced the door of the Longhorn Ball office, took a deep breath, unlocked it, and stepped inside.

The best way to describe what she saw would be "unorganized chaos." The Longhorn Ball offices—an entry foyer where a paid assistant usually sat, two executive offices, one of which would now be Amanda's, and a file room—looked as though they had not been cleaned in weeks. As Amanda wandered through the rooms, she was shocked to see stacks of unopened mail, file folders all over the floor, and a layer of dust on top of everything. It looked as though the place had been ransacked and the burglars, finding nothing of value, had simply left everything all over the chairs, desktops, and floors. It was obvious that there had been desktop computers, judging from the discoloration on the desks where the computers had once sat, but they were gone. What exactly had Susie been doing all that time in the office? Or had she ever even come to the office? It was hard to say.

Amanda, speechless, walked into Susie's office, now hers, and the mess here was the same as in the other rooms—papers strewn all over the floor, envelopes everywhere. The only signs of life or color in the office were a pair of Jimmy Choos under Susie's desk and a cocktail dress hanging on the back of the door that Susie must have kept for sudden social emergencies.

Amanda didn't know where to begin. It seemed as though her life had suddenly turned into nothing but cleaning and organizing—in the home she had rented for herself and her children, and now here. Suddenly it dawned on her why nobody had wanted to take on the responsibility of being Ball Chair. Everybody else in town must have known the exact dimensions of Susie's reign of error. The gossip mill must have let everyone in Hillside Park know just how crazy the situation in the office was, just what a mess would have to be cleaned up before any attention could be turned to next year's Ball. No wonder everybody was so convinced that the Longhorn Ball might never recover from Susie's year.

"Where do I begin?" Amanda was muttering to herself when she heard a knock at the door. Opening it, she found, to her surprise, her mother.

"No way I was going to let you do this all by yourself," Elizabeth said by way of greeting. "I heard through the grapevine how messed up it was in here. I'm so sorry, honey. I wanted to get here before you did so we could go in together. Wow, it's even worse than I thought."

"It's bad, all right," Amanda said, looking gratefully at her mother. The idea that her mother would actually show up and help her out with something was so hard to process that she could barely think of anything else. "Where do we begin?"

"At the beginning," her mother said, surveying the wreckage with a cool eye and arms folded. "I see a lot of unopened mail. Let's find out what the hell is going on. There might be unpaid bills, checks—who knows what? Let's just start off by making piles, and then we can figure what's what."

"Sounds like a plan," Amanda said, but all she really wanted to do was put the keys on the desk, run out of the office, and never come back. That wasn't her nature, though. She was far too responsible a person to do a thing like that, and she knew it. The only way out was to push through.

For the next hour, Amanda and Elizabeth attempted to organize the envelopes, documents, file folders, and all the other messes from Susie's time as Ball Chair. They went through all the papers on the floor, on top of the desks, and on the filing cabinets. When they were done, they had three stacks of envelopes, each a foot high, and several hundred file folders, half of which were empty. Then came the biggest surprise of all, when Amanda opened the drawers of Susie's desk and found the bank books for the organization—along with stacks and stacks of hundred-dollar bills.

"Mom, you've gotta see this," Amanda said. "Take a look."

Elizabeth came into the office from another room and saw the stacks of cash, which Amanda was now piling up on the desk. She emitted a low whistle. "All hundreds?"

Amanda rifled through some of the stacks. "It looks that way," she said.

"I can't believe this. That must be fifty thousand dollars in cash. We've got to get all that to the bank."

"This is nuts."

"This is beyond nuts," Elizabeth said, shaking her head disgustedly. "I always thought Susie was a little stupid. Now I think she's the biggest idiot I've ever seen. Dumber than dirt! This is just unbelievable."

"What are we gonna do? This is a little beyond my experience."

"You know how I met your dad, right?" Elizabeth asked.

Amanda shook her head. Of course she did, but she had no idea which of the many versions of the story she'd hear today.

"I was his bookkeeper," Elizabeth said. "I told you that. I studied bookkeeping in college, because I looked at the way all the marriages of my friends' parents ended in divorce. I figured I'd need to know how to keep track of money if I was going to survive. Besides, my father was a banker, and naturally, he insisted. So I was temping as a part-time bookkeeper one summer, and that's how I met your dad."

"You know what to do with all this stuff?" Amanda asked, waving a hand at the cash, the envelopes, and the files.

"You don't need to be a bookkeeper to know that you've got to open the envelopes and see what's inside. Let's start by counting the cash, and then we'll move to the envelopes, and then we'll move to the files. That's probably as good a starting point as any."

"You're the boss."

Elizabeth shook her head. "I'm not the boss," she reminded her daughter. "You are. I'm just the hired help."

The women grinned and started to count the hundred-dollar bills. Twenty minutes later, after counting and recounting the money, they came to the total of eighty-two thousand, five hundred dollars. Elizabeth went into the file room and emerged with a shopping bag. She stuck all the cash in it and brought it back to her new office.

"Why would Susie have that kind of cash lying around anyway?" Amanda asked.

"Beats me. She must have been running this thing like

her own personal bank account. She's lucky they only arrested her for trespassing. If she was siphoning cash from this thing, she could go to prison. Not even that billionaire husband of hers could help her then. Actually, he probably wouldn't even want to. If she went to prison, life's got to get better for him."

They both laughed, but then Amanda turned serious. "I still don't understand how anybody could be so . . . thoughtless. I mean, didn't she think at some point somebody would see what was going on?"

"Not everybody's responsible. If you don't believe it, take a look at the world around you."

Amanda nodded glumly. "I guess you're right. Let's dig into these envelopes."

For the next two hours, they sorted through the stacks of unopened mail. To the surprise of neither of the women, the envelopes contained hundreds of uncashed checks and hundreds of unpaid bills, nasty letters, and threats to turn off the electricity and phone. Suddenly it dawned on Amanda that she had not even tried to turn the lights on, because the office was so flooded with morning light through its picture windows. She tried the switch. Nothing happened.

"No power," she told her mother.

She picked up the phone. No dial tone.

"No phone?" Elizabeth asked.

"There's a shocker," Amanda said sarcastically. "What hath Susie wrought?"

"I admit I'm kind of blown away," Elizabeth said. "I expected it to be bad, but not this bad. Let's get the checkbook out and start writing checks. We've got a whole bunch of angry creditors. I'll do that while you add up the checks. Between the cash and the checks, we ought to have enough to pay off the bills. I hope."

Amanda went to work. Then she thought of something else.

"Don't let me forget," she said. "I've got to get to Neiman's and turn in this gift card." She took it out of her bag and put it on the corner of her new desk.

"How much was it for again?" Elizabeth asked, glancing at the card.

"Around ninety-eight thousand," Amanda said.

Elizabeth shook her head. "What's this guy gonna do once you start showing him a little attention? Buy you an island?"

"No attention, no island. I don't have the bandwidth for a relationship right now, Mom. I've got my hands full right here."

"Bandwidth! Is that how people in California talk?"

Amanda glanced at her mother. "That's how Bill talked," she admitted. "He liked all that technical jargon."

"Well, let's not go off on Bill right now. We've got work to do."

Two hours later, Amanda had compiled a list of all the checks that had come in and had endorsed them all over to the Longhorn Ball cash-management account. The checks ranged from a thousand dollars for individual tickets, to ten to fifteen thousand for tables in the back, to twenty-five to fifty thousand for tables up front and to even larger amounts for straight donations to the Ball itself. In all, the checks totaled more than three hundred thousand dollars. Some of them were six months old, and Amanda wondered how many of them would still be honored by the bank. She also had to wonder how much Susie's husband would have really had to contribute if Susie had just bothered to open the mail.

At about the same time, her mother finished opening

the bills, which covered electricity and phone at the office, the rental fee for the ranch where the Ball had taken place, the fee for the entertainment, security from the Dallas Police Department officers who had moonlighted to patrol the perimeter of the ranch and keep party crashers out, and everything else, including food and drink suppliers. The women sat opposite each other in Amanda's office and compared notes. The bills came out to just over three hundred thousand.

"We'll be in the black, but only barely," Amanda said, "if all these checks clear."

"I don't think Susie paid one single bill," Elizabeth said. "How could she have gotten away with it?"

"You know better than me, Mom. Who's gonna go up against the reigning Longhorn Ball Chair in this town—especially when it's Susie Caruth?"

"You're right."

"Why don't I go to the bank," Amanda suggested, "and take in the cash and checks, and you can pay the bills? Just don't mail any off until we find out how many of these checks actually clear."

"Sounds good to me. There might be some money in the account, which would help if not all those checks are okay, but somehow I doubt it."

"See you in a bit." Amanda hoisted the bag of cash and a manila envelope full of checks and deposit slips. "They used People's Bank. It's just two blocks from here. I ought to be right back."

A knock interrupted them. Amanda and Elizabeth glanced at each other. Who could that be? To Amanda's surprise, it was Sharon Peavy.

"Hi, honey!" Sharon chimed, charging toward Amanda and

giving her an awkward hug. Sharon glanced over her shoulder at the newly straightened-up offices. "Looks like you've had a busy first morning!"

"Did you see this place?" Amanda asked in disbelief. "Can you believe what a state it was in?"

"I could not," Sharon said, looking sheepish. "You have to forgive me for not telling you. If I had, you would never have taken this on."

"You got that right. Well, come on in."

Amanda thought about how strange the whole situation was. There is an unspoken understanding about leadership among volunteer groups. The vast majority of women who are willing to share their time and talent for charitable causes know that most women who are elected to positions of leadership handle the responsibility well.

They approach their responsibilities with humble hearts, deep senses of duty and commitment, and they put the welfare of the organization above any personal desires or agenda. Rarely is there a chairman who almost immediately transforms into a ruthless, self-promoting, Bridezilla-type character, one who worries only about "her year" and gives no thought to what might be best for the organization as a whole. Susie was that kind of "leader," and that came as a disappointing shock to all. No one could wait for her year to be over, which was another reason she could never have been Chair two years in a row.

Sharon looked around. "Mmm-hmm. Looks like you've gotten this shipshape in a real hurry," Sharon said. "Oh, hi, Ms. Smith," she said when she noticed Elizabeth. She tugged nervously on her shirtsleeve. "Are you helping out?"

Elizabeth looked up from the bills.

"I am," she said. Elizabeth had never been a big fan of Sharon's back when Amanda and Sharon were growing up. There was always one child in a group who led the rest of the children into trouble, be it alcohol, drugs, sex, or whatever else. Among Amanda's peers, Sharon had been that one girl. Elizabeth had never had much use for Sharon and had never been shy about saying so. The coolness that had existed twenty years ago when the girls were both teenagers had not lost any of its frost in the intervening years.

"That's really nice of you, Ms. Smith," Sharon said. "Whose Neiman's card?" she asked, noticing it at the corner of the desk. "Was that Susie's?"

"It wasn't Susie's," Amanda said. "It's mine. Why would you think it was Susie's?"

Sharon shrugged. "I didn't mean any harm," she said, backpedaling. "I just figured maybe you found it in one of the desk drawers. If it was Susie's, I could return it to her."

"It's not Susie's," Amanda repeated flatly. "Anyway, what brings you here? Is there anything I can do for you?"

"Actually," Sharon said, still eyeing the Neiman's card, "I was wondering if maybe there was something I could do for you. I spent a lot of time in this office trying to give Susie a hand. I know where a lot of the bodies are bur—I mean, I know a lot of the computer systems they used. I know where a lot of the stuff is around the office, the important lists, and so on. I could show y'all some of that stuff if you wanted."

"Computer systems?" Elizabeth asked. "Where exactly are the computers?"

Sharon gave a pained look. "Oh, they got repossessed," she admitted ruefully. "I kept telling Susie they were leased computers, they weren't ours. And she kept telling me, 'Possession is nine-tenths of the law,' whatever that means."

"It means Susie's an idiot."

"Well, you won't get much of an argument from me. Do you want to see where some of the hard copies are of the donor lists? We've got 'em going back twenty years."

"Why don't you show my mom?" Amanda said. "I was just heading over to the bank."

"The bank? How come?"

"There was a bunch of cash and checks in the office that hadn't been deposited," Amanda explained. "Take a look."

Sharon glanced in the shopping bag holding the cash and her eyes went wide.

"Oh my God! There must be fifty thousand bucks in there!"

"Eighty-two five, to be exact," Elizabeth said. "What was Susie doing with all that cash anyway?"

"It's as if she lost her mind," Sharon said, shaking her head disapprovingly. "I kept telling her she couldn't be cashing checks and getting cash for herself. I'm telling you, I don't know what day this stopped being the offices of the Longhorn Ball and became Susie World."

"I'm going to the bank," Amanda said, tired of the conversation. Now she was starting to wonder whether the damage Susie had created could ever really be undone. "Mom, do you want to go look for those files with Sharon?"

"Sure," Elizabeth said, getting up.

"I should be right back," Amanda said. "I know it's just two blocks, but I'm going to drive. I'm a little nervous about walking with all this cash."

"Mmm, I don't blame you," Sharon said. "I'd be nervous, too."

"Back soon." Amanda headed out of her office, to her car, and on to the bank.

# 14

✳

At the bank, the very friendly teller took one look at the name on the account, frowned, and became much less friendly, but still very professional. "Just a minute. I've got to call a manager."

Amanda, holding the bags of cash and checks, was surprised. "A manager? How come?" The teller said nothing else.

"Is there something wrong?" Amanda asked, puzzled.

"Would you mind stepping to the side so I can take care of the next customer?"

"Um, sure." Amanda was now deeply confused. A few minutes later, a bank officer who could not have been more than twenty-five approached Amanda.

"I'm Lewis Johnson," he said. He looked like he had played fullback for his college football team. Amanda wondered whether he was really a bank officer, or actually a security guard in a white shirt and tie. "Would you step over to my desk, if you please?"

"Okay."

He led her to one of the desks opposite the tellers' windows, ushering her into a chair. He sat opposite her with a pained expression. "I'm sorry, ma'am. We're no longer authorized to accept deposits for the account of the Longhorn Ball."

"How come?" Amanda asked, surprised. "What's wrong?"

"There were some . . . irregularities with the account," Lewis explained, choosing his words carefully. "I'm afraid our bank no longer has a relationship with the Longhorn Ball. I'm sure you understand."

"I'm sure I don't understand," Amanda replied, experiencing a sinking feeling. "Why don't you just cut to the chase and bring me up to speed."

Lewis Johnson looked as if he would rather feel the weight of another football team's entire front line crashing down on him than continue this particular conversation. "Ma'am, it's kind of a long story. . . . We just don't want that business anymore. That's all I'm really authorized to say."

"Authorized?" Amanda stood, defeated. Normally, she'd ask for someone with more authority, but she had a feeling it'd be useless. "Okay. Well, I'm really not that surprised. Thanks for your time. I'm sure it's nothing personal."

Lewis smiled, clearly relieved that the conversation had ended so quickly. He had obviously been prepared for worse. He must have dealt directly with Susie a lot, Amanda thought.

"Have you been thinking about refinancing?" he asked helpfully.

Amanda couldn't believe his nerve, but knew how to shut him down. "I rent."

Suddenly Lewis's entire demeanor changed. "Have a nice day," he said dismissively.

Amanda figured that Lewis was likelier to get transported to another galaxy by aliens than to make enough to own a home in Hillside Park, but he had clearly bought into the general disdain that everyone in the community had for renters—even renters themselves.

"Thanks for everything," Amanda said tartly, turning to leave.

She sat in her SUV for a few moments, thinking about the bizarre encounter. What must Susie have done at that bank to screw things up the way she did? Well, there were other banks in town. Amanda drove a couple of blocks until she came to the branch of another large commercial bank and she went inside.

"I'd like to talk to an account manager," she told the girl out front, "about opening a corporate account."

"Wonderful," the perky receptionist said. "Someone will be with you in just a moment. Let me get you an officer."

A gentleman Amanda's age introduced himself as Rick Stevens and showed Amanda to a desk. She explained her business, beginning, "I'd like to open up a corporate account."

Rick immediately reached into his desk and took out the appropriate documents. "Do you have anything identifying you as an officer?" he asked.

Amanda shook her head.

"How about a certificate of incorporation? Tax filings? You know, the usual sorts of things."

Amanda sat dumbstruck. "I hadn't thought of any of that. I'm the new Chair of a philanthropic organization. I should have thought of all that. I guess I need all those things to open up an account, right?"

"Sure," Rick said, still friendly. "Congratulations on taking the helm. May I ask the name of the organization?"

"The Longhorn Ball," Amanda said proudly.

The smile vanished from Rick's face.

"Um, did you say . . . the Longhorn Ball?"

Amanda felt a sense of mounting alarm. "Yes," she said cautiously. "Why?"

Rick looked flustered. "Ma'am . . . please don't take this the wrong way, but I know there's no way our bank would be willing to do business with the Longhorn Ball."

"What do you mean?"

"I'm sure you're going to do an excellent job," he said cautiously, "and everybody here in Hillside Park knows what a wonderful organization it is, what a great event it is, and how much money you guys raise for pediatric illness."

"Why don't you just get to the point?" Amanda's patience dwindled.

Rick hesitated sadly. "I can't imagine a single bank in Dallas that would want to have anything to do with the Longhorn Ball at this point. They burned every supplier in the city, many of whom are our customers. They've alienated every business that's done business with them in the past. A lot of us here at the bank were wondering if there would ever be another Longhorn Ball after what happened this year. And you're running it now? God bless you."

"It can't be that bad," Amanda objected, flustered. It was one thing for the crisis within the Longhorn Ball to be private knowledge among the membership of the women involved with it. It was another thing to see the ramifications of Susie's actions reflected in the words and demeanor of a banker Amanda had never even laid eyes on before. It's worse than I thought, she thought.

"What am I supposed to do?" she asked, bewildered.

"It's not for me to say, ma'am," Rick said, shaking his head. "But if I were in your shoes, I'd head right back to the office, type out a letter of resignation, leave it on your desk, and run away from that job like your hair is on fire."

Amanda stood to go. "Thanks for the advice."

"No offense intended," Rick said, standing as well.

"None taken. The reality of this is just a little harsh, as you can imagine. It's all a little difficult to process, that's all."

"I can indeed, ma'am. Good luck."

"Thanks. I'm gonna need it."

As the afternoon progressed, Amanda went to four other commercial banks in the neighborhood. The experience was repeated each time. The problem wasn't that she lacked the appropriate corporate documents. The problem was that no bank wanted to touch the Longhorn Ball. From a banking standpoint, it had fallen to leper-like status. Dejected and unsure of what to do next, she returned to the office to find her mother finishing up the last of the bills.

"Where is Sharon?" Amanda asked, seeing her mom was alone.

"Oh, she took off a while ago. She gave me all the donors' lists, the articles of incorporation, all the important stuff. It was hidden way in the back of one of the files. You know, I can see how Sharon's managed to keep her foot in the door with some of the right people all these years, in spite of herself. While you were out, she was sweet, very helpful and knowledgeable . . . one-on-one with her I found myself having to remind myself of how much I dislike her. She can be very charming."

"Yes, and 'Charm is deceitful,' says the Bible."

"Well, we'd have never found those things in a month of Sundays without her, so let's be grateful that Sharon's nosy, always wants to make herself useful, and be in the middle of things. It sure helped today."

"That's great, I'm glad you found all that stuff, especially the articles of incorporation. I'm going to need them if I'm going to open up an account somewhere."

"What do you mean open up an account?" Elizabeth asked. "Don't we have one? I mean, what are all these checks?"

"Nobody wants to bank with us," Amanda told her.

"What do you mean?" Elizabeth looked up from the check register. She had seated herself behind Amanda's desk.

"Our account's frozen at People's Bank. Then I went to four other banks and nobody wants to touch us. Susie really has screwed this up worse than we imagined, Mom."

Elizabeth let out a sarcastic laugh. "Too bad we sold all our banks! Sounds like our only hope would be to open an account with some out-of-state bank or a bank on the Internet that's never even heard of us. Unless there's some sort of central register for deadbeat philanthropies."

"We need a computer," Amanda said. "Can I take some of this cash and buy one?"

"I'd be careful. We don't want people accusing you of sticking your hand in the till, which is exactly what people are accusing Susie of. Or will be, once Sharon tells everybody in Hillside Park about the cash."

"You think Sharon's going to do that?"

Elizabeth merely stared at her daughter.

"As always . . . hope springs eternal," Amanda said, sitting in the chair opposite the desk. "I guess I could go home, get on the computer and find an online bank. But I still don't know what I'm supposed to do with the cash."

"Keep a thousand for petty expenses," Elizabeth advised her, "and then go to a bank and get a cashier's check so you can deposit the rest. And that way you won't have to carry it around. Although with Sharon's big mouth, you're probably already a marked woman, having all that cash on you."

"That's just great."

"I'll tell you what. I'm not much for the Internet, and you're the one who's so big on bandwidth or whatever you call it. Why don't you go home, go online, and get an account set up, and I'll take care of the cash?"

Amanda nodded. "I can hit Neiman's on the same trip." She looked on the corner of the desk where she had left her Neiman's gift card. "Mom, didn't you see me put my Neiman's card right there?" she asked, pointing to the spot on the desk where she thought she had left it.

"Uh-huh. Did you put it back in your purse?"

"No, I'm certain I didn't, but . . ."

Amanda checked through her handbag anyway, just to be sure. "It's not there," she said, shaken. The women looked at each other and realized at the same time—"Sharon."

# 15

✦

The difference between an evildoer and a martyr is spin—it's not what happens that matters. It's how people perceive what happens that makes the difference.

Such was the case for Susie Caruth, whose husband, in spite of the rumor, promptly bailed her out of jail even before she had so much as set foot in a holding pen or drunk tank. Word reached Edward's office of Susie's arrest even before she and her two police escorts reached the station house for processing. One phone call from Edward to the desk officer ensured that Susie would spend her entire "incarceration" in the women police officers' lounge, an astonishingly lavish facility donated to the department by the husband of a repeat drunk driver who got sick and tired of hauling his wife out of the drunk tank and thought that a major gift might smooth troubled waters the next time she got pulled over.

While the police department was naturally elated with its over-the-top new lounge, which featured a huge flat-screen TV and large leather swivel chairs, the donor's wife's habit of driving while intoxicated continued unabated, and her rap sheet continued to grow until finally her husband was quietly convinced by his attorney to move to their spread north of

Lubbock. There, she could drink and drive all she wanted, putting at risk no one but herself and a lot of prize cattle.

Susie was not fingerprinted, photographed, cavity searched, or subjected to any of the other indignities that an arrested person normally faces. Instead, she sat watching *Days of Our Lives* until her husband came and collected her. But that's not how the story was spread around town. Instead, rumor quickly took flight throughout Hillside Park, conveyed by voice, texting, instant messaging, furtive whispers, and a variety of other high- and low-tech methods of communication, that Susie had been (take your choice) strip-searched, locked in a holding cell with candidates for deportation, roughed up by police officers, roughed up by fellow inmates, assaulted six ways to Sunday, or, according to one feverish instant message that rapidly made the rounds, that she had all but been murdered behind bars. None of this had happened, of course, but the overall effect was to create a wave of sympathy for Susie, the "innocent victim of vicious police brutality," that far outweighed any remaining outrage the women felt toward her for screwing up the Longhorn Ball. Adding to the drama was the fact that Susie was nowhere to be found. Her husband had spirited her away on a ninety-day round-the-world cruise, to keep her from blabbing to friends, enemies, frenemies, and even the local media about what she had done or not done with piles of cash, some of which she had brought home in brown paper bags from the office, much to the consternation of her husband. Edward rightly feared that criminal proceedings could be instituted against Susie, not just for stupidity, but for malfeasance and for sticking her hand in the till. In his mind, it made more sense to get her out of the country until the whole thing died down.

Edward knew she had left behind a trail of wreckage starting with the Ball itself and extending outward to all the banks, donors, and vendors involved with the event. All he could do was hope that the three and a half million dollars he had donated would cover any shortfalls or accounting irregularities, of which, he felt certain, there were tons. His fondest wish was that people could forgive, forget, and move on.

The rumors of Susie's brutal incarceration, combined with her sudden disappearance, created an unexpected halo effect for the train-wrecked socialite. As her cruise ship steamed toward Gibraltar, people back home were raising her to the level of Christian saint, a victim not of her own arrogance and bloated ego but a victim of the "system," whatever that meant. The upshot of all this was that the absent Susie had somehow managed to accrue, as a result of the rumors swollen out of proportion around her arrest and "confinement," the kind of warm and loving thoughts that she had never generated in person. And the more Hillside Park loved the absent Susie, the more likely they were to judge harshly whoever filled her strappy sandals at the office of the Longhorn Ball, namely Amanda Vaughn.

Amanda's first indication of the canonization of Saint Susie occurred when she went to pick up her children from Hillside Park Middle School at three o'clock. Thanks to the documents her mother had given her, she had successfully opened an account with an Internet bank and had FedExed the checks and a cashier's check for all of the cash, minus a thousand dollars for petty expenses. Elizabeth would have to write all of the checks once they came in from the Internet bank, but they both figured that the creditors had waited this long for their money—another week wouldn't kill them.

Things only got strange at school, where a woman Amanda

did not recognize approached her and said, out of the blue, "I think what you've done to Susie is hideous."

Amanda, stunned by the unexpected criticism from this unknown source, stared at the woman, who promptly turned her back on Amanda and went off in search of her children. Amanda, puzzled, stared after the woman, trying to figure out what that was all about. She collected Will and Sarah, who both looked pleased with their first day of school.

"How was school today?" Amanda asked, after kissing Sarah and punching Will playfully on the shoulder.

"Beats me," Will admitted. "I spent the whole day skateboarding."

"You did what?"

"I spent the day skateboarding," her son repeated. "I don't like school. Dad didn't like school, either, and he said he ditched all the time. And now he's a millionaire."

Amanda's head swam. Putting what to do about Will's truancy aside for the moment, she turned to her daughter. "Sarah, how was it for you?"

"One of the girls told me there's a Whole Foods here in Hillside Park," she said. This was clearly the first piece of good news she had received since she had moved to Dallas. "Can we go and get dinner there? Can we? Can we? Please, Mom!"

"I don't see why not."

"And there's a church retreat this weekend," Sarah added enthusiastically. "Can I go? All the girls in my grade are going."

"That sounds nice," Amanda said, happy that her daughter was already in the middle of the social whirl. "Of course you can go."

They started to walk home, Will skating, his ears plugged

with his iPod buds, and Sarah chatting about the personalities of the teachers and students. From the way she was talking, it sounded as though her transition would be relatively smooth. Amanda had worried enormously about how Sarah would fit in with the materialistic Texas girls at Hillside Park, but coming from Newport Beach . . . well, one place wasn't really that different from the other. Sarah had indeed found some other children just as committed to eating healthy and watching their weight as she was, so it looked like her situation was handled.

Will, on the other hand—ditching all of his classes on the first day to go skateboarding with the other truants—that was another matter.

As they walked the six blocks home, Amanda had the strange sense that someone was following them. She turned around, and a Bentley with Texas vanity plates was crawling behind them. The driver was a huge military-looking man in his early thirties. He rolled down his window. "Are you Amanda Vaughn?"

Puzzled, she nodded. "If you're suing me, I've never seen a process server driving a Bentley before. You can just drop off the papers at the Longhorn Ball office."

"Nobody's suing anybody," the driver assured her, his tone friendly. He reached his hand out the window to give Amanda an envelope. "This is from my boss."

"Your boss? If you drive a Bentley, what does he drive?"

"This is his car. Please." Amanda took the envelope as he stepped on the gas and the Bentley purred away. "Have a nice day!" he called.

"What's that, Mom?" Sarah asked. Will had been oblivious to the whole exchange, playing air drums as he skateboarded alongside his mom and sister.

"I have no idea," Amanda admitted. She opened the envelope. It contained a check along with a sticky note on it that read: "Congratulations on taking over the Longhorn Ball. Here's something to get you started. Dinner Tuesday night, 7:30, Nobu?"

Amanda lifted the sticky note off the check and gasped. It was made out to the Longhorn Ball in the amount of one hundred and fifty thousand dollars. She looked to see the name of the account holder—General Services Inc., with the address a post office box in Fort Worth. It could have been anybody.

"He just keeps raising the bidding," she muttered, reeling from the size of the check.

"Who gave you the check, Mommy?" Sarah asked. "What's it for? Is it for the Ball? Is there going to be a Ball next year? All the kids in school say there'll never be another Longhorn Ball. What is a Longhorn Ball, anyway?"

Amanda thought back to the days when Sarah was a baby and she couldn't wait for her to say her first words. What had she been thinking? It seemed like Sarah hadn't stopped talking since the day she started. Smiling at her precocious chatterbox, Amanda reached for her cell phone and called her mother.

"Amanda?" Elizabeth answered.

Amanda had never gotten used to the idea that people no longer said "hello" when they answered the phone. Thanks to caller ID, people just skipped the hellos and went right to first names. It was still a little unnerving for her, even though she had been carrying a cell phone for almost twenty years.

"Mr. Black Mercedes just gave us a hundred and fifty thousand dollars for the Ball," Amanda said.

A long pause ensued.

"Did he invite us to dinner again?" Elizabeth inquired playfully.

"He did."

"And are you going?"

Amanda thought back to the incident at the school, when a mother she had never met before accosted her about wrongdoings toward Susie that she had never committed. She was done with worrying what others thought of her. "I'm going," she said firmly.

"Good answer. No offense, but with what I'm starting to hear from some of my friends, we're fixin' to need all the friends we can get."

Elizabeth hung up before Amanda could ask what she meant by that. Amanda and the children were almost at their house.

"Are you going on a date, Mommy?" Sarah asked.

"It's not a date exactly. The ink isn't exactly dry on your daddy's and my divorce. I consider it more of a business dinner."

"I hope you do. Is it with the man who gave you the car and the clothes?"

Amanda sighed and shook her head. Her daughter was smart. Maybe too smart. "That's the man," she said laconically.

"Good!" Sarah exclaimed gleefully. "Is he a health nut?"

Amanda stifled a grin. "I'll have to get back to you on that one, honey. Let's get inside and see if you have any homework." Sarah skipped ahead while Amanda mulled over this newest piece of the puzzle. This mystery man is *some* kind of nut, that's for sure, she thought to herself.

# 16

✦

Hi there," Sharon Peavy said in her friendliest Texas twang to the first male salesperson she encountered at Neiman's. She had on full makeup, and her Versace V-neck plunged extra low, another score from another unsuspecting male she dragged shopping one day. It just so happened that the individual to whom she was speaking was gay, but she definitely had his full attention nonetheless.

"How may I help you, ma'am?"

"I've got a gift card? Actually, it belongs to a friend of mine? And it's her husband who asked me to bring the card in, because he wants to know the balance. That way, since their anniversary is coming up and everything? He can replenish it, if it's gone down below a certain level. You understand, I'm sure?"

"We can do this very discreetly," the salesman answered.

It was six thirty on Monday evening, a time when Neiman's was not likely to be busy, and therefore a good time, in Sharon's mind, to find out how much money was left on the card. Sharon's attitude was that since the card had obviously belonged to Susie, it would be fair compensation for her hard work—not just on the Ball, but also for protecting Susie from the wolves and jackals baying for her to be fired, or worse, prosecuted. And after all, Sharon and Heather were personally seeing to it that Amanda would bear the brunt of all the blame. Susie definitely owed her for that.

Sharon figured that Amanda had found the card in a desk drawer and rationalized that Amanda was going to do the very same thing, taking it as kind of an early bonus for agreeing to try and resurrect the Ball. Sharon found it absolutely outrageous that Amanda would have claimed that the card was her own. Imagine that, Sharon told herself, whipping herself into a frenzy of righteous indignation. It's Amanda's first day on the job, and not only is she stealing Susie's Neiman's card, but she's probably dipping into that big old stack of cash that Amanda had shown her. And if she isn't, well, it sure sounds good and that's how the story will go.

The fact that Sharon had never known Amanda to be a liar didn't make a damn bit of difference to her. Everyone knew Sharon had never let the truth get in the way of a good story.

"Right this way, ma'am," the salesman indicated.

Sharon followed the immaculately tailored young man off the floor, sauntering over to the customer service department and into a private office. He invited Sharon to take a seat, then slid the Neiman's card through a magnetic reader attached to the computer on his desk. He looked with amazement at the figure that popped up on his screen.

"Is it a lot?" Sharon asked, intrigued by his visual response. Neiman's salespeople had a knack of playing things cool, accustomed as they were to high-dollar clientele and their proclivities for massive shopping sprees. But even he wasn't prepared for the number that he was about to share with her.

"There's ninety-eight thousand dollars on the card," he

said, swallowing hard. Even in the rarified world of Neiman Marcus shoppers, that was a pretty large number—or at least it was a large number for a gift card.

Sharon leaned forward. "Did you say . . . ninety-eight thousand?"

She struggled to conceive of so valuable a piece of plastic. Her mind rapidly translated ninety-eight thousand dollars into couture, shoes, handbags, sunglasses, makeup, and other items. Despite all her previous life training at spending unearned money, she still felt herself struggling to come up with ways to spend the whole thing.

Given enough time, though—say, two hours—she knew she could. "That's it," the salesman said, relieved that he could share his true emotions about the number with Sharon. The amount was more than what he made in a year, and it brought home to both of them the wild disparity between what people earned at Neiman Marcus and what other people spent there.

"Do you wanna . . . run that thing through one more time, darlin'?" Sharon suggested, perched precariously on the edge of her seat. "Maybe a decimal point got transposed or somethin' like that."

The salesclerk nodded. "If you like. But I've never seen the reader make a mistake."

"If you don't mind." Sharon held her breath.

"Let's see," he said, running it through again. He pursed his lips as the same number came up.

"Your . . . friend," the salesclerk remarked, "has a very generous . . . husband." It was evident to Sharon that he did not believe for a minute her story about the origin of the card.

Sharon thought hard about her next step. If the young man became too alarmed, he might call security in to have a little conversation with Sharon. He didn't really have grounds to do so, but she was on store property, and she did have one of the biggest gift cards the salesman, or perhaps anyone at the store, had ever seen. So some sort of authoritative action might be appropriate. Sharon decided to stick with her story. "May I ask you—what was your name? I didn't catch it."

"I didn't throw it," he said cheekily. "Travis."

"Mmm. Travis. Do you think you might be able to tell me whether the card was registered in my girlfriend's name or her husband's name?" She tinkered with her Michele watch as her right knee began an anxious bounce.

Travis glanced at the screen. "It's not in any name at all, ma'am. It's basically like cash."

"Really . . ." Sharon was almost drooling. They locked eyes, studying each other intently, like poker players. It was evident to Sharon that Travis knew the card was not hers. It was equally evident that Travis was looking for a way to cut himself in on Sharon's surprisingly good fortune. Many high-end stores had trouble with their sales staff, some of whom ran a scam involving selling expensive items at retail prices, taking them back as cash returns, then reselling them to the same customer at a fraction of the original price, also for cash, which never saw the inside of a cash register. So Sharon had reason to believe that Travis could be tempted.

"When do you think your friend's husband is expecting to get the card back?" he asked cautiously.

"It's hard to say," Sharon replied, equally cautious, not wanting to give away any more than she had to. "What were you thinking?"

"It would just be a pity," he said with a hint of sorrow in his voice, "if your friend's husband couldn't derive maximum value from the card."

"What's that mean?"

"Well, I think it's a little bit dangerous for a woman like yourself to be walking around with such a valuable card. I mean, God forbid if it were lost, right?"

"God forbid," Sharon said, resisting the urge to cross herself. "Perish the thought."

"May I recommend," Travis said, "dividing the card into, say, twenty gift cards of approximately five thousand dollars each. That way, if one of them were lost, nothing bad would happen. It would just be five thousand dollars lost, and not ninety-eight thousand."

"I see."

"In addition," Travis added, in as professional a voice as he could muster, "we see tons of five-thousand-dollar gift cards at Neiman's every day. They wouldn't raise an eyebrow. Whereas, a gift card for ninety-eight thousand—that's almost an invitation for further . . . shall we say, scrutiny?"

Sharon shook her head and gave a slight grin. "Well, we don't want to invite scrutiny, now, do we?"

"Discretion is everything."

"Mmm-hmm, it certainly is. . . . Would there be a fee for transforming this ninety-eight-thousand-dollar gift card into a bunch of five-thousand-dollar gift cards?"

Travis looked at the door to his office, and glanced out into the hallway, checking to see if anyone was listening.

"I think a ten-percent fee is what the store typically seeks in situations like these."

Sharon thought about it. Ninety-eight hundred bucks? And

she'd be left with almost ninety thousand in five-thousand-dollar gift cards?

"If I can count on your discretion," Travis promised, "you can count on mine."

"I think we have an understanding."

"Wait here. I'll be right back."

# 17

✦

Where on earth . . . is Sharon?" Darlene asked in her breathy voice.

It was twenty minutes to nine Monday evening, and Heather and Darlene were sipping iced tea from her fabulous William Yeoward Isabel goblets, seated on the eighteenth-century chaises in Darlene's living room. Heather made a "beats me" gesture. "I've tried her cell a million times," she said.

"Did she not insinuate she was coming at eight?" Darlene asked in singsong, stroking the ruffles on her Hermès apricot-orange dress.

"I thought that's what we all said. I just don't know why she's not picking up her phone."

"It doesn't matter. How do you think Amanda's first day went as Ball Chair?"

Heather took a sip of her iced tea and grinned. "Couldn't have been all that great. Sharon and I spent the whole weekend messing up that office. By the time we got done with it, it looked like a tornado had hit." She reached for a packet of sweetener and checked to make sure she had the no-calorie sugar substitute.

Darlene laughed. "That must have been devastating for poor Amanda."

"Uh-huh. I wouldn't have been too pleased if I had to come in there and make some sense out of all that mess. For all I know, she's still in there, straightening up."

"Susie did leave that place in terrible, discomfitable disarray."

"No doubt, no doubt." Heather tossed her hair. "But it's hard to think of Susie without realizing all she endured at the hands of the police."

Darlene gave her a withering look. "Don't tell me you believe all that BS about her getting attacked or molested or any of that stuff about body-cavity searches."

"None of that happened?" Heather was puzzled. "But it's all over town!"

"Oh, please! None of that happened. She was in and out of there before you could say Martha Stewart."

"Really? But I heard—"

"You heard wrong. Edward got her out in about a New York minute, and then he put her on a cruise. She might have some legal issues stemming from what she did with the money from the Longhorn Ball."

"Sharon told me that Amanda and her mom found a ton of cash in Susie's desk," Heather said, pointing her feet and admiring her Christian Louboutin pumps, a gift from the latest ex. She envied all the other girls who had a closetful and playfully referred to them as their "Lubys." This was her only pair and she'd had to badger her ex to death for these.

Darlene nodded. "Why Susie had to mess with the money belonging to the Longhorn Ball, I'll never understand. How much money was there?"

"I think Sharon said there was something like eighty thousand dollars in hundred-dollar bills. We were sick we didn't find it when we snuck in there!"

"You'd think Susie was running a drug operation with that kind of cash. What on earth was that girl thinking?"

"It's kind of amazing how bad everybody feels for her." Heather sighed, taking out her cell phone and punching in Sharon's number one more time. Again, it went straight to voice mail. "I just don't know where that girl is."

"The irony is that Susie brought it all on herself," Darlene remarked. "All she had to do was just run that Ball with a semblance of professionalism, and she would never have been in this mess. But that whole police brutality rumor? Don't buy a word of it."

"Okay," Heather said, taking another sip of her iced tea. "But who started it, anyway, if it's not true?"

"I did," she replied, grinning wickedly.

"But why?" Heather asked, mystified.

"The more sympathy there is for Susie," Darlene reasoned, "the less sympathy there's going to be . . . for Amanda."

"So that's how the big girls do it, huh, Darlene?" Heather gave an admiring nod.

"That's right, my little student!"

"Well, what's gonna happen now?"

Darlene leaned forward, eyes shining. "Have you heard the rumor," she began wheezily, "that Amanda found one hundred twenty thousand dollars in Susie's desk? But she only tried to put eighty-five thousand in the bank?"

"No!" Heather covered her mouth with her hand. "I haven't heard that rumor at all!"

"That's because I just started it," Darlene boasted. "Just

you wait. You will. She's going to have the devil's own time trying to get any banking done for the Longhorn Ball." Darlene's expression suggested that she knew a big secret.

"Why is that?"

"Let's just say I made a few phone calls." Darlene couldn't conceal her self-satisfied, smug expression. "I called a few contacts of mine in the banking community here in Dallas. They would never want to sojourn on my bad side."

"What'd'ja do?"

"I just told them," Darlene answered, matter-of-factly looking at her fingernails, "that if they did any banking business with the Longhorn Ball, I'd make sure my husband and all of his real estate friends pulled out every dime from their plebeiat banks."

Heather grinned at her friend's masterstroke. "How many banks did you call?"

Darlene closed her eyes and threw a solemn hand over her chest. "All of them," she said, sashaying dramatically toward the iced tea and almost knocking the pitcher over. "Every single bank in Dallas. And even a few in Fort Worth. Just to be on the safe side."

"WELL, MOM, THAT'S the last of the boxes in the living room," Amanda said. It was almost eleven p.m. The women surveyed the living room, the floor of which was now entirely visible for the first time since the movers had arrived. Elizabeth looked admiringly around the downstairs and nodded her head in approval. "It's starting to look like a home," she said.

"It is, at that. Mom, I don't know how to thank you. You've helped me out so much here and at the Longhorn Ball office. I don't even know what to say."

"Well, you helped me out, by bringing my grandbabies back to Texas. Maybe in a few months I can knock some of that California nonsense out of their heads. Skateboarding. Organic foods. Please."

"As if, Mom. People eat some things that aren't chicken fried here in Dallas, too. And it's not like people in Hillside Park have never seen a skateboard before."

"I guess," Elizabeth said grudgingly. "I just don't see why your kids have to be so different."

"It's not worth worrying about," Amanda said, flopping down on a couch. "I'm hungry." She paused. "Maybe even for something greasy," she added, casting her mother a mischievous grin.

"I'm guessing you've got nothing in your pantry except some organic greens," Elizabeth said, sitting in an armchair opposite her. "Am I right or am I right?"

Amanda laughed. "We probably don't even have that," she said. "I've had zero time for grocery shopping. You know that better than anyone."

"We could call out for a pizza."

"How can you eat pizza and stay so thin?" Amanda had to admit—the conversations with her mother about things as unimportant as pizza and weight gain were so pleasurable that it was worth coming back to Dallas just to reestablish their relationship.

"The real question," Elizabeth said, getting out her cell phone to punch in a number for pizza delivery, "is what's going to happen when a bunch of those checks for the Longhorn Ball bounce. The Ball was such a disaster, I'm afraid half the people who wrote those checks may have stopped payment on them for a variety of reasons—they never got their auction item, they were seated in the incorrect level of sponsorship—some of them may just not want Susie to get credit for obtaining any money from them. How are we going to cover those bills?"

Amanda nodded. "Mom, thank God the Longhorn Ball has such a history in this town—it's almost a monster you couldn't kill if you tried, and Lord knows, Susie tried! Our supporters are so loyal and they know that by no means was this year business as usual. I'm sure after all the talk they realize we need their money more now than ever. I can't imagine they would stop payment or have a check come back to us they weren't willing to make good." She watched as her mother ordered a pizza, and she was seized with the kind of giddy notion that she wasn't sitting in a rental house, with no art on the walls, after the dissolution of a long-term marriage fifteen hundred miles away—but that she was just sitting in a dorm room at college, hanging out with her best friend. Mom as best friend? There was nothing in Amanda's past that pointed to that. But she wasn't saying no to it, either.

"What are you going to do about Mr. Black Mercedes's check?" Elizabeth asked, having completed the order. "I hope you like pepperoni. I forgot to ask."

"Mom, at eleven at night, there's nothing I want more than pepperoni pizza. It's perfect. Thank God my daughter's asleep!"

"I thought so. . . . So what are you going to do about his check?"

Amanda relaxed further into the couch. "I thought about tearing it up—but this isn't a car or a bunch of clothes for me. This is a charitable donation, and if he really wants to make it, I shouldn't be getting in the way. And Lord knows we need the money—that way we can pay all of our creditors and still have some money to spare. Obviously, he sent the check because he wants to get my attention, and he's certainly gotten it, so I figured I'd meet him first and see what this is all about. Then I'll go from there."

"Makes sense." Elizabeth stretched her neck to relieve the kinks.

Amanda decided it was time to change the topic. "Hey, what do you think happened to that Neiman's card? I've looked for it everywhere."

Elizabeth thought for a moment. "You really think Sharon swiped it?"

"I'd hate to believe that." She stared at the paintings and prints leaning against the walls, wishing that she could magically nail them into place with a glance. The idea of standing there with a hammer and nails for hours on end just seemed too depressing to contemplate.

"The only other possibility," Amanda said, returning to the subject at hand, "is that somehow the card got stuck in a file folder or an envelope somewhere. We had so much paper flying around."

"We did," her mother agreed, "but my bookkeeperish instincts tell me that that card is nowhere in that office. I went through absolutely everything after Sharon left, just to put everything in order and make sure we'd be able to find what we wanted going forward. I know a gift card's a little thing, but I'm telling you, it was gone."

"That's so disturbing," Amanda said after a moment. "Why would Sharon do such a thing, if she did? I guess I still want to give her the benefit of the doubt."

"I don't," Elizabeth retorted firmly. "That young lady gave a lot of mothers like me fits when y'all were growing up. There's nothing I wouldn't put past her. And that Heather

Sappington. She's another piece of work. Out of all the women in Hillside Park, how did you immediately hook up with the two of them now that you're back? I always told you there was nothing more dangerous than white trash with nothing to lose. Especially when it comes to our neighborhood."

"Mom," Amanda pointed out, "they picked me. After Sharon Peavy didn't say a word to stick up for me in that Bible study, I had no particular interest in even saying hello to her. And as for Heather, I was never drawn to her."

"Social climbers," Elizabeth said, shaking her head dismissively. "It's worse than a disease. At least they did you a favor, making you Chair of the Ball."

"I'm honestly starting to wonder whether it really was a favor. Knowing the two of them, they must have had some sort of ulterior motive. I mean, this ain't my first rodeo," Amanda said in perfect Texan drawl, winking at her mother. "But I'll be damned if I can figure out what it is."

"Karma's a boomerang. Either Sharon's done you a good turn, or she's just setting herself up for even more trouble. My guess is it's the latter. Though I still believe that there's something therapeutic about your being so involved in this whole Ball thing. It keeps you from sitting home and brooding. That's the worst thing a woman can do."

"I suppose," Amanda answered pensively. "But it's turning into a much bigger pain in the butt than I ever imagined. I just couldn't believe all those banks turning me down. I mean, what's that? Did Susie really poison the well that much in this town? Okay, maybe they fell behind on their accounts receivable. But I've never seen a bank want to turn down a few hundred thousand dollars of deposits, including eighty-something thousand in cash. Let alone every bank in town."

"It does set the mind to wondering. . . . Where is that pizza?"

"So we ought to know in a few days what our cash position is, whether we can pay our bills in full or not."

"Worst case," Elizabeth reasoned, "we can go to our creditors and work something out—half now, half later, something. The thing that I don't understand is, if Susie's husband really did give three and a half million or four million or whatever it is, the story changes hourly, to the Longhorn Ball, where'd that money go?"

"That is the question, isn't it?" Amanda had no answer.

"Indeed," her mother mused. "How come there's nothing in the bank, millions of dollars supposedly donated, and nothing to pay the bills with?"

Amanda thought for a moment. "Did you see any checks made out to the Pediatric Foundation?"

Elizabeth shook her head. "I didn't see all of the bank records, but the ones that I saw didn't point toward any four-million-dollar donation. Maybe we ought to call them in the morning and see if they ever got paid."

"Somehow, knowing Susie, I'm starting to doubt it."

The doorbell rang. "Finally," Elizabeth said. "I'm famished. Since we're talking Longhorn Ball business, we could pay for this out of petty cash."

"I don't want to be bothered," Amanda said. "This one's on me." She headed to the door to pay for the pizza.

"If he's cute," Elizabeth called out, "bring him in. I could use a pepperoni pizza and a man right about now."

"Mother!" Friends with my mom? she thought. This is definitely going to take some getting used to. But she liked the sound of it.

## 18

When Travis had returned to his office that evening, it was not with a stack of five-thousand-dollar, anonymous Neiman's gift cards, but instead with three plainclothes security officers and one member of the Hillside Park Police Department. Sharon was not exactly under arrest at that point, but neither was she free to leave. To her shock and dismay, she realized that Travis had been setting a trap since the moment that she had allowed him to run the ninety-eight-thousand-dollar gift card through his magnetic strip reader.

He had failed to share with her that the card had Amanda's name on it, and instead was following the traditional procedure at Neiman's and most other department stores when someone appeared to be using a stolen card.

After four hours of questioning, Sharon was escorted out of the basement security facility to the Hillside Park Police Department, where she was formally arrested, booked, and charged with possession of stolen property and intent to commit fraud. The difference between Sharon Peavy and Susie Caruth could have been measured in the fourteen hours that Sharon spent in the drunk tank, where her physical attributes met with considerably more interest and enthusiasm than they had back at Neiman's.

Sharon finally made contact with Heather Sappington around eight the next morning, after a harrowing, sleepless night, in which she received numerous invitations from the men in the holding tank across the hall to reveal not just some but all two of her charms, a request she steadfastly denied. Her bail was met by a check from Ann Anderson, which Heather Sappington brought to county jail, where Sharon had been transferred at five in the morning. Heather was waiting outside in her Jaguar when a locked door opened and Sharon was unceremoniously sent back to freedom.

"Oh my God, oh my God!" Heather exclaimed as Sharon rushed to the Jaguar and jumped in. "You poor, poor thing! What happened to you?"

"That bitch set me up!" Sharon sank into the seat and began to cry like a baby. "She had to know what she was doing, that conniving bitch! After all we were trying to do for her."

Heather studied Sharon and her seriously rumpled outfit for a moment, then started the car and pulled away from the jail.

"What we were trying to do for her," Heather reminded Sharon, "was to set her up. We weren't exactly trying to do her any favors, remember?" She reached for a packet of tissues and handed them gently to her disheveled friend. "Poor baby," she said sympathetically. "You just look awful."

Sharon blew her nose piteously. "Two wrongs don't make a right," she said. Heather couldn't exactly understand what that expression had to do with the present situation, but she could see that Sharon was in no mood to be corrected.

"If there's any justice in the world, she's going to have to pay for what she did to me. I'm looking at three to five years in prison!"

Heather looked shocked at first, but then dismissed her friend's concerns. "I have no doubt that Ann or Darlene can make a phone call to Neiman's and get the whole matter dropped." She fished around in her weathered Louis Vuitton bag for her lip gloss.

"I hope so," Sharon sobbed. "That was just the worst night of my life!"

They navigated the neighborhood around the jail and headed for the interstate.

"What are you gonna do about it, honey?"

"Do about it! Mmmm, where do I begin?" Sharon had spent the entire night concocting a whole list of things she intended to do about it. "First I'm gonna call Darlene, because I'm sure she can make this whole thing go away. You're right about that. But that doesn't excuse Amanda for what she did."

"How are you so sure that Amanda was trying to set you up?" Heather asked, sneaking a quick peek at her lipstick in the rearview mirror. "Isn't it possible that you just, like, saw a Neiman's card and swiped it, hoping that Amanda wouldn't notice?"

Sharon looked accusingly at her friend. "I just came out of county jail," she sputtered, "and you would dare to contradict your best friend with the truth?"

Heather finally realized just how overwrought Sharon was. "You poor thing. You need a hot shower, a hot meal, and a nap. I don't think you're seeing things clearly."

Sharon blew her nose. "Oh, I'm seeing things just fine,"

she responded darkly, adjusting herself under her sweater. "I'm seeing things perfectly fine."

THAT SAME MORNING, Amanda walked the children to Hillside Park Middle School, where Elizabeth picked up Amanda to drive her to the Longhorn Ball office. Before Amanda could say hello to her mom, her cell phone went off. She glanced at the screen and saw that the caller was "unknown."

"Who could this be? Hello?"

"Ms. Vaughn?" an authoritative male voice drawled.

"This is she," Amanda confirmed, puzzled. Elizabeth glanced at her. What's this all about?

"This is Sam Horn, chief of security at Neiman Marcus," the caller continued. "I hate to trouble you, ma'am, but would you mind coming by the store at your earliest convenience? There are some security questions that only you can answer."

This is odd. What's going on? Amanda asked herself, but then she knew. The gift card.

"Really? Why me? What is this about?" Amanda asked, not willing to reveal too much until she knew who had tried to use the card.

"Honestly, ma'am, we'd only need fifteen or twenty minutes of your time. It would be best," the Neiman's man said, his tone impassive, "if you could swing by the store. We'll explain when you get here. We need you to take a look at a security video. I promise it won't take more than half an hour."

"I'd better say yes before you tell me it's going to take all day. We'll be right over." She hung up.

"What's that all about?" Elizabeth asked.

"It sounds like somebody tried to use my card at Neiman's,"

Amanda explained. "They want me to head over there right now."

Elizabeth checked the dashboard clock. It was just after eight a.m. "But the store doesn't open until ten."

"I guess security keeps longer hours."

"If it means they found your card, I guess it's a good thing." She turned the car around and headed for Neiman's.

Amanda and Elizabeth reached Neiman's ten minutes later, where they were quickly shown into the same basement security facility where Sharon had been interrogated the night before. Sam Horn, the security officer who had called Amanda a few minutes earlier, ushered her and Elizabeth into seats, pushed a few buttons on his laptop computer, and turned the screen toward the two women. Sam leaned over, pushed a couple of more buttons, and the women listened to the conversation between Sharon and Travis. Sam played the entire exchange, culminating in Travis's disappearance with the card, presumably to get its contents registered on a bunch of other cards. Amanda and Elizabeth were predictably horrified, although not altogether surprised.

"I never liked her," Elizabeth said flatly. "She's just wretched," Amanda agreed with a sigh.

"Ladies," Sam drawled, "can you identify the woman on that video?"

You mean the one with the three sixes on her head, just *smokin'*, Amanda wanted to say, but forced herself to suppress the tangent she wanted to go on.

Amanda and Elizabeth looked at each other like a couple of schoolgirls who had shown up unprepared for a pop quiz.

"Do I have to?" Amanda asked.

"It would certainly aid our investigation," Sam replied. "Can you identify her?"

"Sharon Peavy," the women chorused.

Sam glanced at the papers on his desk, checked to see that the name was correct, nodded, then closed the laptop. He seated himself behind his desk.

"Ladies," he began, "do you realize that Ms. Peavy yesterday tried to commit fraud with a gift card, which totaled—"

He paused to check his paperwork again. "Ninety-eight thousand dollars?"

"We didn't know until just now," Amanda said, miserably uncomfortable. Sharon had been her best friend growing up, she had baked Amanda a pie—a chocolate pecan pie, no less—and had even gone to the trouble of getting Amanda the position of Longhorn Ball Chair. Why would Sharon do a thing like this?

Sam wanted to know the same thing. "Do you have any idea how Ms. Peavy came into possession of your gift card?"

"Do I have to say?" The idea of getting Sharon in trouble held no appeal.

"You don't have to tell us," Sam said, "but it would certainly assist us in our investigation."

Elizabeth glanced at Amanda, wondering what her daughter would do. It was her call.

"Let me just make sure I understand what's going on," Amanda said, buying time. She looked puzzled. "Excuse me, Mr., um—"

"Horn," he said.

"Thank you, Mr. Horn," Amanda said. She felt her heart racing. The idea that Sharon would steal her gift card was just unimaginable, and yet it made all too much sense. "What exactly is going on?"

"We just want to understand the circumstances by which Ms. Peavy came into possession of your gift card," Sam explained in an East Texas monotone. "How did she get your card?"

"It's not my card." Elizabeth threw her a confused look.

Sam looked surprised, as well. "It's not your card? It's got your name on it."

"What exactly would I be doing with a ninety-eight-thousand-dollar gift card from Neiman Marcus?" Amanda asked. "We're comfortable, but I don't have that kind of money."

This was a twist that Sam had not expected. Nor had Elizabeth, for that matter, who stared at her daughter, bewildered.

"Why would a Neiman's gift card with something like ninety-eight thousand dollars on it have your name on it?" Sam asked.

"It must be an accounting error of some sort. I've never seen a card with that much money on it in my life." She grinned. "I'd like to."

"I've got one right here for you," Sam said, reaching into a desk drawer, and taking out a plain white envelope. "The original, as you can understand, is being held by the police as evidence in the case being built against Ms. Peavy." Elizabeth shot Amanda a deeply puzzled glance.

"We made up a new one with your name on it this morning," Sam continued. "That's why we called you in so early, and I hope we didn't disturb your day, ma'am. We just didn't want you to be without it. Anybody who had lost a ninety-eight-thousand-dollar gift card would probably be very upset."

Amanda forced a laugh. "I'd be upset if I lost a gift card of that size," she admitted. "Wouldn't you, Mom?" Elizabeth, stupefied, took a few seconds before she could register exactly what Amanda was asking her to say.

"Oh, no doubt!" she finally said, shaking her head in disbelief. Her daughter, she decided for the millionth time, was somethin' else.

Sam Horn's eyes narrowed. "Are you really telling me," he said, amazed, "that you did not have a ninety-eight-thousand-dollar gift card in your possession, that you do not have a store credit with Neiman Marcus in the amount of ninety-eight thousand dollars, and that if I handed you this gift card with that value on it, you would refuse to take it?"

"I didn't say I wouldn't take it," Amanda noted with a grin, "but then I'd be stealing, too, wouldn't I? I mean, it's not my card. It's not my money. I really don't know what this whole thing is about."

Sam looked as bewildered as he felt. A routine investigation had turned into something he could not wrap his mind around. "I'm just a little bit confused, ladies, and I apologize. You're telling me . . . that . . . Sharon Peavy did not steal your card."

"That's what I'm telling you," Amanda said, the picture of serenity.

Elizabeth shot her a glance that asked "Are you out of your mind?"

"You do understand," the increasingly flustered Sam said, "that without your willingness to aver to the fact that Ms. Peavy stole your card, we have no case against her?"

Amanda thought for a long time before she answered. "I don't exactly know what 'averring' means, but if it means the same thing as 'saying,' then yes, that's what I'm saying. I'm saying that I never had a gift card of that size, and Ms. Peavy therefore could never have stolen it from me."

"But the video—" Sam began.

Amanda cut him off. "That video proves nothing. I'm not a lawyer, but it sure looked like your employee was trying to entrap her into an illegal action. I mean, dividing the one big gift card into a whole bunch of little gift cards was his idea. And unless you've got it on tape somewhere that she actually took possession of the smaller gift cards and actually tried to *use* one of them, I don't even know what kind of case you've got against her in the first place."

Sam looked as if he'd lost his best friend.

"Are you sure—" he asked, hoping against hope that Amanda would say something to implicate Sharon with a prosecutable offense.

"I don't mean to get involved with your store's internal affairs," Amanda began, gaining confidence now. "But if you can't figure out what she did wrong, I don't know why you're asking me."

"B-but—" Sam sputtered.

"Is there anything else?" Amanda asked impatiently. "My mother and I have a lot of work to do. I'm the new Chair of the Longhorn Ball. If you'd like to donate the value on that gift card to the Ball as an item for our auction, I'd be very interested in discussing that with you. But otherwise, I think we need to bring this conversation to a close."

Sam was dumbfounded. "That wouldn't be my decision to make. I'm just in charge of security. Or I will be until somebody finds out what's gone on here. You'd have to talk to somebody in, I don't know, marketing or community relations. Or something."

He looked just devastated that his case was collapsing, and with it, perhaps, his entire career in store security. And if the case was as much in free fall as it appeared, then he would have to answer both to the store and to Sharon Peavy for having pressed charges and sending her for a night in county jail. Elizabeth glanced back and forth between Sam and her daughter, quietly amazed by the turn of events.

Amanda stood, and so did Elizabeth, and so, instinctively, did Sam, a Texas gentleman who rose whenever ladies did. "Don't you want your gift card?" he asked forlornly, holding the envelope for Amanda to take.

"I keep trying to tell you," she said politely but firmly. "It's not my gift card. I hope you find out whose it is. I'm sure they'll be really happy to get it back. Unless there's anything else, Mr. Horn, my mom and I'll be on our way."

With that, Amanda led Elizabeth out of the security office, to the elevator, outside the building, and to Elizabeth's car.

Elizabeth handed Amanda the keys. "You'd better drive. I'm too stunned."

Amanda, calm again after the adrenaline rush of the conversation with Sam Horn, unlocked the doors, waited for her mother to get in, adjusted the driver's seat, and drove away from Neiman's and back toward Hillside Park and the Longhorn Ball office.

"What just happened?" Elizabeth asked. "I'm more confused than Paris Hilton at an outlet mall."

"What happened where?" Amanda played dumb.

"Why did you do that?" Elizabeth asked as her daughter nosed the car into traffic. "Sharon stole your card! She just flat-out lifted it off your desk, hoped you wouldn't notice, and took it to Neiman's. And it was her bad luck that instead of ninety-eight dollars or ninety-eight hundred dollars, there was ninety-eight thousand on it. Otherwise, she would have spent it—and unless they videotape every transaction, you'd never have seen that money again and would've never known what happened to it!"

Amanda said nothing.

"Well, why'd you do it?"

"I honestly don't have a good answer," Amanda admitted. "The last thing I want to do," she explained, "is get involved with some kind of criminal charges against Sharon, or against anybody. There's no peace in that. Nothing good can come of it. I'm not looking to make enemies. Besides, Mother, you always taught me it's okay to take on someone smarter than you are, but don't ever take on someone who's meaner than you are. I saw a mean side to Sharon when we were little, but she never turned it on me. I can't say that anymore. You seem to be right once again, Mom . . . there's nothing more dangerous than white trash with nothing to lose."

"You're not looking to make sense," Elizabeth chided. "You just left ninety-eight thousand dollars on the table."

"It was never my money," Amanda said, keeping her eyes on the road. "It's Mr. Black Mercedes's. Let him go after Neiman's. Or after Sharon. Just leave me out of it."

Elizabeth was all but speechless. "As your mother, all I can do is take credit for how well you turned out."

Amanda grinned. "That's the first time you've ever said you were proud of me—but technically, you really said you were proud of yourself."

"It's as close as you're gonna get. So enjoy it." Elizabeth stretched out a well-manicured hand to give her daughter a reassuring pat on the arm.

What an ordeal, Amanda thought. And it just keeps getting crazier and crazier. She stepped on the gas and headed for the office.

# 19

✦

After the unexpected side trip to Neiman's, Tuesday morning at the Longhorn Ball office found Amanda and Elizabeth trying to line up women to take on committee chairwoman roles and other volunteer tasks within the organization. In addition to having an overall chairwoman of the Ball, the planning structure called for chairwomen to be in charge of underwriting, table sales, the auctions, security, entertainment, food and beverage, location selection, and planning the fall and spring luncheons. The Ball held the member luncheons in order to announce the location, the headline entertainer, the underwriting dollars raised, and, as a motivational device, how the money raised for the Pediatric Foundation actually went to help children. One of the first tasks for the Ball Chair each year was to line up individuals to take on these duties. Normally, these people were already in place the previous year, but this year, *everything* was different.

The committee chairs were chosen from the active members of the organization, which comprised one hundred women in and around Hillside Park's social, religious, country club, and school communities. Sharon had helped locate a list of active and inactive members, along with their phone numbers and e-mail addresses. Since Amanda and Elizabeth had no computers and no office phones, their only method of reaching out was by cell phone, so, one by one, they called each name on the list. It was a trip down memory lane for Amanda—she had known most of the women when she was growing up in the community, had gone to college with some of them, had been sorority sisters with others, and otherwise was familiar with most of the names on the list. Naturally, because she had been away for twelve years, there were about two dozen women she had never met or heard of, women who had moved into the community after her departure. She gave those names to her mother and began to work her way down the list of women she had known from the past. As expected, when everyone is too jammed for time even to answer their own cell phones, Amanda reached voice mail with two-thirds of the phone numbers.

With the remaining numbers, a peculiar pattern ensued. Amanda and the committee member she was calling would be very excited to be back in touch after all these years. The committee member would commiserate with Amanda about her divorce and talk about her own status—married, divorced, single, or some unique hybrid thereof. Eventually, the conversation would get around to the question of taking on a leadership role at the Longhorn Ball, and that's when things got more bizarre time after time. Every single woman Amanda contacted said pretty much the same thing, in pretty much the same words—she'd love to do it, it's such a worthy cause, isn't Amanda sweet for taking on the responsibility of running the Ball, but it just isn't a good time. It's the children. Her husband just started his own company. It's other responsibilities in the community or other philanthropic commitments. It was a million things, and it was everything but "yes."

Elizabeth encountered the same level of resistance on her calls. Everybody was delighted to get a call from the mother of the Longhorn Ball Chair, everybody was so excited that Amanda had agreed to rescue the thing, everybody agreed that the Longhorn Ball did such great things for suffering children, and not a single person had a free moment in order to take on any responsibility connected with the Ball. After a fruitless, frustrating morning of voice mail and rejections, Amanda and Elizabeth snapped shut their cell phones, sat down opposite each other at Amanda's desk, and tried to figure out what the hell was going on.

"Susie's got this thing so screwed up nobody wants to touch it," Amanda said, shaking her head. "I can't get a single person to do a single thing. Even the girls who are literally the bottom rung on the social ladder. The ones who the only time they ever heard their mothers use the word 'luncheon' was when it preceded the word 'meat' are actually turning me down."

"I don't think it has anything to do with Susie," Elizabeth said, frowning. "I think the fix is in. I think somebody told everybody to say no."

"Like there's some sort of conspiracy?" Amanda asked disdainfully. "You don't really believe that, do you? Don't be ridiculous."

"Take a look at our collective batting average," Elizabeth pointed out. "Zero point zero. Don't you think somebody in town would want to do something unless they'd all been told not to?"

"By whom?" Amanda still didn't believe it. "And why would

anybody want to sabotage the Ball? I thought Heather and Sharon weren't trying to destroy it. They were trying to save it."

"Nobody's trying to sabotage the Ball." Elizabeth shook her head at her daughter's naïveté. "Somebody's trying to sabotage you!"

"That's ridic—" Amanda began, but then she stopped, rubbed her chin, and thought. "When you look at what Sharon did with that gift card—she's even worse than I remembered her. And Heather, with her 'Ira' ring on her finger. I wouldn't trust either of those girls as far as I could throw them. But I thought they were acting out of some kind of decency when they asked me to help rescue the Ball. They were just trying to reintegrate me into society, or at least that's what I thought."

"I'm actually feeling a little relieved," Elizabeth said, crossing her arms. "You've turned into such a water-walker that I'm amazed to see you misinterpreting anything."

"I beg your pardon? Water-walker?"

"You returned Mr. Black Mercedes's black Mercedes," Elizabeth began, cataloguing Amanda's recent moral triumphs. "You returned all that nice clothing, even though it was absolutely perfect for you. Then you had the opportunity, and some might say the moral obligation, to cooperate with Neiman Marcus over Sharon stealing your card, and you come up with some crazy story and leave ninety-eight thousand dollars of somebody else's money on the table. You've turned into Ms. Perfect. So it makes sense that you'd have a hard time believing that other people aren't treating you just as perfectly as you're treating everybody else."

"I don't know whether I was just complimented or insulted," Amanda replied hotly. "I'm just trying to do what's right. Or is that inappropriate in your moral universe?"

"I'm sorry." Elizabeth waved a hand in apology. "I don't know what I'm being so testy about. I think every decision you've made has been fabulous. It just seems kind of striking that somebody who could know her own mind so well could have such a hard time seeing what other people are trying to do to her."

"And what exactly are other people trying to do to me?" Amanda's patience was waning.

"I'm not exactly sure what it is. But when these women get together, they're meaner than a bunch of rattlesnakes. Whatever they're plotting, I can guarantee you that it's not good."

HEATHER SAPPINGTON HAD dropped Sharon Peavy off at the home Sharon shared on the outskirts of Hillside Park with her aunt—a secret that Sharon shared with very few women. She could tell Heather since she, too, lived on the wrong side of the tracks with an elderly relative. This was the only way for both women to claim an acceptable address in the Longhorn Ball directory. The pricey rent in Hillside Park would've left virtually no money for anything else—surely not tickets to charitable luncheons, and definitely not the right wardrobe. And wasn't that the most important thing? Sharon found it impossible to sleep. After a long hot shower to wipe any trace of the institutional smell of jail off of her body, she had collapsed onto her bed but found herself too exhausted to sleep, too angry, and too caught up in mentally replaying the events of the last eighteen hours. First, the betrayal by the seemingly duplicitous Neiman's clerk, Travis; then the interrogation at the hands of that admittedly attractive head of security, Sam Horn, who proved shockingly impervious to her femininity; and then the indignity of the police station and the booking process, the ghastly smelling drunk tank, and then the sleepless hours she spent in county jail. It had been the worst experience, or worst sequence of experiences, in her entire life, and the more she thought about it, the more she knew there was only one person to blame for the entire thing. Amanda Vaughn.

The ingratitude of that woman! That's what burned Sharon up more than anything else. Here Sharon and Heather had handed Amanda the opportunity of a lifetime to reintegrate herself into the Hillside Park social scene and start her out at the top! And how did Amanda repay her for this extraordinary act of kindness? By leaving that damned Neiman's gift card in plain sight on the desk, tempting her, daring her, inviting her, maybe even inciting her to take the thing and see what it was worth. In her heart, Sharon knew she never would have used the card. She was just curious. You see a gift card, you want to know how much is on it. She wouldn't have taken it if she had thought it was Amanda's. She thought it was Susie's!

Anybody would know that. Even the police should have known that. Even Sam Horn should have. But did they? No.

Twisting and turning on her bed, too emotionally drained to cry anymore, Sharon suddenly figured out what Amanda's whole scheme had been. Leave the gift card out—because if you didn't want somebody to see it or take it, you wouldn't have it sitting out somewhere; you'd keep it in your purse. It was to look like Amanda's quiet way of thanking Sharon for the privilege of running the Ball. Everybody knew Sharon didn't have anything like Amanda's money. Amanda came from money, she made her own, and then she got a whole big chunk of it after she left Bill. This was supposed to look like an act of kindness or charity on Amanda's part, almost a gratuity, not in a condescending way, but just as sort of a little thank-you. Or at least that's what it was supposed to look like, Sharon told herself, so that Sharon would take it, and then go to Neiman's, and one thing would lead to another and she would be behind bars. Sharon slowly worked her way into another seething mass of righteous indignation. She was just so angry at Amanda that there was only one place she could go in order to get herself straight—straight in her own mind, and straight with God. Sharon practically bolted right up out of bed, ran to the closet, and put on the Marni silk blouse and black silk skirt she'd gotten for a steal at a Hillside Park estate sale (her most conservative outfit). She jumped in her old Beemer and drove to the only place she knew where she could find total acceptance, total peace, and a totally receptive audience for the story she was about to tell.

Sharon Peavy headed for Bible study.

✦

## 20

Meanwhile, at the Hillside Park police station, things were not going well for Sam Horn.

"Drop the charges?" asked Mark Robinson, Hillside Park chief of police, his tone incredulous. "You had me arrest a Hillside Park woman and send her to county jail—and now you're dropping the charges? This cannot be happening."

Sam Horn and Mark Robinson shared a background in the marines, and they were afraid of neither terrorists nor conventional enemies. The only thing that struck terror into the hearts of either man was the idea of an angry Hillside Park woman—angry at them, especially when she had cause to be angry.

"She doesn't exactly live in Hillside Park," Sam said, grasping at straws, trying to put up a brave front. He was just as scared as Mark. "And she rents," he added helpfully.

"I don't care if she lives under a bridge or in the Taj Mahal!" Mark snapped. They were seated opposite each other in his office. "Single, married, divorced—they're all the same. They're all hell on wheels if you piss 'em off. And she's gotta be righteously pissed off."

"There's nothing I can do about it," Sam said, shaking his

head sadly. "An absolutely beautiful open-and-shut case, but the woman whose card it was just went south on me. I've got no idea why somebody like Amanda Vaughn would want to protect somebody like Sharon Peavy."

"You know these women?"

"I know who Amanda is. She's been shopping here since she was a little girl. And her parents before that. Pillars of the community."

"And this Peavy woman?" Mark asked, still not believing that he had arrested a woman on Neiman's behalf and now would have to drop the charges.

Sam was desperate. "As far as we can tell, she's never shopped in the store in her life, at least not with her own money. She didn't really look the type, either."

Mark thought about it for a minute. "I see your point. So how exactly would a woman who can't afford to shop at Neiman's, has never shopped at Neiman's, probably never will shop at Neiman's, come into possession of a gift card for ninety-eight thousand dollars, unless she stole it from the person whose name is on the card?"

"That's what I thought," Sam said helplessly. "It made no sense to me, either. There's no other explanation. Now I'm wondering what Amanda's hiding."

"You think maybe Amanda set Sharon up?" Mark tried to figure out some logical explanation for the story Sam had told him about Amanda's refusal to either condemn Sharon or take the substitute gift card.

Sam shrugged. "These women get into all kinds of situations with each other. We're just a store. We're not therapists. Or referees."

"Is she married?" Mark asked. He was two years from retirement, and all he needed now was something like this to end his career prematurely. "To a lawyer?"

Sam had done his homework. Sharon had been arrested a few years ago on shoplifting charges and was told never to come back in the store again as part of her "restitution." He was keeping that card close for now in case he needed to play it later to try and redeem himself. "Maybe that's the only good news I can give you. She's not married, she's never been married, and if she has a lawyer for a boyfriend, she would have made him come down either to the store or to the police station last night. So if it's a lawsuit you're worried about—"

"Of course it's a lawsuit I'm worried about!" Mark snapped. His tone became weary. "I'll call the district attorney and get the charges dropped for lack of a corroborating witness. But Horn?"

"Yes?" Sam found himself unable to look Mark in the eye.

"Please make sure nothing like this happens for the next twenty-four months. I just want to retire and never see Hillside Park again. Or any of the women in it. Am I clear?"

"Abundantly. I read you loud and clear."


TUESDAY AFTERNOON BIBLE study was ten minutes from wrapping up. The leader asked, "Before we close, do we have any prayer requests?"

Sharon quickly raised her hand. All eyes turned toward her. News of her arrest and brief incarceration had already made the rounds in Hillside Park, and there wasn't a single woman in the room who had not heard the story of her degrading and humiliating experiences. They'd all given her the obligatory, disapproving look down their noses when she came in. Sharon smoothed her silk skirt and spoke in a soft, wounded tone. "I'd like to ask all of y'all to pray for me," she began. "I've just been through the worst experience of my life. I need to heal and find forgiveness in my heart for the individual who deliberately, intentionally, and cruelly set out to do me harm. I was in jail last night and I'm lookin' at doing serious time in a state penitentiary, all on account of her deliberately setting me up. I won't name names, because that would not be very Christian of me, but all I can say is what's so extraordinarily cruel about this woman is that she's in a really great place in her life. I mean, she's the individual who has taken over the Longhorn Ball for this coming year, yet she's gone out of her way to destroy me and cause me harm."

A wave of electricity swept through the room. Everybody in Hillside Park knew that meant Amanda. How or why Amanda might have taken steps that led to Sharon becoming branded a criminal was something no one knew. All leaned closer to hear the gory details.

"Yesterday," Sharon went on, "I stopped by the offices of the Longhorn Ball. I went in there out of a sense of Christian duty to Aman—I don't want to say her name. Oh, I've already messed this up, y'all know who I'm talkin' about? There's only one Longhorn Ball, for goodness' sake.

"Anyway, I went in there because I wanted to assist my dear, dear friend Amanda, whom I had not seen in so many years, who has returned home to Hillside Park after a twelve-year marriage to a man who, as we all know, stepped out on her every chance he could, and the good Lord knows what kind of damage he did, not just to the moral fiber of that family, but also who knows what kind of sexually transmitted diseases he might have introduced into his marriage."

She caught herself for a moment. The sleeplessness, exhaustion, and terror she had experienced in the last twenty-four hours had clouded her judgment. She definitely wished she could take back the part about sexually transmitted diseases. But what the heck. It was probably true, anyway. "All right," Sharon continued, her audience rapt, hanging on her every word. "It's not about the STDs. It's what Amanda did to me yesterday in the office. She took a gift card from Neiman Marcus, with a very large amount of money on it, and unbeknownst to me, while I was there trying to help them make sense of things and find documents and otherwise assist them getting the Longhorn Ball off the ground after what happened this past year, well, when I had my back turned, Amanda took that gift card and stuck it in my purse."

There were gasps from the ladies, who had never heard of such a terrible thing happening. What was Hillside Park coming to, anyway?

"When I saw it, I said, 'Amanda, what's this gift card doing here in my purse? Why, it's from Neiman Marcus!'

"And she said, 'It's my gift to you for making me Chair of the Ball. It must have belonged to Susie. I found it here in Susie's desk. She's got more money than she knows what to do with, so I thought this might be a nice gift for you. Why don't you go on down to Neiman's, see how much is on the card, and why don't you just buy yourself something nice with it. Susie's not going to miss it, is she? Just don't tell a soul what I did!'"

The woman leading the Bible study tried to signal Sharon that she was both off topic and taking far too long. This wasn't a request for prayer; it was the plot of a soap opera. But the leader was the only one in the room who didn't want the story to continue.

"Anyway," Sharon plunged ahead, oblivious, "y'all aren't going to believe what happened next. I went down to Neiman's, and they told me the card was stolen. They roughed me up, taking me into an area of the store where they just had all kinds of boxes lying around. And then from there . . ." Now she began tearing up. "It was to the police station, where I was booked like a common criminal, and then they stuck me in a drunk tank and the men from the drunk tank across the way—I could go on and on, but I wouldn't dream of it. Suffice it to say that all of this was Amanda's wicked plot against me.

"She set me up for all of this! I would ask for prayers for her, but frankly I wonder if she's just too far gone for prayer. I know that where there's life there's hope, but I just don't see how God himself could possibly forgive Amanda for what she's done to me. It's me who needs y'all's prayers. I'm the one who has to learn to forgive Amanda for destroying my life.

"I didn't do anything wrong. I hope you all understand that. I was just accepting a gift from a person who I thought was my dear friend. Please keep me in your thoughts and prayers, and please ask God to guide my heart and show me how to forgive someone who will never admit or acknowledge what she's done to me, so she certainly can't ever ask for my forgiveness."

They all prayed for Sharon to have patience, wisdom, understanding, and peace in her heart to forgive Amanda for her devious ways. The Bible study drew to a close as the women chorused, "In Jesus' name, amen."

An hour later, when Amanda went to pick up her children at the school, there was a definite chill in the air that had nothing to do with the still-sweltering Dallas heat. The other mothers barely glanced in Amanda's direction, as if she suffered from a very rare, highly contagious social disease. Even women who came from families far less stable or wealthy than Amanda's, and were therefore way down in the Hillside Park pecking order, glanced at Amanda as if she were the survivor of a traffic accident but they had no interest in stopping to talk or find out how she was. Word had spread from the Bible study that Amanda had first tried to destroy the reputation of poor Susie, and was now going after Susie's innocent best friend, Sharon. This bizarre and inexplicable series of behaviors could have only one possible desired outcome—establishing Amanda as the new queen and arbiter of taste in social matters for Hillside Park.

Who would lie at a Bible study, the women had asked themselves, and the answer that came back to them was surely not Sharon Peavy. So pretty much everyone—all of the mothers involved in the social network of Hillside Park—found themselves believing, and believing fully, every word about Amanda that Sharon had spoken. On top of that, Heather had begun a smear campaign of her own, sending e-mails to everyone she could think of about how strange it was that Amanda could come back to Hillside Park and foster so much discord and even outright hatred in less than a full week.

Amanda had no idea what had transpired at Bible study, and she greeted the other mothers as she had the day before while picking up Will and Sarah. This time though, things were different. No one talked to her. No one even offered eye contact. "I don't understand. Am I imagining things?" she asked herself.

"Why won't anybody even so much as give me the time of day? I know I'm the queen of hurting my own feelings, but this is ridiculous."

Two women Amanda's age approached, and she started to

say hello. But before she could get out a single word, one of the mothers, a recent import to Hillside Park from somewhere else in Dallas, turned to Amanda with a glare. "How could you do that to Sharon?" she hissed. "Don't you have any idea how hard she worked for you?"

Amanda's jaw dropped. She couldn't think of anything to say. But she didn't need to, because at that moment, another woman approached her.

"What you've done is disgusting," this new stranger said. "First, you completely sabotaged Susie, and now you're trying to take down Sharon as well and send her to prison?"

"I don't know what you're talking about," Amanda began, but her accusers had already turned their backs and gone off in search of their children. As they turned away, Amanda heard one of their cell phones ring and couldn't believe her ears. This mean-spirited stranger's ring tone was set with Carrie Underwood's "Jesus Take the Wheel." Oh, *please*! "She might want to rethink that," Amanda said under her breath. "Maybe I'll change mine to Guns n' Roses' 'Welcome to the Jungle' or Bon Jovi's 'Living on a Prayer.' " How befitting, she mused. Amanda wandered around, crushed emotionally, wondering what she had done to deserve these outbursts, looking for Will and Sarah. When she found them, and Will went into his litany of the seventy-nine reasons why Hillside Park Middle School sucked, Amanda didn't even have the energy to tell him to quit using that word.

Sarah had more harsh comments regarding the obesity, lethargy, and nonathleticism of her classmates, but Amanda lacked the energy to respond to her, either. She wanted to work up the strength to tell her that there were plenty of athletic children in Hillside Park, and she would find them before long, and that even a community as intellectually advanced as Hillside Park still existed in the United States, where a vast childhood obesity problem was increasing year by year. But she was just too crushed by the attacks. She dropped the children at her mother's place and went back to the Longhorn Ball office, where she sat alone in the dark.

Suddenly it was just all too much for Amanda—the new house, the new life, the new responsibilities of the Longhorn Ball, and the new accusations that she had done something terrible to the lives of both Susie and Sharon. She sat in her chair behind a desk that had neither computers nor phones, in an office that lacked electricity, and she put her head down on her desk and began to sob uncontrollably.

# 21

✦

Elizabeth, Will, and Sarah looked up with surprise from the dinner table as Amanda entered the kitchen, as dressed up as any of them could ever remember having seen her. Elizabeth suppressed a grin while Sarah and Will stared at their mother, trying to figure out why she would be so dressed up. Amanda was wearing a stunning champagne-colored Roberto Cavalli dress. "You look gorgeous, Mom," Sarah exclaimed. Even Will couldn't think of a clever comeback.

"Glad to see you're going out finally," Elizabeth said. "I thought I was going to have to fill in for you a second time."

Amanda, embarrassed, turned away from her family and busily started moving dishes and plates from the sink into the dishwasher.

"Where are you going, Mom?" Sarah asked. "Some sort of charity thing? Is it connected with the Longhorn Ball?"

"In a manner of speaking," Elizabeth said, her grin spreading. "Your mom has to talk to one of the major donors. See if she can get him to up his donation." She winked at her daughter.

"That's not true," Will said, raising his voice. "Mom! You're going on a date!" His tone was halfway between accusation and betrayal. Amanda could feel herself blushing, and kept herself turned away from her children.

"Are you going on a date?" Sarah asked.

"You're not even technically divorced!" Will exclaimed. "I'm telling Dad!"

That did it. "If your dad hadn't started dating a year after we got married," Amanda retorted, "we'd still be living in Newport Beach!" She put her hand over her eyes. "Why did I say something that stupid?"

"It's true," Elizabeth told Will. "I know you love your daddy, but he was no saint. I understand you're very angry right now, but you've got to let up on your mother, Will."

Sarah closed her eyes and put a hand in the air. "Could we just, like, slow down a little bit? I just feel like we're getting a little too much information over here. Mommy, are you really going on a date?"

She took a closer look at her mother. "Are your eyes red? Oh, Mommy, you look like you've been crying again!"

"Yes, my eyes are red," Amanda admitted. "And no, I'm not technically going on a date. There's a man who gave one hundred and fifty thousand dollars to the Longhorn Ball. He's the same man who—well, never mind that. When somebody gives you that much money, you have to sit down with them face-to-face and find out what their expectations are. How many Ball tickets will they want, is this to underwrite something specifically? You have to ask these questions; it's part of your responsibility. That's just how things work."

"So is it a date or isn't it?" Will asked, getting back to the crux of the matter. He looked less like the tough guy he pretended to be and more like a little boy who suddenly realized just how shattered his world really was. Amanda turned off the water and came to the table. She put her hand on Will's head. "Your daddy and I aren't married anymore," she said gently. "I wouldn't exactly characterize tonight as a date. I'm not in a dating mood, and you're right—technically, your father and I are not divorced. I've got no interest in other men. I've certainly got no interest in your father. But I'm not ready to be involved with anyone else. I promise you that. My primary concern is taking care of you guys."

Will shook his mother's hand away. "Well then, why are you going out? Why not send Gigi?"

Amanda thought about telling her son the truth—that she was intrigued by the extraordinary, even overwhelming generosity of the man she was going to meet tonight, and she had to satisfy her curiosity as to who would seek to give her a three-hundred-thousand-dollar car, a ninety-eight-thousand-dollar wardrobe, and a hundred-fifty-thousand-dollar donation to the Longhorn Ball. Especially when it seemed that everyone in Dallas was running as far away from the Ball, and from Amanda, as they possibly could.

"I know it's all hard to deal with," she told her son quietly. "Believe me, it's hard for me, too."

"There must have been a reason Daddy had all those girlfriends," the boy snapped.

"The technical term is sex addiction," Elizabeth cracked, only to receive an angry glare from her daughter.

"Mother, please. Don't make this worse than it is."

"Why were you crying, Mommy?" Sarah asked, touching her mother's arm.

"I just had a tough day, honey," Amanda admitted with a tiny sigh. "People weren't exactly kind to me, and they just gave me the sense that something was very wrong with me."

"With you? But you're perfect! You eat red meat, but aside from that, who's better than you?"

Amanda could feel the tears coming again, but she forced them back, not wanting to look glassy-eyed at her first encounter with Mr. Black Mercedes.

"Who's sweeter than you?" Amanda asked Sarah, kissing her hair.

"Everyone," Will said tartly, looking like he might burst into tears, too.

"That's enough, Will," Amanda said sternly. "Look. Let's just get this straight, once and for all. I'm not going on a date. I've got to see a man who is donating a hundred and fifty thousand dollars to the Longhorn Ball. I'm going to have a drink with him or dinner or whatever, but I'm sure I'll be back in time to tuck you guys in, say your prayers, and give you goodnight kisses. Gigi's going to stay with you and I'll be back soon."

"You're not going to spend the night with the guy, are you?" Will asked. "You're still married."

Amanda looked at her son, shocked and speechless.

"That didn't stop your father, not for a minute," Elizabeth told her grandson. "I don't care how many Game Boys or Wiis your father buys you. If you're going to be casting blame around, why don't you keep in mind the fact that he was a serial philanderer?"

"Mom, will you please?" Amanda demanded.

"What's a . . . serial philanderer?" Will asked.

"Look it up in the dictionary," Elizabeth told him, grabbing another piece of fried chicken. "You'll see his picture right there."

"Mom," Amanda began, sounding exasperated, "I made up

my mind when I came back here that I would do everything I could not to poison the children's minds against their father."

"I never signed on for that deal," her mother said. "From my point of view, the more poison, the better. Let 'em know the truth. Then they'll get off your case."

"Will you please let me handle this my way?"

"Suit yourself. Sooner or later, you're going to figure out your way's obviously not working. Where are you meeting him again?"

"That Japanese place over off Cedar Springs. I've never been."

"A wise choice," Elizabeth said approvingly. "Muy romantico. And muy discreet."

Amanda rolled her eyes. "I don't have time for this." She got up, grabbed her purse, and kissed each of her children on the top of their heads. "Listen to Gigi," she instructed.

"Have a nice date," Will called out after her. "Don't do anything I wouldn't do!"

"Like smart off? Be disrespectful? I'm probably not likely to do that. Thanks for the advice."

"Love you, Mom," Sarah said, crunching into a carrot. "If you eat the sushi, make sure it's super-hyper-fresh."

"I'll do that," Amanda said, barely suppressing a smile. "But thanks anyway for watching them, Mom. Please, don't say anything more about their father. I think you've done enough damage for one evening."

"I think I have at that." Elizabeth sounded quite pleased with herself.

"Oh, Mom." Amanda glanced at her watch. "I'm late. Bye."

"Bye," her family chorused, and she was gone.

●  ●  ●

HEATHER SAPPINGTON AND Sharon Peavy sat at the bar at Bob's, watching the early dinner crowd arrive and get seated. Bob's was the hottest singles bar in Hillside Park, offering a combination of convenience and discretion that few other bars could match. It was the darkest bar in the community, and it provided taxi service along with the opportunity to leave one's car in the secure private parking lot until the next morning, a service that aided those whose blood alcohol levels were over the limit, as well as those who came in their own cars and went home in someone else's.

Heather and Sharon often joked that they had barstools named after them at Bob's, an assertion that wasn't that far from the truth.

"Shouldn't you go easy on those?" Heather said, indicating Sharon's third double apple martini. "You didn't even get any sleep last night. Have you eaten anything today?" I certainly haven't eaten anything, Heather thought to herself, but the vodka soda she was sipping made for as good a dinner as any.

"What's the point of eating?" Sharon asked glumly. "I'm a convicted felon."

"Honey, honey. You're nothing of the sort," Heather assured her, rolling her eyes. "You had a little trouble at the store. Darlene will get it all worked out. Have you called her yet?"

"What you call 'a little trouble at the store,' the district attorney calls 'three to five years for larceny by trick.'" Sharon tried to surreptitiously fix her boobs for optimal cleavage, but her writhing wasn't lost on any of the men in the bar. Her hot-pink ruffled tunic only attracted more attention. At least it was a Jil Sander—the only one she owned. "And no, I haven't called Darlene," she mumbled. "I'm just too embarrassed."

"Poor baby," Heather comforted, chewing on her lower lip. "I still don't understand how the whole thing happened."

"I told you five times," Sharon insisted, her words slurred. "She set me up. What did I ever do to her?"

"You were trying to destroy her socially. Maybe she caught on."

"It was all your idea. And I never liked it from the beginning. You pushed me into it."

"I did not." Heather's dismissal was halfhearted, though. She had pushed her friend into it, and they both knew it. Sharon glared at her cheap platform sandals. Heather busied herself fixing the strap on her deeply discounted Donna Karan halter top.

"Where do we go from here?" Sharon said. "Do you think they're going to make me surrender my passport?"

"Except for Club Med in Cancun, years ago," Heather noted, "I don't remember you ever leaving the country. Do you even, like, have a passport?"

"Mmm . . . not really." Sharon stared at the mirror above the bar. "But maybe they'll make me get one and surrender it."

"You've been watching too much *CSI*."

"The way my social life's gone," Sharon admitted, "those guys hollering at me from the drunk tank last night? Those were the best offers I've gotten in months."

"Poor baby." Heather stroked Sharon's hair. "It's all gonna be okay."

"Not for Amanda," her friend muttered darkly.

"What do you mean?" Heather checked out a couple of men who looked to be in their early fifties at the maître d's stand. She positioned herself more advantageously on the bar stool, seductively angling her legs to make her thighs look thinner.

"I fixed her wagon but good," Sharon said.

"How?" Heather asked, only paying half attention to her friend.

Those guys were cute. "At Bible study."

Heather saw the two men joined by two women who had to be ten years younger than herself and Sharon. She shook her head, disgusted. "In Bible study?" she asked, tuning back into the conversation with Sharon. "Don't tell me you prayed for her," she added, alluding to one of the favorite surefire methods that a very few Hillside Park women used for getting gossipy information into the public record.

Sharon gave a self-satisfied smile. "Actually," she said, pulling on her drink, "I prayed for myself."

"Huh? What are you talking about?" Heather watched the older men and the younger women smiling, looking unbearably happy in general as they made their way to their table. Isn't that nice, Heather thought bitterly, silently wishing she had a husband or boyfriend or even an underage manservant waiting back home.

"It was so cool. I was genius!" Sharon explained. "I asked the women in Bible study to pray for me. I explained that I was the one who needed their prayers, because I had been set up so viciously after I had extended myself in true Christian fellowship to a woman who turned around and bit me like a snake. I told the whole story about the gift card, and getting arrested, and how the whole thing had been a setup from the start. Now that I think about it, Amanda was probably in with the Neiman's security staff and the Hillside Park police from the get-go. I wish I had thought of that sooner. I could have put that into my prayer request."

"How did it go over?"

"It went over perfectly." Sharon caught the bartender's eye, pointing to her drink.

"Um . . . are you sure you want another one of those?"

"Don't worry about me, darlin'. I'm just in a celebratory mood. I might have gone to jail for a night, but Amanda's reputation is going to be ruined forever. It doesn't get any better than that."

Sharon's cell phone rang. She fumbled in her purse, found it, and flipped it open. The screen read "unknown caller."

She glanced at Heather, as if to say, "I wonder who this could be."

"Hello?"

"Sharon Peavy?" asked a stern-sounding male voice.

"This is she," Sharon said, quickly sobering up.

"This is Detective Paul Martland of the Hillside Park Police Department."

Alarmed, Sharon put her hand over the mouthpiece. "It's the police," she whispered to Heather.

"I think something of an apology is in order," the detective began, sounding embarrassed and contrite.

"What are you talking about? I already apologized."

The bartender placed a fresh double apple martini in front of Sharon, but she quickly waved it away.

"It's actually . . . well, we're the ones who need to apologize to you," the detective continued.

"I beg your pardon?" Sharon asked, thinking that maybe the call was a function of her alcohol intake.

"Ma'am," Detective Martland continued, "I'm just calling to let you know that all charges against you have been dropped."

"Dropped?" Sharon was stunned. She had been playing the role of Christian martyr only for a few hours and had begun to relish her status as such. Was it already being stripped away from her?

"Did you say you're dropping all charges?" she repeated, speaking slowly, as people who've had too much to drink often do—so as to keep others from recognizing just how drunk they really were.

Heather looked baffled. "They dropped the charges?" Sharon waved a hand to silence her.

"Why are they dropping the charges?" she asked into the phone.

"The woman whose card it was?" Martland said, sounding uncertain, as if the story were too hard for him to believe as well. "Actually, the woman whose name was on the card. A Ms. Amanda Vaughn."

"I know whose name it is. Get to the point."

"I'm trying, ma'am. It's a little confusing on my end. But the point is this—the security department at Neiman Marcus asked her to come to the store this morning so that she could corroborate the story. Ms. Vaughn explained that the card was not hers, that she had never seen the card before in her life, that you therefore couldn't possibly have stolen it, and that she was not interested in testifying against you in any way, shape, or form. When the district attorney heard that, he had no choice but to drop the case. I'm sure that Neiman's is going to work out some sort of compensation for you for the . . . inconvenience you suffered."

Sharon's mouth formed a perfect O. Something she had perfected, as she had had much practice and experience.

"Are you . . . are you there?" Martland asked. "Did we lose the connection?"

"I'm here. I don't know if I'm all here, but I'm here. So that's the end of it? It's over?"

"Except for the matter of how Neiman Marcus wants to compensate you for what you went through. Can you come by later this week?"

"This is all very hard to believe," Sharon said slowly, trying to make sense of everything through her slight alcoholic haze. "I just want to make sure I heard you right. It's over?"

"It's over," the detective confirmed. "Sorry for what you went through, ma'am."

"That makes two of us." She disconnected and put the phone back in her purse. Heather stared at her.

"The scoop? What was that all about?" she asked.

"They brought Amanda down to Neiman's, to the security office. And she told them it wasn't her card, even though it had her name on it. So I couldn't possibly have stolen it from her. I guess without Amanda testifying against me, they had no case. So they dropped the whole thing."

"They dropped the whole thing?" Heather repeated in disbelief.

"Except for the fact that the detective said that Neiman's wants to compensate me for what I went through." Sharon thought for a moment. "I guess that's their way of making sure I don't sue them."

"Wow!" Heather said softly.

"Wow, is right," Sharon repeated.

She thought for a long moment. "She never set me up," she admitted sheepishly. "I just swiped that card. I figured it was Susie's, and Amanda would never have even noticed it with everything going on. And she knew it. She didn't have to get me off the hook with the police. I've got no idea what made her want to do that."

"She's just a kind person," Heather said. Sharon pursed her lips and nodded.

"Yeah, she is. Unlike me." Then she realized what she had done earlier, in Bible study, and she felt a sharp pain in her head. "I can't believe what I did. She kept me from going to prison, but I dragged her name through the mud in Bible study. Do you have any idea how screwed I am?"

Heather thought for a moment, as Sharon caught the bartender's eye, and this time raised two fingers, pointing to her drink. The bartender, surprised but not all that surprised, since he had been serving Sharon for years, nodded and set to preparing two double apple martinis.

"I don't know how screwed you are," Heather said, sipping her own drink and watching another two men in their early fifties arriving at the maître d' stand. "But I've got the feeling that if I stick around, I'm gonna find out."

# 22

*✦*

Across town, at Nobu, Amanda nervously handed her car off to the valet, went into the restaurant, and approached the impossibly young, impossibly chic woman at the maître d' stand.

"I'm looking for . . ." She realized she didn't know whom she was looking for.

The girl actually had a photo of Amanda clipped to her reservation book. She smiled. "You are Ms. Vaughn. Please follow me."

Amanda followed her past the main dining room and into one of the private dining rooms in the back. She ushered Amanda into the room, and a moment later, Thomas Harrington, Amanda's high school classmate and the object of her four-year unrequited crush, stepped inside.

"Oh, my God!" she exclaimed, putting a hand to her mouth. "Tom! It's you!"

"It's me, all right," Tom said sheepishly, kicking off his fabulous Armani loafers and taking a seat on the floor at the small table opposite Amanda. "I hope it's okay that it's me."

She shook her head slowly, as if to say, "Nothing could surprise me now."

"Tom, you're a married man! What are you doing showering all these crazy gifts on me?"

He shrugged. "I'm about as married as you are." The news shocked Amanda.

"I thought you guys were great together," she said, overwhelmed with disbelief. "You and Janie are one of the happiest couples in Dallas."

"Don't believe everything you hear, positive or negative, is all I can say," Tom said philosophically. "Our marriage was never right from the beginning. The only good thing I can tell you is that we never had any kids."

"But—but—I heard a lot of stories about what was going on back home when I was out in California. I never heard a word about the two of you."

"We both wanted to keep it that way," he said with a nod. "Janie's starting a new life in Santa Fe with some painter she met. I was going to move out of Dallas for a year and go to Austria for the winter and ski and then just kind of travel around for a few months and figure out what I wanted to do next. And then I heard that you were coming back to town."

"I'm living in your house," Amanda said.

"I know. I'm your landlord."

"That's some coincidence." She was still trying to wrap her mind around the idea that Tom was Mr. Black Mercedes.

"It wasn't much of a coincidence. I told Ann Anderson that if you rented any other house than mine, she'd never sell another house in Hillside Park—and I guess I'm one of the few people who could actually make that happen."

"I guess you are," Amanda agreed, flustered. "I'm sorry. I'm still just trying to come to grips with the fact that you're the guy."

"I'm the guy, all right," he agreed with a grin, studying her to see exactly how she felt about the whole thing.

"Why did you have to do things on such a crazy scale?" she asked. "The Mercedes? The wardrobe? The donation to the Longhorn Ball? Why couldn't you have just, I don't know, sent flowers or chocolate like a regular guy?"

"Well, I know you've always wanted a black Mercedes and I knew better than to give you a watch. How's that for an answer?"

"I'd really hoped everyone had forgotten that story," Amanda said, mortified.

"And as far as the regular guy thing goes, I may be a lot of things," Tom said, a hint of pride in his words, "but one thing I'm not now and I've never been is a regular guy. And you're not exactly a regular girl. And remember, there are some people in Hillside Park who still don't believe I was innocent of the drug smuggling charges—I thought you might be one of them."

"How come you and Janie didn't work out? I mean, if you don't mind me asking."

"Aside from her . . . interest in the fine arts? It's hard to say. She hates Mexico, and I was spending half my time there or more. We have a beautiful place in Mexico City—I have to stop saying *we*. It's a hard habit to break."

"Tell me about it," Amanda said wryly.

"I'm sure I don't have to," he said. "And a place in Veracruz, and a really nice place in Acapulco. And another place in Zihuatanejo."

"You sound more like a hotel chain than a human being," Amanda joked.

"I like nice things," Tom cheerfully admitted. "And nice places. And nice people. Is there anything wrong with that?"

"Not as far as I'm concerned. I feel the same way."

"Janie didn't. She had a very hard time, first with the amount of time my work took, and second, with the success we started to enjoy. I think all that high cotton was a little out of her comfort zone, if you know what I mean."

"I suppose."

"That didn't keep her, or her lawyers, from asking for—and receiving—half of everything I built. But it's okay. I'm sad that things went the way they did, but I don't have any real hard feelings toward her. She definitely knocked me down from eighty-seventh to two-hundred-thirty-fourth on the Forbes list, but I'll get over it. I'll bounce back."

"I admire your resiliency," Amanda said, laughing. At that moment, a startlingly attractive Japanese woman entered with a large bottle of warm sake. She poured cups for the two of them and left through the room's curtains.

"You a sake girl?" he asked.

"Not really, but I could become one for the evening, if that'll help."

"That'll help," he said. They toasted glasses and tasted the warm, sweet wine.

"So in your mind," Amanda began, "a black Maybach, the perfect wardrobe at Neiman's—that's the equivalent of candy and flowers. What do you do if you really like a girl?"

"I don't know," Tom admitted, grinning. "I haven't really liked anybody aside from Janie since I met her. Now that she's off with Leonardo da Vinci over in Santa Fe, I guess I've got some time to find out. Before Janie, it was you, but you had to go run off with what's his name."

Amanda blushed. "Didn't you think maybe you were pushing a little too far, too fast?" Amanda took a second sip of the sake.

"I haven't been in the 'dating scene' for ten years," Tom said sheepishly. "I was never a man for small gestures. In any aspect of my life."

"I've been out of it for a while myself," Amanda noted ruefully. "Who knows? Maybe this is how everybody does things. Dropping off cars and wardrobes. But somehow I doubt it."

"Me too." Tom sipped his sake and smiled.

"Why all the secrecy? Why couldn't you have just come out and said, 'It's me and let's have dinner'?"

"You know how it is in Hillside Park. Tongues wag. It seems like every kind of communication you make can be intercepted. I just thought it might be more interesting if we did it this way."

"Well, you certainly had me guessing. . . . Oh. You're not going to like this. After I sent back the clothes to Neiman's, they gave me a gift card, but I didn't really . . . keep it. It's kind of a long story."

"I'd like to hear it."

"I don't really want to relive it right now," Amanda said shaking her head. "Some other time. Anyway, I can make it up to you."

"It's not enough money for me to worry about," he said, dismissing it.

Amanda paused. She thought ninety-eight thousand dollars was enough for anybody to worry about, but, she figured, maybe she was wrong.

"How do you like the house?" Tom asked.

"It's perfect. It's beautiful. We love it. I guess you miss it."

Tom thought before he spoke. "I miss the house. But I don't exactly miss some of the memories."

"I know exactly what you mean by that."

"I'll bet you do. Rumor has it that you had a pretty tough go of it out in California."

"Well, for once rumor has it correct. It wasn't a lot of fun."

"It never is." An uncomfortable silence settled between the two of them.

He finally broke it. "I didn't even ask you if you like sushi," he said apologetically.

"You didn't even ask me if I liked you enough to have dinner with you," Amanda replied, giving him a small grin.

"Well, do you?"

"Do I what? Like sushi or like you?"

"You can take any part of the question you want."

"I like sushi just fine." Her smile widened. "The jury's still out on you."

"Fair enough." Tom studied the dinner selections. "So you've taken over the Longhorn Ball."

"It's the other way around," Amanda said, studying the offerings. "I think the Longhorn Ball has taken over me."

"Why is that?" Tom asked, closing his menu.

"I wouldn't even know how to begin to answer that question," she said wearily. "First, Susie left the office in the most disgraceful state imaginable. Second, if it were any other organization or business, they'd be throwing her in jail for malfeasance and stealing cash. Third, it feels like there's some sort of conspiracy in town to keep me from succeeding. There's not a single woman in Hillside Park who's willing to help out in any way, shape, or form. And fourth, I don't know if there's a vendor in the state of Texas who will have anything to do with us. I don't think Susie paid a single bill all last year. How's that for starters?"

Tom considered all of those factors. "Well, how'd you get roped into chairing the Ball in the first place?"

"Roped into it is exactly the right phrase," Amanda said. "A couple of women approached me and asked me to do it, and I just figured, I've got nothing else going on. I thought it might integrate me back into the neighborhood. Instead, I feel like I've turned into an untouchable, overnight. It's been really bizarre."

"That's too bad," he said, rubbing his chin. "You're not going to send my check back, the same way you sent back the car and the clothes, are you?"

"It all depends," she answered coyly. "Were you sending the check because you want to support the Pediatric Foundation, or because you were trying to get my attention?"

"Both," he admitted with a smirk. "Is that an acceptable answer?"

"It'll have to be," Amanda said, matching his expression. "Let's order." The waitress appeared.

"I think we're ready," Amanda said.

"I was hoping you'd say that," Tom replied.

"I mean to order. There you go again."

Tom smiled, and they ordered dinner.

# 23

*

Elizabeth was waiting when Amanda returned at close to eleven p.m.

"And the mystery man is?" she asked as Amanda let herself in.

"My landlord," she replied, shaking her head. "And the boy I was crazy about all through high school. Tom Harrington."

Elizabeth pondered the surprising news. "Well, I'll be. And did we have a nice time with our landlord?"

Amanda looked thoughtful. "We did."

"I thought he was a happily married man . . . You want to talk about this for a minute? Or do you want to get some sleep, so we can get ready to be bludgeoned by all the women in the neighborhood again tomorrow morning at the Ball office?"

"Let's talk. I need to debrief."

They headed for the living room. Amanda flopped onto the couch, while Elizabeth took a chair opposite her. "Do tell," Elizabeth said, fighting the urge to straighten the pillows on the sofa.

"I wouldn't even know where to begin," Amanda said. "Tom's wife left him for an artist. She took half his money and went to Santa Fe."

"Leaving your husband for an artist, and taking half your husband's money to Santa Fe," her mother repeated, impressed. "Why didn't I ever think of that?"

"Because you were too good a wife even to harbor such thoughts."

"I'm not quite as good as you think, but that's a story for another day."

Amanda wanted to ask what she meant, but thought better of it, filing it away for another time.

"So we just had a really nice time," she went on. "He's actually pretty shy, for someone as successful as he is, which explains those crazy gifts. It didn't seem to bother him at all that he wasn't getting his ninety-eight thousand back from Neiman's."

"My kind of guy," Elizabeth said admiringly. "Is there a future between the two of you?"

"If I want there to be one," Amanda answered with a sigh. "I just feel like the timing's off. The ink isn't dry on either of our divorces. You know what I mean?"

"Ink can dry in a hurry. I wouldn't let this one get away."

"It's weird living in his house." Amanda glanced around the living room. "It's almost a little creepy."

"As long as he's got half of his money left, he could donate this house to the Longhorn Ball and buy you fifty more. He's incredibly wealthy, you know."

Amanda nodded. "His divorce knocked him from the top half of the Fortune 400 to the bottom half, but that's still pretty impressive territory."

"It impresses the hell out of me," her mother said. "There's more to a man than money, but if you want my opinion, there's not much more. So what did you guys talk about all that time? You must have been together for three hours."

Amanda leaned back on the couch. "This and that . . . Our marriages. Our divorces. Our exes. Mexico. Italy. And the Longhorn Ball."

"What about the Ball? . . . Oh, and I checked our account. Most of those checks we deposited didn't clear. I hope you're going to accept his donation. Otherwise, we're so upside down, it's not even funny."

"I am. And I think he's going to help out with the Ball."

"Help out? How?"

"It doesn't look like we're getting any support from the ladies. It looks like I've been totally frozen out. Even the paranoid have real enemies, right? So he wanted to know if he could get together with a bunch of his friends and get things lined up. He said he and his buddies could have the ball organized in a New York minute."

"But what about the members?" Elizabeth asked, looking concerned. "How are they going to feel about a man taking a leadership position in the Ball?"

"If they're not willing to get involved," Amanda said flatly, "I don't see where they get to have an opinion."

"I suppose you're right. So how did you leave it?"

"We're just going to take it slow."

"No more cars?" Elizabeth asked, teasing. "No more shopping sprees at Neiman's?"

"None of any of that. I told him the ground rules. No presents, normal dates. And we both decided we wouldn't meet anywhere near Hillside Park. I want to keep this out of the gossip mill for as long as humanly possible."

"I wouldn't be surprised if there was already a video of you guys on TMZ.com."

"Mom, how do you know about TMZ.com? You're not exactly an Internet person."

"Will was showing me all kinds of stuff on the computer," Elizabeth said. "I've got a feeling you don't want to leave that boy alone with a laptop. I don't know what he's liable to download."

"That's just great . . . another thing to add to my long list of problems with Will! I'm starting to feel completely overwhelmed by all this, Mom. I've never had this much difficulty in all areas of my life simultaneously.

"What do I do with Will, how do I run a women's nonprofit and have a Ball with no women wanting to help, and how do I keep Tom and me off the Internet?"

Elizabeth grinned. "All of a sudden, it's 'Tom and me'? My, don't we work fast?"

Amanda waved a hand dismissively. "Just stop it . . . I don't know about you, but I'm exhausted. I gotta get to bed. We've got another long day of rejection and failure ahead of us at the Ball office."

"I'm worn out just thinking about it," Elizabeth said as they both stood. "You know, I bet he kept a key," she added, picking up her purse and heading for the front door.

"A key to what? And who are you talking about?"

"Tom, of course. And I'm talking about a key to this house. I'd use the dead bolt. Unless you want to just leave the door ajar."

"Mother!" Amanda feigned exasperation.

"Sweet dreams!" Elizabeth called over her shoulder as she headed out the door. "In Tom's bedroom, no less!"

"Mom, you stop it. I'll see you in the morning."

She shook her head in mock disapproval at her mother and headed upstairs to bed. *My mother is hilarious and awesome,* Amanda thought gleefully. *How has it taken me this long to figure that out?*

ACROSS TOWN, PHONE lines were burning. Amanda and Tom had been seen together, and by midnight, almost everyone in Hillside Park knew about it.

Heather hesitated to call Sharon, because she knew how deeply Sharon had always fantasized about being Mrs. Thomas Harrington, but Heather figured if she didn't break the news, someone else would. On top of that, there was a certain sick thrill in passing along news that was potentially devastating, even to a friend. Not that she didn't love Sharon wholly and completely—she'd give her right arm for her best friend. But after all, what were best friends for, if not to impart a little suffering here and there?

"Sharon, honey?" Heather asked when Sharon answered.

"Is everything okay?" Sharon sat up in bed, yawning.

"Something you need to know." Heather went right to the point. "It's, like, kind of a big deal. Amanda's mystery suitor. It's Tom."

Sharon blinked repeatedly. "Tom? As in Tom Harrington? Am I dreaming?"

"No, no, sweetie. It's true. She was at Nobu with Tom. In a room in the back. Obviously trying to keep a low profile. As if that were possible."

"Of all the men," Sharon said, unable to keep the shock she felt from affecting her tone. "How sure are you about this?"

"I'm absolutely, positively, one hundred percent sure. Dead certain."

Sharon was livid. "This just won't do," she said bitterly. "Of all the men! I never even had a chance with him!"

"Do what you gotta do."

"You bet I will. Now it's personal."

"As if it wasn't before?" Heather purred.

"Now it's really personal."

# 24

✦

The next morning, the only woman in Hillside Park who did not know about the blind item in Ellen Salter's society column in *Hillside Park People* was Amanda herself. She and the children had fallen into a familiar rhythm of getting ready for the new school day—getting dressed; getting lunch together; for Sarah, last-minute homework review; and for Will, making sure that his skateboard, Game Boy, and iPod were all in perfect working order. Elizabeth, however, took the *Hillside Park People*, a weekly neighborhood publication. It fell to her to deliver the unwelcome story to Amanda, whose cell phone rang just as she and the children were stepping outside to begin the six-block walk, or, in Will's case, skateboard ride, to school.

"I'm just getting the children out," Amanda told Elizabeth. "Can it wait?"

"Not really," Elizabeth said as the Vaughns left their house and began the short journey.

"If it's about last night—" Amanda began, but Elizabeth cut her off.

"It's not about last night," Elizabeth said flatly. "Just listen."

"Listen to what?"

Elizabeth read aloud, "'Hostile takeover at the Longhorn

Ball? Amanda Vaughn, who recently ankled multimillionaire hubby number one in sunny SoCal, has elbowed her way to the top of one of Hillside Park's most important soirees. Since then, it's been handcuffs and leg irons for anyone who gets in her way. Both Susie Caruth and Sharon Peavy found themselves in the grasp of the long arm of the law in recent days, and Hillside Park ladies are shying away by the droves from any involvement with the Ball, lest the same thing happen to them.'"

Amanda's jaw dropped as she listened in horror. Her children looked at her, as if to say, "What's wrong?"

"But wait, there's more," Elizabeth continued.

"'Tales of stacks of cash and high-dollar gift cards from many top Dallas emporia going missing are also a highlight of the new reign. Where does it end? What price philanthropy?'

"Are you still there?" Elizabeth asked when she was finished.

"Barely," was the only word Amanda could muster. She felt dizzy, as if the whole world were spinning and collapsing onto her. "How could anybody write something like that?" she asked when she was able to start breathing again.

"Write what?" Sarah asked brightly. Will was lost in his own world of skating and music, oblivious to his mother's plight.

"Don't worry about it," Amanda told her daughter, trying to sound brave. "It's nothing."

Sarah studied her mother. "Whatever it is, Mom, it's something and it's not nothing."

"Mom, I'm with the kids," Amanda said into her cell phone. "I'll meet you at the office at eight thirty. We'll figure it out then. Where did that appear?"

"Ellen Salter's column. The good news is that nobody believes a word she says."

"As I recall, that's why everybody opens the paper to her column first," Amanda replied sarcastically. "So they can find out what they're not supposed to believe for the week."

"Try and look at it this way—at least it's not like it was Alan Peppard's column in the *Dallas Morning News*, thank God."

"But, Mom . . ."

"Whatever. Stiff-upper-lip time. See you at eight thirty."

Amanda disconnected. She was seething, and she was scared. The article made it sound as though she were responsible for the arrests of both Susie and Sharon, which was absurd, because she hadn't even been involved with the Ball when Susie was marched out of the office by the police. As for Sharon, the truth was that Sharon had been headed for state prison when Amanda essentially destroyed the case against her single-handedly. But what was this about bags of cash and gift cards? It had to be Sharon giving Ellen Salter the information, because she was the only one who had any knowledge that there was cash in the office, or that Amanda had taken it to the bank.

If the article should have been smearing anyone, Amanda thought, it should have been Susie. She's the one who was using the Longhorn Ball as her own personal ATM machine. Once again, no good deed goes unpunished. Amanda, glum, did not even notice that her daughter had been trying to get her attention for two whole blocks.

"What's wrong, Mommy?" Sarah asked, taking her hand. "What did Gigi tell you? She was talking for such a long time."

"A lady wrote some things about me in the newspaper that aren't true," Amanda explained, deciding that telling her daughter the truth was the fastest way to end the conversation. If she appeared to be holding back, Sarah would be after her like a bloodhound to get the facts.

Sarah thought about it for a moment. "If it's not true, then you don't have to be sad! Nobody will believe it!"

Amanda looked down at her daughter and shook her head sadly.

"I'm gonna tell you how some adults can be sometimes. The less truth there is in something, the more people want to believe it. It's like there's a really dark side to some people—the worse they can think of someone else, the better they're allowed to feel about themselves."

"I don't understand," Sarah said, bewildered.

Amanda noticed as Will, oblivious, skated out into the street without noticing the early rush-hour traffic cutting through Hillside Park. "William Armstrong Vaughn," Amanda yelled, "you've got to pay attention!"

Will looked back at his mother, his expression saying, "They didn't hit me, so don't worry about it," and went on skateboarding.

"It's an ugly thing about human nature," Amanda told Sarah. "Sometimes, the worse the thing you say, the more people want to believe it. And then they can't wait to repeat it."

"But gossip's a sin," Sarah said, still not getting it.

Amanda sighed. "You're right, Sarah, it is. Gossip's nothing more than evaluating and exploiting other people, and it's wrong but very easy to participate in, unfortunately. Too many people get their value from being the one 'in the know' and more often than not, they have bad information—and it's very hurtful and damaging to people. Everyone's entitled to their own opinion of someone, but no one's entitled to their own set of facts about someone. So often, gossip is presented and then repeated as fact, and it can be devastating to someone's reputation. Your reputation's your most valuable asset, so when people

are being cruel, they're also being very irresponsible and care-
less."

Sarah pondered that and looked around. She noticed that
one of the new friends she had made in school, a girl named
Lacey Wood, born and raised in Hillside Park with family who
had been friends with the Smiths for decades, was approaching. "Hi, Lacey!" Sarah called out. "Wanna walk with me?"

Lacey eyed Sarah and her mother. "My mom says your mom's
a bitch," she said, crossing the street without another word.

Sarah burst into tears.

"And everybody says your healthy eating is just a cover for
your anorexia," Lacey called back. "Nobody wants to room
with you at the church retreat this weekend because they say
you're going to be making yourself throw up the whole time!
It's disgusting!"

"That's so not true!" Sarah wailed, burying her face in her
mother's skirt. "Mommy, how can they all just tell lies about
me?"

"Those little girls said you're anorexic?" Amanda asked,
astonished.

Sarah nodded, her tears flowing freely. "They all said that."

Amanda had to suppress the urge to scream or to kill someone. It was one thing to mess with an adult. It was another
thing to start a rumor about a defenseless child. That was un-
forgivable. Heartbroken and furious, Amanda grabbed her
daughter's hand and stalked after the other girl.

"Lacey Wood!" she yelled. "You get back here this instant,
young lady!"

Lacey turned and glared insolently at her. "Well, it's all true!"
she retorted. "My mother said it. You were even in the newspaper! And we're not letting you in the gymnastics carpool,

either! They're gonna tell you we don't have room, but we have room. We just don't want *you*!"

Sarah, bawling by now, was shouting, "I don't want to go to school!"

Will, piling on, had taken the ear buds out of his ear to listen. "That's 'cause you're a big baby!" he shouted at his sister.

Sarah wailed louder.

"Lacey," Amanda railed, "I'm gonna tell your mother what you said, and she's gonna wash your mouth out with soap!"

"Oh, then let me guess . . . you're gonna have my mother arrested?" Lacey shot back.

Amanda was shaking all over. It was hopeless. Suddenly she felt an enormous urge to call packers and movers and put everything on the next moving van back to California. It might have been the land of fruits and nuts, but at least nobody got into your business the way they did here.

"I can't go to school, Mommy," Sarah said through sobs. "They're gonna crucify me."

"Only if they've erected two crosses and not one," Amanda said, thinking quickly. "Will, you go on ahead. You go to school. Sarah's staying with me today."

"That's not fair!" Will exclaimed. And then he brightened. "It's okay, Mom. I was gonna ditch all my classes anyway." With that, he darted ahead into the growing crowd of skateboarders and students making their way to school, and he was gone.

Amanda was *desperately* trying to suppress an outburst that would've terrified the devil himself. Anorexia? Shutting her out of a carpool over this ridiculous Longhorn Ball nonsense? And let's see . . . who were the moms we were carpooling with? Oh, that's right, one was famous for having an affair with the married father of one of her kindergarten students while she was teaching at Hillside Park Elementary. The other was famous for shutting herself in at home alone every night, drinking so heavily she knows better than to ever answer the phone past seven p.m., chain-smoking twenty feet from her child who has asthma so bad she's on a nebulizer for home breathing treatments, and for being the *only* mom in the history of Hillside Park to be cited for endangering a child by trying to drive carpool while still under the influence of Ambien! By all means, ladies, please feel free to take my inventory! I can certainly see how you'd think you were in a position to judge me and my family! Amanda was seeing red, she was so angry, but she *had* to keep it together for Sarah's sake.

"Come on, sweetheart," Amanda told Sarah, lovingly stroking her hair. Amanda made a mental note to talk with Will about his school attendance. As if I don't have enough on my mind already, she told herself. "They want to go after me, that's one thing. But if people are going after you, well, this means war."

"War?"

"It's just a figure of speech. I'm not going to let you go to school and be humiliated. You're just gonna hang around with Gigi and me today at the Longhorn Ball office. Incidentally, I've got a feeling today might be my last day as Chair."

Sarah stopped walking. She wiped her tears away and looked up at her mother. "You mean you're gonna let them run you off? But the Ball helps sick kids, doesn't it?"

Amanda realized she had no comeback. "You're right. I'm not going to let them run me off. You, Gigi, and I are going to go to the office. We're going to put in a full day of work, and we're going to get this Ball off the ground. So help me God."

Sarah brightened. "That'll teach grown-ups to believe everything they hear."

"How did you ever get so smart?"

"I'm a Cali girl. We don't take crap off nobody!"

"Sarah!" Amanda exclaimed. "Where did you ever learn an expression like that?"

"From Gigi."

"I should have known." Amanda laughed, set on salvaging the day and forcing it in a better direction. With a determined expression, she took her daughter's hand, and they headed back to the house to get the car.

# 25

·✶·

When Amanda, Elizabeth, and Sarah arrived twenty minutes later at the office of the Longhorn Ball, they were surprised to find a chauffeur-driven Bentley idling in the no parking zone across the street, in front of Hillside Park Presbyterian. As Amanda's SUV pulled up, the Bentley's driver went around to the back of the car and held the door open. Tom Harrington emerged.

"Tom!" Amanda exclaimed, surprised. "What are you doing here?"

"Who's he?" Sarah asked her grandmother.

"That's Mr. Black Mercedes himself," Elizabeth said.

"Really! He's much younger than I imagined."

Elizabeth glanced quizzically at her granddaughter but said nothing as Tom crossed the street and joined them. "I saw the paper this morning," he said, totally disgusted. "I figured you could maybe use some help or another person to bounce ideas off. Or maybe just somebody with a gun."

"You packin'?" Elizabeth asked Tom.

Tom grinned. "I'm not, but he is." He gestured toward his driver, a man who clearly tipped the scales north of three hundred pounds and bore a striking resemblance to Hoss, the character played by Dan Blocker on the old *Bonanza* TV show.

"I hope you're not paying for him by the pound. That's a big boy."

"Even if I did, he'd be worth every penny. . . . Am I invited in? Or is a man unwelcome in the sacred precincts of the Longhorn Ball office?"

Amanda glanced at Elizabeth. "I think it's time to pass an emergency bylaw to admit men."

"All in favor, say aye," Elizabeth said.

"Aye," chorused Amanda and Sarah.

"Good news!" Amanda told Tom. "You're in."

Tom returned a smile, Amanda unlocked the door, and the four of them went into the office.

Elizabeth turned to Sarah. "Let's you and I go out and get coffee and doughnuts, okay? I think we ought to let these two do the high-level strategizing without our company."

"But Gigi—" She took one look at her grandmother and knew that resistance was futile. She and Elizabeth went around the corner to get coffee, but not before Elizabeth gave Amanda a big wink, to which Amanda responded by rolling her eyes.

"After you." Amanda held the door for Tom.

"Wouldn't think of it. Ladies first." The two of them headed into Amanda's office, and Tom took a seat opposite her desk.

"We've still got no lights," she said apologetically. "I'm hoping that maybe by next week, once we get our bills paid, we can get the power turned back on."

"I think the lights are the least of your worries," Tom replied, looking around. "So this is the nerve center of the mighty Longhorn Ball operations."

"I'll tell you who has a lot of nerve," Amanda said, settling into her seat. "Sharon Peavy. How could she have said all those things about me to that reporter? Doesn't she realize I kept her out of jail?"

"You want to walk me through that gift card thing? That's the only piece of the puzzle I don't think I have."

Amanda summarized the events surrounding the Neiman's gift card. "So I feel like I've got a world of trouble, and for no reason," she concluded.

"Yeah, you do. What are you going to do about all this?"

"Honestly, I've got no idea. I'd like to tell all these people to go to hell, or much worse, but I don't see what good that's going to do. I'd really like to walk away from the Ball, but I don't know what kind of example I'd be setting for my children. I feel like I'm damned if I do and damned if I don't."

"I think you've described the situation exactly right."

"Well, what would you do?"

"Well," Tom began, "I know a guy in San Antonio who could make all your problems go away. You just put the names of the people who are bothering you on a piece of paper, and they'll be floating down the Rio Grande before you can say 'plausible deniability.' "

Amanda gave a rueful smile. "Don't think that thought hasn't crossed my mind. But I don't really think that's the best approach."

"I honestly don't see the difference between that and the kind of character assassination they're doing on you. I could even go get my driver to take care of business," he joked, "but then I'd have to find a new driver."

Amanda laughed. "Three-hundred-fifty-pound marksmen

who can drive a Bentley aren't a dime a dozen," she said, grinning. Her smile quickly faded as she became serious again. "I don't know what to do, Tom. About anything."

"Well, let's take stock," he said, his tone simultaneously gentle and businesslike. "What do we have?"

Amanda wanted to say, what we have is two people, one very recently divorced, one still pending, who've gone on one "date," one living in the other's house, and you seem to know me so well that you can pick out nicer clothing for me than I can. But she thought for a moment longer and said, "We've got an event that was the highlight of the social calendar in Hillside Park for over thirty years, and it was screwed up so badly by the last person to run it that nobody wants to go near it."

Tom nodded.

"And we've got a whispering campaign that's actually hit the newspaper," Amanda continued, "whereby there's not a single woman in Hillside Park who wants to lift a finger to help me. If anything, it seems like the whole town has closed ranks against me."

"Check. That's how I see it, too."

"So I'm running a Ball, with no support, no volunteers, nobody who wants to chair a committee, no electricity, no computers, and no phone. And somehow, I'm supposed to spin this straw into three or four million dollars' worth of gold for the Pediatric Foundation. Is that how you're seeing it?"

"That's how I'm seeing it."

"What would you do," Amanda asked, "wise and all-knowing developer of half of Mexico?"

"Punt," Tom said teasingly. "And get on the next plane to Acapulco."

Amanda gave him a dirty look.

"Thanks a lot. Seriously. I'm not going to quit. I'm not going to give them the satisfaction of destroying my reputation, harming my children, *and* running me off! You should have heard what one of the little girls said to Sarah this morning." Tom waited. "I agree with you about what you said, that character assassination is like murder without a weapon," she continued, sitting back in her chair. "And I'll tell you what the problem is. Every single one of the women who've given me the most trouble in this whole thing—they're all supposedly fine Christian women. Heather Sappington. Vodka bottle in one hand, Holy Bible in the other. Never misses a party Saturday night. Never misses services Sunday morning. Never misses a doctor's appointment to get some more diet pills—at least that's what my mother says.

"Sharon Peavy. My best friend growing up, but now she's gotten so bitter and jealous about my life—which is a joke, because I'm the one getting over a divorce, not her. But I've got some money and she doesn't, and I might not have those perfect knockers she has, but I'm not so bad for a woman who's—oh, well . . . never mind. But she's another one. Going to Bible study and looking all squeaky clean and religious, when the reality is that she's slept with every man in Dallas who's got a positive net worth."

"Present company excluded," Tom interrupted.

"Oh, I'm sorry. Your loss," she cracked.

"I might still be on the Forbes list," Tom said, with monumental understatement, "but I still wouldn't spring for a night with that nasty girl."

Amanda's grin widened. "No, you wouldn't," she agreed. "And behind them has got to be Darlene Cockburn, because you know the three of them are thick as thieves and you know she's been the info source for Mom's age group—five marriages, four divorces, four massive settlements, and number five ready to be cashed in whenever she gives her lawyers the nod, and yet she has a whole building at the church named after her.

"And then there's Ann Anderson," she concluded. "Heather must have pictures of her with a Thoroughbred in a stable somewhere. Otherwise, I don't understand for a minute how the two of them could be friends."

She took a deep breath, and Tom waited for her to continue.

"The thing is," Amanda went on slowly, "if these women want to go after me, fine. I'm a big girl. I can take it. I'll do just fine whatever happens. But tear up my daughter's heart? No way. Now this stuff is affecting my children. Sarah now, Will next. And that's where I draw the line."

"So what do you want to do?"

"I wish there was some way to teach them a lesson . . . It's like my dad always said—you don't ever want to start a fight, but it's sure okay to finish one. I only took on the Longhorn Ball because it does good work and it raises so much money for the Pediatric Foundation, and I figured it would be a good thing to occupy my time. But it's not only about the Ball any longer. There's one thing these women just don't seem able to grasp."

"And what's that?"

"You can be a good Christian," Amanda said slowly, thinking it through. "Or you can be a bitch. But you can't be a good Christian bitch."

Tom threw back his head and laughed so hard he brayed like a donkey. "I love the expression and I'm sure I've known a few, but why don't you give me your definition of a good Christian bitch."

"It's pretty self-explanatory," Amanda said, "as a matter of fact. If you're professing to be a good Christian, you're claiming to have a desire to be like Christ, to have a heart like His. When a good Christian hides behind the cross while putting herself and her worldly desires ahead of her desire to be like Christ, at any and everyone else's expense when she deems it necessary, she becomes a good Christian bitch. I mean, for heaven's sake, don't let Jesus get in the way of a good agenda. Does that make sense? Do you understand what I'm trying to say?"

"Actually, I do. My mother used to say some of the meanest people she'd ever met, she met in church," Tom said. "So, how can I help?" Tom asked. "This is a cause I'd like to sign on to. I've taken my own share of heat from the 'good Christian bitches.'"

"We all have, believe me . . . This Ball is supposed to be run by women," she pondered, "but except for Elizabeth, Sarah, and me, we don't have any. They've all been scared off. So I guess it's time to enlist the services of a man."

"If I'm that man," Tom said, grinning, "the answer is yes."

"Only one thing, though."

"What's that?"

Amanda paused before she spoke. "We both know that you could write a check right now to the Pediatric Foundation big enough that we wouldn't even have to hold the Ball. But that's not the point. I don't want you to step in and save me. What I want you to do is help me get this Ball back on its feet so it actually thrives, not just survives. And if you can do that, maybe I can focus on setting things right. These . . . if you'll pardon the expression . . . bitches need to learn a lesson. They've gone after me for no reason other than the fact that I'm theoretically in their way, and they think I've caught all the breaks in life and they've caught none. Which is a whole 'nother story, because as nice a man as you are, I'm truly not ready for any involvements."

"I understand."

Amanda thought she could hear disappointment in his voice. "All I'm saying is," she said earnestly, "let's take care of the Ball and the bitches first. And then we'll figure out where you and I stand. How is that?"

"That's a deal." They shook hands.

At that moment, Elizabeth and Sarah arrived with coffee and doughnuts.

"Looks like some sort of major deal went down in our absence," Elizabeth told Sarah, seeing the handshake.

"This is better than school!" the little girl exclaimed.

"Don't get too excited, honey," Amanda told her daughter. "This is only going to last for a couple of days, until I get things squared away here in the community. Anyway, Mom, I'm pleased to announce the formation of the Men's Auxiliary of the Longhorn Ball. And here's the Chair of the Men's Auxiliary, Tom Harrington."

Elizabeth nodded approvingly. "Wait till the ladies hear about this."

"Wait till the ladies find out I'm about to fix their wagon."

Elizabeth's eyes narrowed. "How?"

Sarah's eyes lit up. "This is way better than school."

Amanda glanced at Tom. "I haven't exactly figured out how just yet. But if I don't find a good enough plan, Tom here says he's got a guy in San Antonio who can make all our problems go away."

"That's the spirit. Shoot 'em all and let God sort it out. Amanda, your daddy would be proud of you."

"Mommy, are you really going to have those ladies killed?" Sarah asked, alarmed.

Everybody laughed. "Of course not, honey," Amanda said. "But something tells me they're about to get a lesson they'll never forget."

# 26

✦

Lunchtime found Sharon Peavy and Darlene Cockburn huddled in Darlene's favorite booth at Tizio's, a neighborhood bistro-type restaurant in the middle of Hillside Park Village, a half block from the movie theater. In Hillside Park society, as in the Mafia, there are two types of restaurants—the ones to which you bring your wife, and the ones to which you bring your girlfriend. This was definitely a "wifey" type of restaurant, due in part to its location. You would never take your girlfriend to lunch in a restaurant favored by "ladies who lunch," because the chances of word getting back to your wife from three different sources before you left the restaurant about whom you had squired to the restaurant approached 100 percent.

Tizio's drew a solid lunchtime crowd from the businesses, law firms, and financial institutions that ringed Hillside Park Village, catering to its wealthy clientele. You could slip in for a burger and a beer, or a salad that met with the guidelines of the nearby Cooper Clinic (a rehab center for the overfed), but it was no place to take a girlfriend.

Sharon and Darlene ostensibly studied the menus, but since they knew them by heart, they spent more of their time absorbing the kind of sociological detail that was so close to their hearts—who was lunching with whom, who was wearing what, who got a good table and who got relegated to a second- or even third-tier table, and who had already knocked back a few too many even at this early hour. The restaurant had been featured a few months earlier in the *Wall Street Journal* as a "power lunch" spot, complete with a diagram showing which tables were considered most desirable. Until the diagram had run, most people really didn't know better. But now that something as august as the *Wall Street Journal* had declared new levels of status depending on where one sat, the maître d's job had become radically more difficult—and more lucrative—as the financially stable members of the community, which is to say, pretty much all of them, jockeyed for favor.

"Mmm-mmm-mmm," Sharon was saying, indicating with her eyes a woman two tables away. "I mean, really . . . did she actually look in the mirror when she got dressed this morning? Bright orange short-short shorts with gold high-heeled wedges at her age? How did she stand there and think 'I look really cute today'?"

Darlene suppressed a grin. "It isn't a look I would favor," she said, petting her shoulders in her St. John suit. "And she's obviously not from around here."

The only part of the menu that held any attraction at all for Sharon was the wine list. Her night in jail had given her the kind of headache that she normally associated with Saturday nights when she permitted herself to be overserved with red wine, vodka, or, if neither of those was readily available, tequila. Her temples were throbbing with pain from a headache that was a function of sleeplessness, frustration, and upset over the whole state of affairs with Amanda Vaughn.

"I feel like the world's biggest idiot," she admitted, looking at the names of the wines as if they were a menu of prescription drugs especially selected to ease her pain. "I should never have kicked up this whole hornets' nest with Amanda."

"For heaven's sakes, why not?" Darlene glanced around the room, filing away mental notes about various clothing labels, or lack thereof, seating locations of various parties, and other vital information. "I thought your plan was working out marveliciously."

"It was never even my plan." Sharon jerked angrily on her chain necklace, a barely passable Ann Demeulemeester replica she'd bought for less than ten bucks at TJ Maxx. "It was Heather's idea. I just went along with it."

"If you didn't think it was a good idea," Darlene asked, sweeping her outstretched hand across the table and almost toppling Sharon's ice water, "then . . . why did you get involved?"

"Are you kidding me? Think about Amanda for a minute. I had an old score to settle with her over Bill anyway. Even though I'd never told her about it, we were good enough friends, she should've known I had a crush on him when he started pursuing her and then she goes and *marries* him! She's beautiful, she's a genuinely nice person, she's got plenty of money—her family's and Bill's—she's single or she's on the verge of being single, and she's available. Doesn't that make you just wanna throttle her? Adding insult to injury, I've had a thing for Tom my whole life and he's after her."

Darlene shook her head. "Truth be told, her demographic and mine don't exactly . . . overlap. I'm interested in a slightly older archetype of man than she is."

"That's easy for you to say," Sharon moaned. "A guy who's interested in somebody your age—that's one thing. There are tons of older guys. But if you look at the concentration of men from thirty-five to forty-nine who are independently wealthy, available, or soon to become available, you're looking at a very small pool indeed. Throw someone like Amanda into the mix and she's going to draw all the attention away from somebody like me just like she did all through high school. I knew what to expect the second I heard she was coming back. I mean, I've been around here so long, everybody knows me."

"Not in the biblical sense, I hope," Darlene said, giving her a coy smile.

"Close enough. Sometimes I feel like I could write a *Zagat's Guide to the Private Parts of the Men of Hillside Park*."

"I'd buy a copy of that."

"What are you talking about? You never have any trouble getting a man to marry you. I wish I knew your secret."

"I've gotten inquiries from the Learning Annex about doing a seminar on that very topic," Darlene said with a laugh. "But tell me . . . why are you so upset about what's transpired with Amanda?"

The waitress arrived at their table. Sharon glanced at her and sized her up, relatively accurately, as a fifth- or sixth-year college student who was tired of school and no longer fit in with the world of sororities and cheerleading, who didn't come from a ton of money, and who just wanted to meet some guy who had a few bucks so she could forget about the whole college thing, live in a big house, have a bunch of babies, and then come eat in restaurants like this as a Mrs. in the Neighborhood. Sharon knew the type; she had been one herself. Unfortunately, that strategy seemed to have worked for just about everyone *but* Sharon and, of course, Heather.

"We're not ready," Sharon said in a tone that revealed a measure of her competitiveness with the waitress, who could easily have picked off any of the men in whom Sharon felt any interest with just a glimpse of her unlined, perfect skin.

She nodded at Sharon, glancing disapprovingly at the outward display of cleavage, and headed to another table.

"You don't like our waitress, I can tell," Darlene noted.

"Don't even start. Everything I've done has been disastrous. We both know it was Heather's idea to have Amanda take over the Ball. I just went along. I figured it would keep her off the streets, keep her from competing for what men there are before I even knew about Tom."

"And?"

"And? What do you mean *and*?! The one thing she didn't have in the community was power, and now she does. And the first person she used it against was me. She had me arrested, you know that."

"You're the one who swiped the card from her desk," Darlene gently reminded her.

"It wasn't her desk," Sharon said defensively. "It was Susie's. I figured it was Susie's card and—"

Darlene waved her hand, speaking with unusual clarity. "We've been over this six ways to Sunday. Let's try to deal in reality here. You swiped the card, you got in trouble, and then out of the goodness of her heart, Amanda bailed you out."

"Mmm. I guess . . . But it gets worse. You saw Ellen Salter's column this morning?"

"About how Amanda got both you and Susie arrested? Wasn't that a little bit much? She hadn't even unpacked her bags in Dallas when they took Susie in. She had nothing to do with that. You'd better hope Amanda doesn't sue you for libel, or slander, or . . . whatever it's called."

"That's the thing," Sharon admitted. "I really screwed up.

A bunch of times. When I took the card, when I called Ellen—I'm just so jealous of Amanda that I'm not thinking straight."

"How about thinking of apologizing?" Darlene asked. She adjusted her noisy row of diamond bangles and glanced at the salad selections on the menu she knew so well.

"Uggh, I don't know," Sharon said, disgusted. "Because I just don't want to, I guess. It seems like Amanda got all the breaks in life and I didn't. She came from money. She grew up in a beautiful home in Hillside Park. She's got everything a girl could ask for in life—"

"Including a philandering husband," her older friend reminded her. Darlene was making a surprising amount of sense. "As a veteran of at least three and possibly five such husbands, I want to suggest that their value is completely overrated."

"Maybe so. But it's not fair! I've never been married, not even to a guy who can't keep it in his pants. I'm never going to get to have children. At least she had the choice."

"And that was Amanda's fault how? So, what are you thinking of now? Since you're not planning on apologizing to her."

"I just can't apologize." The waitress moved back into view. Sharon glanced at her, despised her, and had the awkward sensation that she was really despising herself.

The waitress, for her part, glanced at Sharon's décolleté. Her look clearly said, "Is that all there is to you?"

"I'm still not ready," Sharon told her. She turned her attention back to Darlene. "It's just all her fault. If she hadn't moved back to Dallas, none of this would have happened. Why couldn't she have been the devoted mother she pretends to be and kept her children closer to their father in California? *That* would've been the right thing for Miss Perfect Amanda to do—not uproot those poor kids and drag them back to Dallas and away from Bill! Bill's business is there—he has no choice but to be where his business is and how else is he supposed to provide that ridiculously large, I'm sure, alimony and child support check she's gonna cash every month. But he's supposed to send it knowing he has such limited access to his kids because she just had to come back to Dallas!"

Darlene just glared at her. It was times like this that even she had a hard time really understanding what kept her in a close friendship with this tragic, pathetic, bitter woman. Over the years, she'd had to defend her friendships with both Sharon and Heather to a multitude of her better groups of friends.

"Maybe, just maybe," Darlene continued, "one of Bill's indiscretions had produced an unplanned pregnancy that turned a meaningless one-night stand into the mother of his child, as she was in search of those very same said checks. This other woman had a child from a previous marriage at Will and Sarah's school. It was just too awkward, too incestuous, too hard to explain to children their age, so she came home. She thought it was best for her children to remove them."

Sharon sat there, finally speechless. "Oh my God! Why didn't you tell me all that before?"

"I just found out this morning, myself. Amanda hasn't even told her own mother yet. Elizabeth just found out through a mutual friend in LA who has mutual friends in Newport."

Sharon was stunned and hated herself even more. "Well . . . what do you want me to do?"

Darlene made another broad gesture across the table, this time narrowly missing the ketchup bottle sitting precariously near the edge. "You know I'm in your corner."

Sharon studied the wine list and wished she lived in one of the romantic-sounding places from which the award-winning wine collection had been assembled—Napa Valley, the south of France, or Zinfandel. Where was Zinfandel, anyway? Maybe an Italian isle?

"Mmm. I want to start another rumor about Amanda." Sharon took a quick glance down her shirt for affirmation of her remaining assets. "Something juicy. Something people will hate her for."

"Chicken salad," Darlene told the waitress, who gave one last unimpressed look at Sharon. Sharon glumly shook her head to indicate that she didn't want anything, and the waitress flounced off.

"I don't have a dog in this fight," Darlene noted. "You wanted me to make her head of the Ball. I did that. But you, my dear . . ." She took in a great gust of air. "You are the one who had to steal that noxiferous gift card and then call Ellen Salter. If you want to do anything further to Amanda, other than apologize, you can just count me out."

"Some friend you turned out to be." Sharon shot Darlene a dirty look. "Where is that waitress? I think I need a drink."

"You might want to reconsider that drink." Darlene cast an equally chilly look on her lunch partner, her voice oozing with disdain. "I think it's more the root of a lot of your problems than you realize or are willing to admit right now."

"If I want that kind of advice," Sharon retorted sharply, "I'll go to AA. Not to lunch with you. Okay?" She began tapping her fingers furiously on the table. "Now, where's that waitress when you need her, anyway?"

# 27

---

✦

We've got to make some decisions here," Amanda told her mother. "Are we going on with this Ball? Or aren't we?"

Before Elizabeth could answer, there was a knock at the door. It was Tom, bearing lunch from Whole Foods. "That's the biggest health food store I've ever seen," he exclaimed, handing out salads and sushi. "I think I'd like to buy it."

"You want the whole . . . Whole Foods?" Sarah joked, pleased with herself.

"I want the whole of anything I get into," Tom told her, grinning. "I don't do things halfway."

"Well, if we're not going to do this Ball halfway," Amanda said, "we need a plan."

They opened up the various boxes and set to their meals.

"What's this book?" Sarah asked, holding up a thin volume titled *Longhorn Ball Rules and Regulations*.

"Oh, that's something boring," Elizabeth told her. "It's just about how this whole Ball thing is organized. I don't think you'll find it very entertaining reading."

"I'll be the judge of that," Sarah said, expertly tweezing a piece of sushi into her mouth with the chopsticks while opening up the rule book. Elizabeth watched her, amazed.

"Hey, Mom!" Sarah suddenly exclaimed. "Your picture's in here!"

"Where?" She looked over to the page Sarah was holding open. Sure enough, there was a picture of Amanda at a Ball a dozen years earlier, toasting glasses with Bill and another couple.

"In brighter times," she said, eyeing the picture.

Elizabeth peered over her shoulder. "You kids look happy as a gopher in soft dirt. Guess that was before you realized dirt gets you, well, dirty."

Amanda cast her mother a playfully reproachful glance. Then she looked back at the picture and let out a soft whistle. "Can you believe how young we looked?"

"I think you look pretty young now," Tom said gallantly.

"At your age," Elizabeth cracked, "every woman looks young."

"Thanks a lot," he retorted good-naturedly. "Actually, we've got to decide a couple of things. First, what to do about the Ball, and second, what to do about all these women ganging up on Amanda over here. It's just not ladylike."

"It's all too ladylike," Elizabeth corrected him. "Unfortunately, it's what ladies do."

"Women, maybe," Amanda countered. "But not ladies."

"This is interesting," Sarah said as she made her way through the bylaws of the Longhorn Ball. "I never knew there were so many rules."

"That girl could find interesting reading in the telephone book," Elizabeth said, with a mixture of pride and puzzlement over her granddaughter's voracious interest in all printed matter. "If only her taste in food was as varied as her taste in information. Amanda, you gotta explain to her that a little beef won't kill her."

"I don't really know what to do about these women," Amanda said, ignoring the comment about her daughter's eating habits. "Short of moving. Although I'll say this—if they're going after me, I can take it. But when it starts trickling down to my children, that's when I start to get upset. It's true what they say—you're only as happy as your unhappiest child."

"All right," Tom said, rubbing his hands together. "First things first. Let's figure out this Ball thing. Is it worth preserving?"

"Of course," Amanda said flatly. "It's hard to imagine Hillside Park in the fall without the Longhorn Ball. It's been a fixture for as long as I can remember."

"And it raises so much money for the Pediatric Foundation," Elizabeth added. "If you took it away, the women here would have even more time to gossip instead of doing something constructive with their time."

"So we've got to preserve the Ball," Tom said. "But we've got almost no money."

Amanda nodded. "I just got an e-mail from the bank—almost all of the checks failed to clear. I guess people canceled them after everything that went on with Susie. So not counting your check, we have about a hundred and ten thousand in the bank and—Mom, how much do we owe on unpaid bills?"

"Just call it an even two hundred thousand," Elizabeth said. "If it weren't for you, Tom, we'd be ninety thousand dollars short."

"Okay," Tom said. "We don't have money. Volunteers?"

Amanda shook her head. "I told you," she said. "Everyone I talked to who is active said no. Not a single woman on active status is willing to chair a committee this year. That's why I think either Darlene or Ann Anderson or somebody got to them all."

"How many active members do you have? How many inactive?"

"It always comes out to a hundred. I either spoke to or left messages for all the active members, and I haven't gotten a single woman interested in stepping up and doing something significant."

"What about the inactive members? Did you contact them?"

"By e-mail."

"And?"

"Either my e-mails didn't get through their spam filters," Amanda said tartly, "or somebody got to them, too."

"Sounds like somebody's playing a little Texas freeze-out," Tom said, shaking his head. "If this were happening in a business setting, somebody would be looking at a big fat lawsuit for restraint of trade or interference of contract or something along those lines. This is nutty."

"It may be nutty," Elizabeth interjected, "but it's definitely how things work in Hillside Park. It's worse than junior high school. In fact, it's like being trapped in junior high school for the rest of your life. And *this* situation has really been more like *Alfred Hitchcock Presents: Mean Girls on Steroids.*"

"I'll have to agree with that!" Amanda snickered.

"Is there any way to get rid of the membership and start over?" Tom asked. "That's what I would do. Just clean house."

"You can't throw a hundred women off the Longhorn Ball Committee," Amanda said incredulously, looking as if Tom had suggested the most ridiculous thing in the world. "Some of them are the biggest donors. You alienate them, and you have no Ball."

"As it is, we have no Ball anyway," he pointed out. "You mean there's really no way to get rid of them?"

"No way on God's green earth," Amanda answered flatly.

"Once you're part of the Longhorn Ball membership, you're in for life, as long as you pay your annual dues."

"Unless you read bylaw sixty-seven," Sarah said.

"Not now," Elizabeth told her. "We're discussing serious business."

"But I'm being serious!" Sarah replied, indignant.

"Gigi's right," Amanda told her daughter. "Maybe you just want to go in the other room and read some more. I sure wish we had a computer going. Then you could play games or something."

"I don't play computer games, Mom," Sarah said firmly, digging in her heels. "I've told you they're a waste of time. Will you all please listen to bylaw sixty-seven?"

"I'm all ears," Tom said. Amanda glared at him. Don't interfere with what I tell my daughter, she thought.

"Bylaw sixty-seven," Sarah said, pouncing on the invitation to join the adults' conversation, "reads as follows, 'Any active member who fails to participate, when asked, in preparation work for the upcoming Ball may be dismissed by the Chair at her discretion.' Mom, what's discretion?"

"It's a loophole big enough to drive a tractor trailer through," Tom said, grinning. "Amanda, why don't you just fire your members? Your daughter just told you that you could."

"I can really do that?"

"If that's what the bylaw says." Tom leaned over Sarah's shoulder and read the relevant passage. "Your daughter's right as rain! You've got the power!"

Amanda sat up a little straighter in her chair. "By the powers vested in me as chair of the Longhorn Ball," she declared, "I hereby fire every active member of the Longhorn Ball Committee. All one hundred of those lazy heifers. They're gone."

"Seconded," Elizabeth said.

"You don't really need to second me, Mom," Amanda said, embarrassed. "I've got all the power."

"Well, it never hurts to be seconded," Elizabeth said, miffed.

"But what about the inactive members?"

" 'Bylaw sixty-eight,' " Tom read aloud. " 'Any inactive member who fails to keep her dues current as of September thirtieth of any given year may be dismissed from the committee at the discretion of the Chair.' "

"I can get rid of the inactive ones, too?" Amanda grinned. "I'm starting to like this whole power thing!"

"If they didn't pay their dues . . . Elizabeth, did they?"

She shook her head. "I didn't see any checks marked dues. All the checks I saw were for tickets or donations."

"Susie probably forgot to send out bills for dues for the inactive members and the active members," Amanda remarked.

"In that case," Tom said, "you can chop them, too!"

"Consider them chopped!" Amanda pointed a finger in the air. "Off with their heads!"

"What do you think of that?" her mother asked. "We started off with a hundred-plus members ten minutes ago who didn't want to lift a finger. Now we're down to just one. Amanda over here. And then we've got Tom, in the Men's Auxiliary. That's not bad work."

"You just fired ninety-nine people," Tom said to Amanda. "How does it feel to be ruthless?"

"It's great, except for one thing. Now we don't have anybody to do anything."

"We just have to divide up the committees among ourselves," he said. "But before we do, I think we should grant honorary membership status to Sarah, because she's the one who found the bylaws that let us do all this trimming of unnecessary fat."

"Done and done. Sarah, congratulations, sweetie. You're an honorary member of the Longhorn Ball Committee."

"Yippee!" Sarah exclaimed, delighted. "Do I get a Neiman's gift card?"

Everybody laughed. "Not just yet. But if you keep finding bylaws like that, I'm sure somebody's going to buy you something."

"Okay," Tom said, turning back to business. "What are the committees that these women were supposed to be heading up? Because we've got to divide them among ourselves."

"Underwriting's first," Amanda began. "Raising money is what this whole thing is all about, anyway."

"I'll take that. I can make a few phone calls. What's next?"

"Food and beverage," Amanda said, reading from the list on her desk.

"I'll take that," Elizabeth said. "With help from Sarah, of course."

"It's going to be vegetarian and organic," Sarah promised.

"Better not tell the donors," Amanda told her.

"Or the Texas Cattlemen's Association," Tom chimed in. "I guess I can't hit them up for a donation."

"Guess not. Okay, next one is security. I'll take that myself. According to the *Hillside Park People*, I've got so much clout with the police that I'm the perfect one for that job."

"That's fine. What's next?"

"Entertainment." Tom thought for a moment. "I've got some pretty good ties to the entertainment community. If you could have anybody, who would you bring in?"

Amanda thought for a moment. "George Strait. I used to love his music back in the day. I've been away from Texas so long I don't even know who's big in country anymore."

"George Strait would cost a fortune," Elizabeth said. "We could never afford him."

"I could make a phone call," Tom said. "I'll take entertainment."

"Well, that's pretty much it," Amanda said. "There are some other jobs, but there's nothing Mom and I can't handle. Our finances are pretty simple—'cause we're broke."

"Not for long," Tom said. "Not after I make a few phone calls. By the way, what's the date for the event? If I'm going to ask George, I need to know that."

Amanda gave him an "okay, sure" look.

"It's always in September. By then, everybody's back from wherever they went, and it's a chance for everybody to catch up on what they did over the summer. That's eleven months away."

"'Bylaw seventy-nine,'" Sarah read aloud. "'The date of the Ball, typically the first or second Saturday in September—'"

"That's what I'm talking about," Amanda told Tom.

"'—may be set at the discretion of the Ball Chair if there is a compelling reason to pick a different date.'"

Amanda ran a hand through her hair. "I never knew that."

"So," Elizabeth mused, "you could have the Longhorn Ball pretty much anytime."

Tom wasn't listening. "Hang on a minute," he said, dialing a number on his cell phone and going into another room.

"Damnedest thing I've ever seen," Elizabeth said. "A Ball with no committee, no money, two women, one billionaire, and a nine-year-old. That's something new."

"I wonder who Tom's calling?" Amanda mused.

Tom rolled back in to the room and closed his cell phone.

"I'd like to propose a date for the next Longhorn Ball."

"Shoot," Amanda said, her pen poised above her date book.

"Four weeks from tonight." Tom's suggestion was greeted with consternation by both Amanda and Elizabeth.

"You can't have a Longhorn Ball so soon after the last one!" Amanda exclaimed.

"I really think that's a good night for the Longhorn Ball," Tom said firmly. Something about his tone made both women wonder why he was so fixed on that date.

"You know what we should have?" Amanda hit on an idea. "We should have a thank-you party, for all the donors and vendors and all the other people Susie wronged. Let all of them come and celebrate. If you really want to have this party so soon after the Ball."

"That sounds like a plan," Tom said, nodding. "Maybe we can get back in a few people's good graces."

"Who did you just call?" Elizabeth suddenly asked.

"Let that be my surprise."

"But this whole thing is impossible," Amanda said, shaking her head. "We're supposed to have a luncheon in November to announce the entertainment—this isn't the way it's done."

"It's a new approach," Tom admitted. "I'll grant you that. But as head of the Men's Auxiliary, I promise you that there are compelling reasons why you want to have the event four weeks from now. And besides, if we can pull off a decent thank-you party then, maybe we can get people interested in doing it the right way for next year. With somebody else stuck with the job of Ball Chair."

"It's a little unorthodox," Amanda admitted, "but there's

something pleasing about the idea of not having this responsibility hanging over my head for the next eleven months." She sighed. "Okay. As the Chair of the Longhorn Ball, I use the power vested in me to declare that the party to thank all the people who got screwed—sorry, Sarah—by the last Ball Chair will take place—are you kidding me? Okay. Four weeks away. All in favor?"

Tom, Elizabeth, and Sarah chorused, "Aye."

"All opposed?" Amanda asked.

Silence.

"Then that's it," she said, banging her pen down on the desk like a mock gavel. "I hope you know what you're doing," she said sincerely to Tom. "I hope we all do."

Her cell phone rang. She unfolded it, saw that the caller was "unknown," and said to no one in particular, "I wonder who this could be."

"Hello?" She listened intently, a look of frozen horror appearing on her face.

"What happened?" Elizabeth asked.

"It's Will," Amanda said as she hung up, stricken. "He got into a fight at school, and he's in the hospital. Come on, let's go."

The four of them, ashen, looked at one another and practically ran out of the office and jumped into Tom's car.

✦

## 28

"Where's my son?" Amanda demanded, trying to remain calm as she ran into the emergency room at Southern Methodist Hospital, two blocks from Hillside Park.

"Are you Ms. Vaughn?" the attendant asked.

"I am."

The woman nodded reassuringly. "Your son's gonna be fine. Just some lacerations. He looks worse than he is."

Amanda felt her heart stop at the word *lacerations*, but she found herself relieved by the attendant's sense of calm. "Where is he?"

"In back . . . down the hall on the right."

Amanda turned to her mother, daughter, and Tom, and repeated what they had just heard the attendant say.

"He's gonna be okay," Amanda said, trying to convince herself but unable to believe it until she saw her son. The attendant showed them inside. They passed several other casualties, who looked as though they had had far worse experiences than just a few lacerations, before finally coming to Will's room.

"Will?" Amanda asked. Her son's head was covered in bandages, and an IV ran into his arm. A bank of monitors beeped arrhythmically in the background.

"Yeah, it's me," her son said. "I guess I forgot to duck."

"What happened to you?" Amanda asked, sitting on his bed and gingerly touching his face. "You got in a fight?"

Will nodded, wincing from the effort. "I had these Texas kids all wrong," he admitted, sounding groggy. "The guys here sure know how to fight."

"Nothing's broken on you?" Elizabeth asked.

Will shook his head, wincing again. "Nothing got hurt except my pride. They told you it looks worse than it is, right?"

Amanda nodded, slightly relieved. "How did this happen, Will?"

"It's all about that stupid article in the newspaper," he said disdainfully, as if the whole matter were not really worthy of any further discussion. "Some people were making some cracks about you—actually, about me, too. They wanted to know if I'd have you get them arrested if they didn't give me their skateboards. I didn't even want their lame skateboards. I like mine."

Amanda glanced at Elizabeth and Tom. "It was because of the article?" she asked, her heart sinking.

"Sure. It's actually the only reason I went to all of my classes today. It's like you're a celebrity."

"A celebrity? What are you talking about?"

"Half the kids in school think it's really cool that you get people arrested," he explained. "The other half think you're a raving bitch." He added hastily, "That's not my word. That's theirs."

Normally Amanda would have castigated Will for using such inappropriate language, especially about her. But her greater concern was the fact that the newspaper story had broadened the dispute, such as it was, between the good Christian bitches, as she had taken to calling them in her mind, and herself. It was one thing to talk about her. It was another thing entirely to have her children be part of it. And obviously, it wasn't just girls Sarah's age. From what Will was saying, the whole school was involved.

"Did they say how long you're going to be in the hospital?" Amanda asked.

"Not for long," Will replied. He jerked a thumb at Tom. "Who's this guy?"

Amanda reddened. "Um, it's our landlord."

Will looked at his mother, entertained. "A landlord who makes house calls! Hey, Mom—you work fast. Who is he, really? Does he know you're technically still married?"

"And I'm just recently divorced, myself," Tom told Will, before Amanda could say anything. "It's something we like about each other."

"So some guy hit you in the head with a skateboard?" Amanda asked, taking the conversation back to a more comfortable topic. "At Hillside Park Middle School?"

Will rubbed his head. "It was either that or a two-by-four. I'm standing up for your honor, Mom. Which may be more than this guy is doing," he added, glancing at Tom.

"Let's just stay out of my business. I'm just glad you're okay."

"Me too. But I think I want to move back to California. It's safer."

Just then, a doctor entered Will's curtained-off area. Embroidery on his long white coat identified him as Dr. Elliott.

"You're the parents?" he asked, turning to Amanda and Tom.

"I'm the mother," Amanda said quickly.

"Your son's got a thick skull," the doctor told her. "Lucky for all of us."

"That's what I've been saying for years," Amanda replied. "Looks like it finally did him some good for a change."

"That's not saying very much," Sarah cracked.

"Mom! Make her stop!" Will exclaimed, pained. "I'm in a hospital, for Pete's sake!"

"Okay, both of you, that's enough," Amanda said. "I'm just glad you're okay, son. But I'm not okay with the women who were behind this whole hate campaign to do me in at all costs! Mom, why don't you and Sarah stay here? I've got to talk to Tom for a minute. I've got to take care of something."

Elizabeth studied her daughter. "Sounds like something's up. I'll stay with them."

Dr. Elliott studied Will's chart, leaned in, and examined the wounds under the bandages.

"The only guy I know with a thicker skull," he said, "is the guy who runs this hospital. And look at you. You'll be fine. See y'all."

Dr. Elliott left, and Amanda and Tom headed out of the room after him.

"I just can't stand this," Amanda, infuriated, told him. "I know why they're doing it. They're obviously threatened, and they're trying to ruin me. I just never imagined my own best friend from childhood would turn on me."

"What do you want to do about it?"

An idea struck Amanda. It was brilliant. It was doable. And it just might work.

"What I've got in mind for them," she said slowly, formulating her thoughts, "is the perfect brand of payback. I'm going to stop all this nonsense, and I'm going to do it by taking the higher road." So far she'd proven to herself that you can take the high road and still wind up a grease spot on it. She smiled.

It was almost too obvious, it made so much sense. "What time is it?"

"Quarter to one," Tom said, glancing at his Cartier watch.

"Perfect," Amanda said, starting down the hallway. "Oh, um . . . can I borrow your car?"

"What's mine is yours," he responded, intrigued. He tossed her the keys to his Bentley. "Just be careful."

"Thanks," Amanda said gratefully. "Hold down the fort at the hospital for a little while, would you?" She took a deep breath. "These good Christian bitches are gonna regret assuming my children were fair game."

"Where are you going?" Tom asked, watching Amanda's confident gait with wonder and admiration.

"Where am I going?" Amanda flashed Tom a perfect smile. "Why, I'm going to Bible study, of course."

## 29

Amanda had smoked some in college, mostly when she drank, but had never considered herself a smoker. For some odd reason, throughout her life, whenever she found herself under immense pressure, she always reached for a cigarette. Just one, and she always immediately regretted it and wondered why she thought she had to have one in the first place. Today was no different. On her way to the church, she flew by the package store in Hillside Park Village and grabbed a pack of Marlboro Lights. She realized how horrified Tom would be about her smoking in his Bentley, so she rolled down the windows and turned off the air conditioner, trying to limit the odor.

She turned into the parking lot, a little faster than she should've been driving, and squealed to a stop. She didn't see the minister at Hillside Park Presbyterian standing across the parking lot, hardly believing what he was seeing.

She took one last, long drag off the cigarette, then flicked it out the window and onto the concrete parking lot. Dr. Wilkes stood there with this mouth open and when she opened the door, all he saw was tanned, bare legs and red-bottomed stilettos.

Amanda suddenly noticed the reverend and quickly and sheepishly bent down and threw the extinguished cigarette butt in the trash, and smiled and waved as she scurried off. Dr. Wilkes had to laugh—he'd known Amanda her whole life and he'd always referred to her as "God's wildest child." That seemed to be even more true these days than when she was in high school. Where angels go . . . trouble follows, as they say.

Amanda hurried inside the building and headed for the Bible study classroom. When she entered, she was disappointed to see that neither Sharon nor Heather was there. She was hoping they'd be present. If Bible study class wouldn't allow you to feel safe and provide a place where you could tell the truth and have people around you love you anyway, then where else could she possibly hope to confront these two? In a very loving and Christian way, of course. She also knew the value of being able to tell her story with them there, but then again, another one of Amanda's all-time favorite books was *When God Winks*. It's a book about coincidence, or really that coincidence is nothing less than God's purposeful plan. She decided that she would speak no matter what.

They opened in prayer, went over a few items of business, and Amanda asked the lady who was leading that day if she might be allowed to address the group as a whole. She was happy to let Amanda have the floor.

Amanda took her time explaining all the drama, the nonsense, and the happenings of the days since she'd arrived back in Dallas, backing up a time or two to give more details about how she made her decision to leave her husband and come home. She shared more than she intended to, but their faces seemed interested and sympathetic, and she thought this would be the only time she'd have the floor on this topic, so she might as well make the most of it. She explained how difficult this had all been not only for her but also for her mother and especially for her children. She asked for prayers from all of them and then made an astonishing confession.

"I wanted to share with all of you some things I've learned these last few weeks as I've been fighting off all the accusations, gossip, the rumors—all the trouble I've had. I've really had to examine my own heart due to all of this and acknowledge how guilty *I've* been in the past of listening to rumors that people told me. I would have *no* idea where their information had come from and certainly had no way to gauge its accuracy, yet if they were a reliable enough source and sounded sure of themselves, I would believe them.

"I've realized there have been many times in my life when someone else was under attack and I'd be so grateful it was her and not me that I'd be happy to go along with the lynch mob, in hopes I'd be spared at a later date. I realized how often I've given someone that sideways glance when I knew *she* was the topic of the moment, but what she really needed was for someone to stop and ask her how she was or at least smile and say hello, but I wouldn't dare because someone might see me speaking to the current persona non grata, and then what? I know how guilty I've been of treating other people the same way I have so vehemently objected to being treated myself.

"I ask you to please pray that God will continue to open my eyes and my heart—to help me make better decisions when I find myself involved in, but not the focal point of, such hurtful behavior in the future. I'm so grateful for your prayers for my children and hope you'll continue to pray for them as I plan to join you each week now that I'm so glad to be home.

"As far as Heather and Sharon are concerned, I'd really love for you to ask God to put it in their hearts that I'm here to renew old friendships, not create new enemies. I'm really looking forward to being an integral part of this Bible study and having the opportunity to give back to all of you as much as I've already gotten from being involved in this group in such a short time."

The women responded with shouts of affirmation and support for everything she'd said. Amanda smiled, thanked them all, then hurried back to the hospital. As she left, she noticed the whispering had already begun. Her confession would be all over town by that evening, she was sure.

BY THE TIME she got back to the hospital, Will, Sarah, Elizabeth, and Tom were all engrossed in a game of Texasopoly, the University of Texas version of Monopoly. Sarah was winning, as always. She had all the real estate and all the money. She had everyone on the verge of ruin, even Tom.

"Well, what have we here?" Amanda asked as she came back into Will's room.

"What we have here is a genuine ass-kicking, ma'am," Tom admitted with a laugh. "I'd like for Sarah to come to work for me immediately, if you don't think they'd mind her leaving school at such a young age." Tom winked at Amanda, and she was so genuinely proud of her daughter.

Will had to interrupt, of course. "Hey, that's not really fair! You know, I have a head injury."

A few minutes later, the nurse came in and announced that Will had been released by Dr. Elliott and could go home and spend the night in his own bed.

Elizabeth wasn't so sure. "Are you sure he's okay and they don't need to keep him overnight for observation?"

Amanda wasn't exactly looking forward to spending the night in the hospital, so she quickly jumped in. "No, Mom. If they say he's released, that means he's done really well since they've been observing him. We can continue to observe him from the comfort of our own home."

"Well, I'd feel better if you'd let me come spend the night. I'll sleep in Will's room. With all these people suffering what seem to be minor head injuries that end up—"

"Mom, I completely understand what you're saying and I'd really appreciate it if you'd come and spend the night with us tonight, okay? Wouldn't we love that, kids?"

Will and Sarah both immediately responded with, "Yes, Gigi, please come home with us."

Tom jokingly said, "Why, thanks, I'd love to come, too, I just love slumber parties, but oh, wait—I don't have a bag. I'd better not. How about I come get everybody in the morning for breakfast at Buzzbrew's, though."

"Sure!" the kids chorused.

"But what's a Buzzbrew?" Sarah asked.

"I'm not exactly sure," Tom answered, "but we'll ask them when we go tomorrow. How's that?"

"Great!" they all agreed, and the nurse put Will in his wheel-chair for the trip down to the car.

Everyone was exhausted, so they were pretty quiet on the way home. Amanda quietly said to Tom, thinking both children were sleeping, "You know you don't have to take us to breakfast in the morning. I know you lost half a day today be-ing at the hospital with us, so please don't feel—" when all of a sudden, she was interrupted by the two children she was cer-tain were sound asleep.

"No, Mom!" and "Speak for yourself, Mom. We want to go to breakfast! On a school day, at that, so we'll probably need to at least miss first period."

"Well, wait a minute," Tom said. "I was planning to be back here at six thirty so I could have you to school on time—I didn't invite you to brunch. Unless you'd rather wait till the weekend and we can go to brunch, if you'd rather."

"Yeah, okay, let's have brunch this weekend instead. Who wants to wake up at six thirty?" Will said.

"And what are your plans for tomorrow?" Tom asked Amanda.

"I'll be at the Longhorn Ball office all day tomorrow and would love for you to come by and keep me company at some point, if you're in the neighborhood." Amanda exaggerated batting her eyelashes at him, since thanks to Latisse, they were quite extraordinary.

"I fully expect to find myself in the neighborhood, so I'll call on my way to see if you need anything." As he spoke, they pulled into her driveway.

Amanda helped Sarah get into bed and Elizabeth, who had driven back with Tom's driver, Guy, headed upstairs with Will. Amanda loved putting her children to bed at night. You could always really get them to talk to you at bedtime. They might ignore you or give you one-word answers all day long, but when it came to bedtime, they were full of all kinds of information.

Sarah was really exhausted tonight and asked to say the "short version" of prayers. As she walked down the hall, Amanda heard Will and her mother both snoring already. It had been a really long, challenging day but wound up being a really good day, after all.

# 30

✦

The next morning, Elizabeth got up first, put on coffee, and made a really big breakfast for everyone. Sarah and Will were out the door to school a little earlier than usual and as soon as they were gone, Elizabeth stopped to have a word with Amanda.

"I just wanted to tell you how incredibly proud I am of you," she said with all sincerity.

Amanda laughed. "What's that about, Mom? Are you feeling okay? I thought Will was the one hit in the head yesterday, not you." She smiled.

"No, I'm serious, I really am. The way you handled all of that yesterday—from the office to Will ending up in the hospital to your visit to the Bible study class—which I'm still dying to hear more about it, by the way, but I know it went well or I'd have heard otherwise—I was just really proud of how well you handled yourself. With poise and grace and never even once hesitating as if to say, 'I wish there was a man in this picture to take care of all of this for me and make this all go away.'"

"Well, thanks, Mom. You know, I hadn't thought about it, but now that you mention it, I didn't think about it. I just did it," she reflected.

"I don't think I was the only one impressed. I noticed Tom seemed quite content to just sit back and watch you handle it all so well," Elizabeth said.

By now she had gathered her things and was heading toward the door to go to her house.

"What I appreciated was that no macho beast raised its head and tried to act like there needed to be a man in charge to take over. He seemed perfectly fine with letting me take care of my family myself."

"I know, but it sure is nice to know he's gentleman enough to jump in there had you asked for his help." Elizabeth leaned over and gave Amanda a kiss on the cheek.

"Oh, I bet he would've been there for me, but fortunately it was easy to handle and I want Tom to know I'm not looking for someone to rescue me," Amanda declared.

"I think he's probably already figured that out," Elizabeth said, and was out the door.

By 9:30, Amanda had already stopped at Starbucks, had the usual "old home week," which is unavoidable at that Starbucks, and was at the office. She immediately got on the phone and decided it was time to call Nancy McRae and take her up on her offer to let her know if there's anything, anything at all she can do. The greatest thing about Nancy was she was still the most authentic person she had ever met and was *not* the type to offer something she didn't fully intend to back up. On the other hand, she wasn't sure that Nancy had included charity work in that offer and it had just been limited to family stuff. Amanda was about to find out.

She took a couple of deep breaths and said a little prayer out loud. As Nancy's phone was ringing, all Amanda could hear was herself saying, "Please, God. Please, God. Please, God," and about the time she had said the third, "Please, God," Nancy answered.

"Hey, Amanda! I'm so glad you called! I was beginning to think you had decided you didn't like me anymore," she said, and Amanda busted out laughing.

"No, of course not, I've just been ridiculously busy, but when you hear why I'm calling, you might be convinced I don't like you anymore."

"Oh, no," Nancy teased. "What's going on? Is something wrong?"

"Well, yes, no, and maybe. Nancy, you know how hard it is for me to ask for help and you know I never ask unless I'm desperate and also because people who know me, know that I don't ask unless I'm desperate and that if they tell me no, I get my nose out of joint?" Amanda finally took a breath.

Nancy sat there for a minute and finally said, "Oh, yeah, we were both working on that at one time, but I see you've not had any success with improving that part of your personality, either, so go ahead. What do you want me to do that I'm not going to want to do but am going to go ahead and do anyway because I love you and I know you wouldn't ask me if you weren't desperate?"

"I'm desperate for your help with getting a thank-you party pulled together in a very, very limited amount of time and I need your help with *everything*, Nancy. Every area, every category, every possible way you can imagine. I'm not asking you to chair underwriting, I'm asking you to *be* underwriting with me. I'm not asking you to chair the silent or live auction, I'm asking you to *be* the live and silent auctions with me, I'm not asking you to chair reservations—"

"Okay, okay, okay, Amanda." She was laughing hysterically

by now. "I get it. I'm there. I'm sorry I was out of town when you called for volunteers a few days ago, but I'm here now and ready to help in any way. Where do I need to be and when?" Nancy asked, and Amanda was relieved she could hear her smiling as she spoke.

"At the Longhorn Ball office as soon as you can get here," she cringed as she answered.

"Let me make a few calls like you just made to me, first, and I'll be there right away, okay?" Nancy already had written down several names on a scratch pad before she'd finished the sentence.

"Nancy, I have to tell you, I just can't thank—"

"Save it, Amanda. Let's skip the sappy stuff, it's as hard for you to say as it is for me to hear and thank God we're the kind of friends where all that's not necessary. I'll see you in a bit." Nancy was serious and Amanda knew it.

"OK, thanks so much, Nance, and I'll see you when you get here." Amanda hung up and immediately started jumping up and down, screaming.

By the end of the day, Nancy had come to the office with three other girls who had older children and were stay-at-home moms—"a chairman's answer to prayer," as this meant they at least had from nine or ten to at least three o'clock every day to help. Amanda remembered two of the girls from high school. She didn't know them well, they were more Nancy's friends, but she'd always liked them. They just didn't have any classes together or didn't live near one another in the neighborhood. One was Mary Voss and the other was Kathleen Duffy. They were both gorgeous blond bombshells, and if it were possible, Amanda was sure they were even more beautiful now than they had been in high school. The third was someone new to the neighborhood since Amanda lived there, but a good friend of the other three girls. Her name was Dallas Kelly, and she was a stunning brunette. The best part about all four women was that they were just as smart and sweet as they were gorgeous. They were all the call to arms type of friends, and the other great thing about them was that if Amanda was Nancy's friend and she needed them, they were there. Amanda wondered why she'd been so close to Sharon in high school instead of befriending this group.

They spent the next couple of weeks working twelve hours a day, which was possible because these girls had great husbands who adored their wives and who were happy to take over the minute the nanny left every day. There would be breaks here and there to run carpools, but everyone understood what a tight time frame they were on and everybody rallied to help them be as productive and successful as they could possibly be each day. People were calling the office and offering their time and talent every time they turned around, and Tom kept his office crew and his cronies really busy as well. The first weekend, the girls worked straight through and the husbands took the children's weekend schedules or bribed the nannies to work through the weekend. Tom had business to tend to in Austin that weekend but promised to get some Ball business done while he was there. Amanda was grateful, as she knew she'd be too busy to see him that weekend anyway, so it all worked out for the best.

Since Nancy had been a cochair in charge of outdoor production just three years ago, she handled finding the place. The location, Amanda was thrilled to learn, would be South-fork, which for years now had been the most logical choice. As the original family home of TV's fictional Ewings of the series *Dallas*, it was a tourist attraction with all the proper facilities needed for a grand outdoor event. It also happened to have one particularly appealing characteristic: The location was exactly thirty-five minutes from the heart of Hillside Park.

Dallas's husband knew some of the biggest sponsors, so she was in charge of the silent auction. It wouldn't be the size of a regular year's auction, but Amanda knew she could still raise a decent amount of money, and she was pleasantly shocked by the community's generosity.

When it came time to do table reservations and placement of the really big donors, Nancy, Mary, Kathleen, and Dallas proved to be invaluable. Amanda had been away for so long, and Elizabeth's older crowd didn't really do the Longhorn Ball like they did the first twenty-five years it was on the social calendar. Table reservations were always the biggest pain because, unfortunately, on the night of the Ball, you found out who had a gracious heart and who had an ego the size of Texas. Thank God these girls knew whom to seat where, whom not to seat together, and whom not to seat in front or behind someone or you'd never hear the end of it. Those women were worth more than their weight in gold in this department.

Of course, these girls made an event of shopping for their ensembles. They spent the day with a car and driver, chauffeuring them from one promising source to another. They were such fun and not the types to mislead one another. There was not one among them who wouldn't encourage another to look her absolute, very best. They took turns trying on one amazing outfit after another. They were very free with opinions and wouldn't hesitate to gladly hand over something that someone seemed to adore or suggest that something one tried might look better on another. All the girls were joining in gathering accessories and jewelry to add that special touch. The outing was full of laughter and joy and by the time they called it a day, they were all deliriously happy with what they had all helped choose for one another. It was an exceptional day and they all would have fond memories of their time together.

Once outfits had been selected, the worker bees from Tom's office were kind enough to do the set-up work in the auction tents and the girls had a spa day together, Tom's treat.

Amanda had the driver drop off all the other girls before he took her home and Tom was waiting for her at her house when she arrived.

"Well, how was it? Is everyone all cowgirled up and ready to go?" Tom had a big smile and watched as Amanda led the driver up to the front door, loaded down like a pack mule with packages, garment bags, shopping bags, and even a hatbox.

"Tom, you wouldn't have believed it! We had the most amazing day!" Amanda was talking a mile a minute, and Tom could see she really meant it.

"Looks like things are working out pretty well," he said, smiling. "I think I know a few people who are going to have fun at the Ball, no matter what happens."

## 31

⋆

The night of the Ball, Amanda, Nancy, Mary, Kathleen, and Dallas all got adjoining hotel suites at the only non-motel near Southfork, a gift from Nancy's sweet husband. They had someone come out and do their hair and makeup—another gift from Mary's and Dallas's husbands, and each suite was full of flowers and champagne, a gift from Kathleen's husband.

Tom had his driver pick the girls up and drive them to the ranch in a limousine stocked with lots of champagne, Patron (if they really needed it to take the edge off), and several non-alcoholic beers for Amanda to feel like a "big girl" that night.

They entered the VIP room and the air kisses were flying all over the place. It was a beautiful night—not too hot, not too humid, and there was a genuine excitement in the air, as well as a disbelief that these women had managed to pull this makeup Ball together in four short weeks. It was amazing.

Tom had a special surprise for entertainment at the live auction stage that he claimed would rival the surprise on the main stage. Elizabeth was going to bring Will and Sarah out for just a little while, so they could get the full effect of what Mom had been so absorbed with lately. They couldn't stay long—there was a steadfast rule about no one under twenty-one being allowed at the Ball—but of course, Tom had friends on the local police force. He had promised to take personal responsibility for Will and Sarah, so they were going to be allowed to stay for a couple of hours. As the VIP party got in full swing, the girls were all toasting their success and promising one another they'd never do this again, all at the same time.

All of a sudden, it was time to kick off the set that would eventually lead to the live auction. Amanda could hear the band start, but with the density of the crowd it was impossible to see, but who needed to—when you heard the words "Whiskey River, take my mind," they all knew exactly what Tom had been doing in Austin last weekend. He'd been securing none other than Willie Nelson for the live auction entertainment. Willie had played the Longhorn Ball many times before, but never on the live auction stage. Willie was an icon years before the very first Longhorn Ball, so him playing the smaller stage was a real coup!

Willie was smiling and waving at Tom and giving him a thumbs-up, nodding at Amanda. She threw her arms around Tom's neck and was fighting back tears of joy—she couldn't believe the lengths he'd gone to in order to guarantee her success tonight and she was moved beyond words. She stopped and gazed up at him, looking very dapper in his cowboy cool ensemble, and said, "Tom, I just don't even know how to begin to thank you, not just for the things you did for tonight, but for the unwavering support you've shown me since we ran into each other again."

Tom laughed. "Well, whatever you do, sweetheart, don't start thanking me yet!! That's just the first of many, many surprises you have before tonight is over, so you just relax and enjoy yourself—that's what tonight is about for me. Watching *you* have more fun than you've had in as long as you can remember—that's when I'll know I've had a good time."

Amanda couldn't believe it. He really was almost too good to be true. Suddenly she felt a huge pang of regret. How could she ever have believed those unfounded rumors? And to think, she'd been so unbelievably wounded to think people had done the same to her? She would have liked to think her heart was as big as Tom's, though her gestures might not be as grand. But Tom Harrington was without question the kindest, sweetest, most thoughtful, amazing man she had ever met and he'd gotten a bum rap, obviously. Why was it so hard to believe the same thing could happen to her?

She was shaken out of her daydream by yet another person coming up to congratulate her on everything being so perfect. Every time someone had, she had immediately directed them to Nancy and the girls, explaining that they were the ones who really deserved all the credit. At one point, she turned around and they'd all disappeared with their husbands. An hour later, they reappeared and they all headed to the live auction stage together as Willie started his very last rendition of "Whiskey River." The girls were going to make the obligatory announcements, thank-yous, etc., and start the live auction.

A local celebrity news anchor, Meredith Land, who was a beautiful, bubbly, yet no-nonsense newswoman, was going to emcee and all the girls introduced her together. The live auction started with a trip on Dallas's plane to their fabulous home on Red Mountain in Aspen, Colorado. The trip was for eight people for five days and they had thrown in their personal chef for the stay. The auctioneer started the bidding at ten thousand dollars and it sold for twenty thousand in no time. You would never know the economy had been so lousy over the last few years. People had been incredibly generous—to donate, to buy—it was almost surreal.

In the midst of this fun and excitement, suddenly Nancy elbowed Amanda and said, "Take a look over there."

Amanda followed her gesture toward the ladies' bathroom. "What am I looking at?" she asked.

"A pretty pitiful sight, if you ask me," Nancy said as she took another sip of her margarita.

"I'm still not sure I see what I'm supposed to be looking at." Amanda was serious. There were people everywhere, so she really couldn't figure out what Nancy was pointing out to her.

"On the hay bale—sitting down to the right of the exit door to the restrooms?" Nancy gestured again.

This time, Amanda saw exactly what Nancy was talking about, but she really couldn't believe her eyes. There on the hay bale, totally isolated from everyone else at the party, sat none other than Heather Sappington and Sharon Peavy. They were a pitiful sight. It wasn't even ten o'clock yet and they both looked so drunk, the kind of drunk where you're *so* drunk your facial features are distorted because they look like they've fallen. They were back to back, as if they were literally holding each other up. They were both wearing very un-fabulous outfits in general, and looked absolutely miserable. Heather was wearing something that she must have purchased at a resale shop. It was a turquoise suede dress but had an uneven coloring, as if the suede had been dry-cleaned too many times and not by a dry cleaner that specializes in cleaning leather and suede. It was ill-fitting as well and obvious they'd just gotten close to her size. She looked like a stuffed sausage, and even the seams looked like they might give. When your outfit is turquoise, are you really supposed to wear that much turquoise jewelry with it? And it was that awful greenish tint that really clashed with her outfit.

Sharon had on a beautiful white blouse but it didn't close exactly right at the bust. The buttons pulled and, as they say, there were boobs everywhere. Amanda had to do a double take because yes, she had seen what she thought she saw: a denim prairie skirt. Her skirt was so long, it literally dragged the ground and she'd probably given up and sat down to get a break from other people stepping on her hem all night. Even though "Rhinestone Cowboy" had been last year's theme, it looked like Sharon had purchased and worn every faux diamond in the city.

They were a ghastly sight.

Amanda watched for a few minutes and as different people would walk by—either a girl headed to the ladies' room or a couple walking in that direction—Sharon, Heather, or both would almost perk up for a moment and speak. No one stopped and very few even really spoke, just gave a halfhearted wave and moved on. The girls would then deflate back to their original position.

Even as awful as those two had been to her, Amanda was a better hostess than to sit there and watch someone have such a miserable time. It took a few minutes, but Amanda finally made her way over to where Sharon and Heather were sitting.

"Hi, girls! How are you?" Amanda yelled out as she approached them.

They immediately perked up. "Oh, hey, Amanda!! We're great! Good job—this is really phenomenal what you've done.

We were just sitting here talking about how we wished you'd asked us to help you," Heather said in the sweet Sunday school tone that only she could muster in a situation like this.

Sharon, of course, flipped her head around like it was on a swivel and looked at Heather with an absolute glare her drunkenness couldn't disguise and said, "What in the hell are you talking about, Heather? We were not."

To which Heather gave her a swift, very obvious kick to the shin with her cowboy boot and said between clenched teeth, "*Yes*, we were, Sharon."

Amanda decided she should probably break this up before it got even uglier. "Oh, girls, that's so sweet of you. I thought you'd probably had enough after last year and didn't want to put you on the spot. Since last year was technically just last month, I figured you were still recovering, I'm sorry. You know you could've called me and offered and I'd have gladly set you to work."

They looked at each other and rolled their eyes. Amanda couldn't decide who they were more disgusted with, her or themselves.

"Where is Darlene? I haven't seen her all night," Amanda said.

This was the first time either one of them seemed a bit pleased since Amanda first spotted them.

They both looked at each other with big, goofy grins, then just busted out laughing.

"What? What's so funny?" Amanda asked.

"Oh, let's not go there," Heather ordered.

"Oh, why not?" Sharon wondered. "She'd not hesitate a minute if it were one of us."

Heather gave her a dirty look, then almost fell off the hay

bale as she turned away from her, having to put her hands out and steady herself on the ground before she could raise back up.

Sharon gave a shrug and said, "Well, it seems her husband was always going to be out of town tonight, but she had a surprise phone call from his current affair. You know, the kind where they finally get impatient and call the wife? Only it turns out the other woman was another man this time."

"Oh, no. I hate that for her. I can't imagine . . ." Amanda's voice trailed off.

All of a sudden, Heather started to get a little aggressive.

"Oh, do you, really? Sweet little Amanda, do you *really* just *hate* that for her?"

Amanda was totally caught off guard, but quickly recovered. "Well, of course I do, Heather. You're her dear friend, don't you feel for her, too?"

"I'll tell you what I think," Heather started, but was interrupted by the auctioneer calling Amanda's name.

Everyone around started saying, "Amanda, he's trying to get your attention!! Amanda, look up at the stage." It seemed everyone around her was telling her to look in that direction and like they'd been trying to get her attention for a minute or two.

Amanda looked up, bright red in the face. She put her hand over her mouth and was laughing when she saw Nancy, Dallas, Mary, Kathleen, and Tom all walking toward her.

They all walked up and hugged her, Tom put his arm around her, and she could hear Sharon say very loudly, "Oh, I think I'm going to be sick," then she heard Heather say, "Shut up, Sharon."

Amanda was really confused now. She looked at Tom and Nancy and said, "I'm so sorry, I didn't hear what was going on! Did you need me?"

Nancy looked at Tom and grinned really big. "Well, Amanda, we had to stop the auction because we didn't want you to miss this."

"Miss what?" Amanda said. "What item are we on?"

"The one we told Tom you've been coveting since it came into the office last week," she said. All four girls smiled and nodded, as if they were finally letting Amanda in on a big secret.

"Oh, no, you didn't. I'm so embarrassed." Amanda wanted to die.

"Don't be. We wouldn't tell him the first hundred times he asked because we knew you wouldn't want us to, but the man is persistent." Nancy gave Tom the nod as she spoke.

The next auction item was a magnificent, one-of-a-kind platinum and diamond cross donated by Mary's dear friend of many, many years, Jude Steele of the Jude Frances Jewelry Company. It was enormous and the design was incredible. The cross had about five carats of diamonds, total, and half-carat diamonds were set every few inches in the chain. It was a fabulous piece, and Amanda adored it. The auctioneer started the bidding at ten thousand dollars and there was a frenzy of bidding. Amanda stuck her fingers in her ears and playfully shook her head back and forth at Tom and Nancy.

Amanda turned her back to the crowd and looked up just in time to see what she thought was fire coming out of Heather's eyes. Sharon gave her an equally disgusted look. When she heard "*Sold*" and everyone started clapping, Nancy, Mary, Dallas, and Kathleen all came over and gave her a group hug, very pleased that they'd managed to surprise her.

She gave Tom a big hug and kiss and as she pulled away from him, caught the backsides of both Heather and Sharon stomping away.

"Oh, Tom, I think Sharon's upset." Amanda felt genuinely bad for her.

"Amanda, look. One of my favorite things about you is that you care about how other people feel, but one thing you have to realize, or I guess Sharon has to realize, is that I still wouldn't be interested in her if you were still happily married, living in Newport."

"I know, Tom, I guess it's just easier for her to blame me than believe that, so let her. I just can't worry about it."

"No, you can't and neither can I, for that matter. Now, I told you there were lots of surprises tonight, so let's go to the main stage. The live auction only has a few more items, and we want to beat the stampede."

Tom took her hand and they walked past the other people watching the rest of the auction and headed for their table in front of the main stage. As they sat at their front-row table, they waited for the live auction to end and the main stage act to begin, which at this point was still a mystery.

They looked up and saw the girls and their husbands heading toward the table. It was a constant stream of conversation about how "so-and-so can't believe we pulled this off, they said we couldn't do it and we did," or "so-and-so says this is the best Longhorn Ball ever and it's not even a Longhorn Ball, technically," and "I've had a million people tell me tonight these are the best auction items we've ever had."

Tom made a toast before the band started, while you could still hear, to Nancy and the girls for rallying and for knowing what it really means to be there for a friend when they really need you. Amanda made one to the husbands for being such great guys and for being so supportive when they could've been anything but. It was a "love fest," all in all.

They looked up on the stage and there was Guy, Tom's driver. He announced, "Ladies and gentlemen, would you please help me welcome to the thank-you party for the Longhorn Ball . . . Mr. George Strait!" and the crowd erupted in applause.

Tom grabbed Amanda and said, "You owe me a dance!"

She jumped up, took his hand as he led her to the dance floor, and said, "I believe I do," and they danced together for the first time since they met.

AFTER THE CONCERT, everyone headed back over to the other side of the party for the late-night dance band. Tom and Amanda stayed at their table, still just taking in the whole thing, enjoying some time to themselves. They were the only people left in that whole, huge concert area.

"Tom, I just can't believe how completely perfect this entire evening has been, from beginning to end! My heart is so touched by the immeasurable kindness and generosity of people who were near strangers, just a month ago."

"Yeah, it kind of renews your faith in people in general, doesn't it?" he said, smiling and kissing her on the head.

"It really does—I was just thinking about how grateful I am for my mom, my children, for Nancy, and for my new friends. I'm even so grateful for their husbands, even though I can't remember half of their names right now, I'm so tired!" and she and Tom both laughed.

"What do you say we walk on over to the late-night party just to make sure everything's going okay, and then we'll sneak out," Amanda suggested.

Tom stood up quickly as if to say, "I thought you'd never ask," and they headed to the other side of the ranch.

• • •

AMANDA KNEW TOM could never understand how truly happy she was to be home. It was so wonderful to be back in her old neighborhood, especially the familiarity of everything about it. Sure, it had changed some in the years she'd been gone, but there were so many things about it that were the same. It gave her a comfort and joy she really hadn't anticipated when she was considering the move back from California. There was something magical about the neighborhood that Amanda never could appreciate or understand until she'd moved away. She'd always been a little puzzled by the fascination outsiders had with Hillside Park—especially the Dallasites who had their own history in their own neighborhoods. It really never made sense to her that they all seemed to have an almost "let's move to Camelot, where it never rains till after sundown" idealism about Hillside Park, but after being away and coming home, she had more empathy and less curiosity for these people.

Her relationship with her mother had never been better. Amanda didn't know whether to attribute the new ease in their relationship to time lost, the fact that Amanda was now a mother, herself, or maturity on her part, but regardless, she was so very delighted to be close to her mother again—literally as well as emotionally. Will and Sarah would learn things from Elizabeth that they should learn from a grandmother. Family history and stories should really come from their grandmother. They were too important for Amanda to share when she was so unclear on the details. Also, the unconditional love and traditional spoiling that are a grandmother's duty would've been missed had Amanda not brought the children back home. This environment was so nurturing for them—something lacking when they were in California, and Amanda was so excited to establish new family traditions that would include their Gigi.

Elizabeth would never know how it warmed Amanda's heart to have her mother rally around her and lead the defensive against the "good Christian bitches." She had given sound advice and encouraged her to maintain a cool head while carefully traversing the potential pitfalls of social life, just within what seemed like the first few minutes of her being home. Amanda had needed a mentor for this, and her mother proved to be the perfect ally to survive such a senseless attack. Amanda had always been such a mother bear with her own children, so it did her heart good to see her own mother react the same way to her struggles. Having lived in the middle of the social swirl her entire life and having seen it all at her age, Elizabeth not only took her daughter under her wing and protected her, she also stood firm behind her and protected her to the nth degree.

Her mother, like most mothers, had the typical advice of, "Honey, five years from now this won't matter at all," but at the same time, Elizabeth had been around long enough that she had seen people's lives destroyed by spiteful, mean-spirited gossip and wasn't about to let her daughter's fate be determined by jackals. It's true that the high road is always the best route and you can still prevail by doing the right thing. With success truly being the best revenge, Amanda had triumphed over the "good Christian bitches" with her dignity intact.

TOM AND AMANDA decided to skip the after-party, and headed home, with Guy driving. Tom dozed off before they were off ranch property, and Amanda decided maybe he was the only person who had worked harder than her mother these last few weeks. She stared at him, holding her breath, praying that he wasn't a snorer. "Oh, thank God," she laughed to herself, when he stayed quiet. Tom was such an amazing man. He had more than proved himself in so many ways. Maybe he was the man for her, but maybe he wasn't—but right now, she was just thrilled to feel something she hadn't experienced in years: contentment. She knew that come what may, she would be absolutely all right because she was home. This time for good.